外教社
博学文库

默温诗之欲望
与无限性

DESIRE AND INFINITY
IN W. S. MERWIN'S POETRY

冯 冬 著

上海外语教育出版社
外教社 SHANGHAI FOREIGN LANGUAGE EDUCATION PRESS

图书在版编目(CIP)数据

默温诗之欲望与无限性／冯冬著.
—上海：上海外语教育出版社，2017
（外教社博学文库）
ISBN 978-7-5446-4637-6

Ⅰ.①默… Ⅱ.①冯… Ⅲ.①默温–诗歌研究
Ⅳ.①I712.072

中国版本图书馆 CIP 数据核字(2017)第 002645 号

出版发行：上海外语教育出版社
　　　　　　（上海外国语大学内）　邮编：200083
电　　话：021-65425300（总机）
电子邮箱：bookinfo@sflep.com.cn
网　　址：http://www.sflep.com.cn　　http://www.sflep.com
责任编辑： 李健儿

印　　刷：上海信老印刷厂
开　　本：890×1240　1/32　印张 5.625　字数 197千字
版　　次：2017年 2月第 1版　　2017 年 2月第 1次印刷
印　　数：1 100 册

书　　号：ISBN 978-7-5446-4637-6 / I · 0366
定　　价：20.00 元
　　　本版图书如有印装质量问题，可向本社调换

博学文库编委会成员

出版说明

　　上海外语教育出版社始终坚持"服务外语教育、传播先进文化、推广学术成果、促进人才培养"的经营理念,凭借自身的专业优势和创新精神,多年来已推出各类学术图书 600 余种,为中国的外语教学和研究作出了积极的贡献。

　　为展示学术研究的最新动态和成果,并为广大优秀的博士人才提供广阔的学术交流平台,上海外语教育出版社隆重推出"外教社博学文库"。本文库遴选国内的优秀博士论文,遵循严格的"专家推荐、匿名评审、好中选优"的筛选流程,内容涵盖语言学、文学、翻译和教学法研究等各个领域。本文库为开放系列,理论创新性强、材料科学翔实、论述周密严谨、文字简洁流畅,其问世必将为国内外广大读者在相关的外语学习和研究领域提供又一宝贵的学术资源。

上海外语教育出版社

For Merwin

A man
sat by the side of a river
listening to the turning of the wheel
only there was no wheel to turn
he just sat there listening
day and night passed
the first light of dawn
traveled through the green trees
he looks up at the unnamed sky
waiting for
the alien blessing
to come

CONTENTS

ABBREVIATIONS

In this book the following abbreviations will be used, all of which are fully documented in the Works Cited.

BF	*The Book of Fables* (2007)
EE	*The Ends of the Earth: Essays* (2004)
FF	*The First Four Books of Poems* (1975)
FH	*Flower & Hand: Poems 1977–1983* (1997)
FI	*Finding the Islands* (1982)
LU	*The Lost Upland: Stories of Southwest France* (1992)
MV	*The Mays of Ventadorn* (2002)
P	*The Pupil* (2001)
PC	*Present Company* (2005)
RM	*Regions of Memory: Uncollected Prose, 1949–82* (1987)
RS	*The River Sound* (1999)
RT	*The Rain in the Trees* (1988)
SD	*Summer Doorways: A Memoir* (2005)
SF	*The Second Four Books of Poems* (1993)
SS	*The Shadows of Sirius* (2008)
ST	*Selected Translations 1948–1968* (1969)
T	*Travels* (1992)
UO	*Unframed Originals: Recollections* (1982)
V	*The Vixen* (1995)

前　言

　　本书诞生于一种迫切要求,即将诗学研究从长久以来的新旧历史主义与形式主义的框架中解放出来,让诗学(语言之生成)充分切入当代哲学与精神分析的争执地带,其中之一则是"他者"(陌异性)之观念得以丰富开展的区域。本书涉及的一些关键概念,如无限性、欲望、创伤、实在、神圣、匿名性、踪迹、自然、荡力(jouissance)等等,因其对诗意生成过程中未具专名力量的指向,一方面超越了以修辞学为基础的传统阐释框架,另一方面也与当下流行的形式、流派、族裔、生态、意识形态、全球化等外部批评拉开了距离。法国哲学家巴迪欧认为文学提供了一种"思想的形式",它甚至是关于"思想的思想",即对思想本身进行反思的某种带有绝对性质的思想。这样一种对文学的思考显然很难通过一般意义上的"文学研究"来达到,因它要求阐述的不只是一个"学理问题"(这样的问题通常被设定起来以维持学术生产),也不仅仅满足于"批评范式"的转变(解构、精神分析因被化约为一门"文学批评方法"而失去真正的干预力量)。对诗歌和诗学来说重要的是,如何进入一种黑格尔所言的理念层面的源出性思辨,以达到对具体的诗意之物的横贯辨识,即如何让诗学与他者之思充分交锋,以带出诗的心理、伦理与政治的潜能——诗的陌异潜能。

　　同时也出于一种当下性的要求,本书选取了当代美国诗人默温(W. S. Merwin, 1927-　)作为讨论对象。由于反对学院派形式主义,默温早期诗作就已经显露出比同时代美国诗人更为彻底的对异质存在的思考与探寻。无论从列维纳斯他者哲学还是拉康精神分析来看,默温诗作都呈现出某种崇高的不可毁灭的精神特征,当然,这种寄寓于时代精神之匮乏的"精神",不可避免地显出想要突破人类符号关系从而直达真实的迫切欲望。默温虽积极投身社会运动,他的诗作却展现出超越美国社会现实的诸多向度——既不遵循垮掉派对现实的对抗性宣言,也与深度意象派对自然力量的主观召唤有所差异。默温在诗中打开的乃是一个超越二元对立结构的无限纵深的世界;该世界在诗人的知觉领域内不断回撤,将自我带入历史与社会现实之外的未名之物的遭遇,引发其创伤性的欲望、愉悦与荡力。这种带入的姿态本身即暗含了超越既定历史与现实规定性的潜能。本书阐述的重点即默温所欲望的这种匿名神圣性(无限性)如何是成问题的,如何具有"设定"与"解设定"的双重性。

具体来说,本书将从神话、宗教、爱欲、记忆四个方面展开对默温诗作无限性质的论述。这四种模式并非相互并列,而是彼此交替、渗透、映照。第一章讨论默温诗中"力比多固着"的心理成因以及默温早期对流动性、无形性以及幻影的追寻如何发展成突破"父名"与社会象征关系的紧迫感与内驱力。第二章讨论犹太—基督教他者与匿名他者在默温诗中的相互替代。20世纪60年代,面对由越战引发的历史终结感,默温放弃基督教神学的单义拯救主题,转向匿名的遥远荒野以求精神漫游之场所,在与自我、逻各斯、上帝以及可命名之物相异的事物的遭遇中,默温诗作表现出的激进被动性与深沉虔敬暴露了"技术"与"认知"的不充分。第三章讨论默温如何在爱情诗中获取"父名"之外的另类荡力,以超越父名对于"施爱的主体"的限制。默温的爱情诗遵循中世纪游吟诗的传统,将女性呈现为神秘的不可把握的对象,但其后期诗作却越来越聚焦于自然与爱欲的颇为问题化的结合。默温的爱情与自然诗,在无意识的层面上,并非如生态批评所揭示的那样寻求人与自然的和谐,它更接近对人与自然之结构性差异或内在"非一致性"的某种见证。第四章从默温晚期诗作中一再出现的"阳光"意象入手,追溯背后复杂的心理、记忆、情感因素。在突破"父名"及其所代表的社会—象征秩序的过程中,默温一方面在诗的想象中任意享受遭遇异质存在引致的荡力,一方面也因为此荡力而生发出对父亲的负罪。自20世纪70年代中期父亲的逝世,默温不断在诗里召唤早期的记忆碎片来哀悼他,同时,为弥补违越"父名"所带来的负罪与悲痛,默温重复地唤醒早期记忆与家族起源以通向史前的匿名他者,以此解开记忆的缠绕。

在一个资本化与管理盛行的时代,诗似乎难以维系其精神性而渐渐落入同一的逻辑和权力的领地,诗之精神性愈发紧迫。默温诗作在日常现实之边缘展开进而趋向无限的外部,如此诗学路径无疑给予当下诗学研究与诗创作一种转换的可能。默温诗作的多重性远非一、两种解读所能穷尽,其蕴含的精神潜能也非纯粹的学理研究所能把握。对诗的倾听本质地先于对诗的言说甚至分析,无论在列维纳斯还是拉康的意义上,在海德格尔还是巴迪欧的意义上,默温诗作都不失为思想在诗中实现自身的一个特例。通过阅读默温,我们不仅可以谈论一种"思想之诗",更可以期待一种"诗的思想",即吸收、横贯并替补了哲学与精神分析的非整合性的源出之思。甚至,我们或许最终能提出一个与"感官的诗学""政治的诗学""伦理的诗学""生态诗学""物质诗学""DNA 诗学"等等相对的"诗学的诗学",即决定所谓"诗意之物"的位置究竟何在,这取决于诗学的跨界拓展和它回返自身的能力。

本书在我的博士学位论文基础上修改而成,在此我要感谢南京大学外国语学院杨金才教授对该论文的悉心指导,他对论理的强调引导我在思考上力求客观,在论述关键点上达到集中与连贯。另外,我还要感谢台湾 *Concentric: Literary and Cultural Studies, NTU Studies in Language and Literature* 以及美国 *College Literature: A Journal of Critical Literary Studies* 的匿名审稿人,他们关于方法论的批评意见让我更为严谨地参与学术讨论,也更为批判地看待哲学与精神分析的理论框架。此外,美国诗人 Scott Alexander Jones 帮我校对了书稿,他对语言的敏锐也直接感染了我,让我体会到英文写作的冒险与愉悦。最后,感谢上海外语教育出版社将本书纳入"博学文库",并在遴选过程中提出宝贵意见。

Introduction

A modern disciple of high Romanticism, with all its remoteness, ghostliness, shadows, dreams, fantasies, ecstasies, and nostalgia, William Stanley Merwin (1927 —   ) achieves a unique status in the contemporary literary scene of the United States. Despite his concern for and involvements with major social issues such as the anti-Vietnam War movement, protests against nuclear arms, and the environmental movement starting back in the 1970s, Merwin's writings have maintained another dimension beyond immediate US social realities. To readers accustomed to urban lyrics, Merwin's poetry may sound anachronistic, for much of it does not refer to the current postindustrial consumer society. Rather, he sings of skylarks and nightingales in the remote villages of southern France, where he lived intermittently for years, or of the fauna and flora of Majorca and Maui. Like the migrant birds he loves and writes about, Merwin himself has traveled extensively during his life, from New Jersey, where he was born, to Portugal, Spain, France, England, Greece, Mexico, and finally to Hawaii. He has lived in Hawaii for the past forty years. Like the Knights Templar of the Middle Ages seeking the Holy Grail, Merwin over his entire poetic career exhibits a strong and persistent spiritual quest for the distant, the transcendent, and the infinite. His unquenchable spiritualism puts him in the same camp as such poets as P. B. Shelley, W. B. Yeats, and Friedrich Hölderlin. In the age of mechanical reproduction of artworks, Merwin's writings have curiously retained that long-lost "aura" associated with the enchantment of words and fascination with origins.

Merwin can be described as a post-romantic in that he has de-romanticized Romanticism; he keeps the basic gesture of Romantic

2

transcendence while discrediting both Byron's self-aggrandizement and Whitman's appropriation of nature. Merwin also questions the grand narratives of equality, freedom, and brotherly love, which constitute the ideal of human emancipation since the French Revolution. Indeed, in the 1960s Merwin's poetic vision was so bleak and apocalyptic that he was in the paradoxical position of being considered either the most Romantic or the most anti-Romantic of contemporary poets. Robert Pinsky, after reading "Whenever I Go There" in Merwin's *The Lice* (1967), cries that it "embodies an extreme Romanticism: a pursuit of darkness, of silence" (94), while Thomas Byers, reading the same book and comparing it with the poems of Walt Whitman, concludes that "Merwin not only disbelieves the Romantic position but finds it immoral and destructive" (*What I Cannot Say* 88-89).① The controversy points to the inherent contradiction between Merwin's deconstructive voice and what Laurence Lieberman calls "a sustained inner urgency" (qtd. in Folsom and Nelson 10), a poetic yearning for what is "higher" than the experiential world.②

The problematics of transcendence and historicity in Merwin's poetry have long perplexed his critics. Reviewing *The Lice* in 1967, Laurence Lieberman hastened to crown Merwin the poet-prophet by announcing that the book "has perfectly captured the peculiar spiritual agony of our time" (qtd. in Perloff 122). Now it has become commonplace to consider Merwin's poems from the 1960s to be dark, sparse, and pessimistic, because the historical time did not seem particularly hopeful for poets. Lieberman's praise actually demotes Merwin to a representational / representative poet of a certain historical condition, inexorably pinning him down by historical repercussions. Although Merwin admits that "it was possible for [*The Lice*]

---

① Byers draws the vital distinction between Whitman and Merwin, arguing that "Whitman's encounters with nature often involve dominance and submission" while Merwin holds "a belief in the intrinsic value of that which is different from us" (*What I Cannot Say* 82, 84).

② Merwin's deconstructive use of poetic language has been a shared discovery among his critics. See Carl Nelson, "The Resources of Failure: W. S. Merwin's Deconstructive Career"; Walter Kalaidjian, "Linguistic Mirage: Language and Landscape in Merwin's Later Poetry," *W. S. Merwin: Essays on the Poetry*, ed. Cary Nelson and Ed Folsom (Urbana: Illinois University Press, 1987), 78-121; 198-223. Also see Thomas B. Byers, "W. S. Merwin: A Description of Darkness," *What I Cannot Say: Self, Word, and World in Whitman, Stevens, and Merwin* (Urbana: Illinois University Press, 1989), 79-110.

to be considered as a reflection of its historical context," he soon adds that "readers continue to share with us something of history that is not strictly historic" (*SF* 1, 2). It seems that what concerned Merwin then was not the process of national history but the end of history — eschatology, the "coming of extinction," as one of his prophetic poems in *The Lice* is titled.[1]

Cary Nelson, commenting on another typical poem "Beginning" in *The Moving Target* (1963), says, "It is an eschatology of origins; it binds the course of history to a single core of emptiness" (107). Dismantling the master narrative of history as progress and Enlightenment, Merwin presents the final impasse of man's age-old hegemonic control over each other and over the natural world, calling for a spiritual journey into "the white plain / under the white sky" (*SF* 218), a pre- or post-historical site where "its beginning is a true origin — an end" (Nelson 107). Thus Merwin had gone further than any "spiritual agony" to the "No Man's Land," to the kernel of history that is non-historical, where "spiritual agony" is largely swallowed up by the biblical pre-creational chaos. Reading *The Lice* along with Merwin's mythopoetic poems of the 1950s helps to clarify Merwin's continuous effort to break out of man's anthropocentric obsession with *his own story*. In *W. S. Merwin the Mythmaker* (1986), Mark Christhilf finds that "Merwin often describes the present in images suggesting the mythical apocalypse: things are falling, broken, ending" (24); Merwin's transcendental vision is thus bound up with the prophesied end of human history.

Not every critic is ready to credit Merwin's apocalypse. After laying bare the elaborate metrical devices in several exemplary 1960s poems of Merwin, Marjorie Perloff dismisses Merwin as a "fastidious poet, whose gift is perhaps less for revelation than for delicate resonance" (142). Merwin was indeed "fastidious" in his early discursive poems, such as "Dictum: For a Masque of Deluge," "East of the Sun and West of the Moon," "Leviathan," and "Grandmother Dying," in which he was working more with dramatic invention than with poetic reduction. To characterize *The Moving Target* or *The Lice* as "fastidious" on the sole ground of metrics, however, is to mistake Merwin's built-in sense of meter

---

[1] Here Merwin's vision of eschatology due to the Vietnam War should be strictly differentiated from Francis Fukuyama's proposition of the predominance of Western liberal democracy as "the end of history."

(Merwin started writing regular hymns at the age of five) for the ostensible manipulation of the poetic process, something Merwin highly suspected in the 1960s and eventually discarded after the 1970s. The innate poetic resonance does not handicap Merwin's transcendental reverie but reinforces its enchantment. Revelation need not exclude resonance.

Harold Bloom, less enthusiastic than Lieberman and more lenient than Perloff, dictates in a half sympathetic and half condescending tone that "Merwin's predicament … is that he has no Transcendental vision, and yet feels impelled to prophesy" (14). What Bloom has in mind is the Emersonian transcendentalist, a self-confident, optimistic eyeball viewing the whole phenomenal world. Merwin's dark defeatism in *The Moving Target* and *The Lice* obviously does not fit into this paradigm. Therefore, Bloom considers Merwin incapable of "a belief in an influx of light and power," and the light Merwin presents is "wholly meaningless" (16). However, one is tempted to read Merwin in the opposite direction and argue with Bloom as to the meaning of the adjective "meaningless." Jarold Ramsey, commenting on *The Lice*, observes that "the speaker ultimately looks *beyond* man to a natural world as desolate as T. S. Eliot's vision of the end," yet what Merwin opens up is more like a "posthuman world" than a wasteland (32; emphasis original). What Bloom has overlooked or misrecognized is exactly this "beyond" emphasized by Ramsey. Merwin's transcendental vision is "meaningless," not because it is too dark or despairing, as Bloom finds, but because it has crossed the border of human signification and passed into a psychotic state in which the naïve dichotomy of optimism and pessimism no longer applies. The vision is more pathological than historical.

Like the German Romantic poet Friedrich Hölderlin, Merwin often perceives human reality from a nonhuman or divine vantage. Charles Molesworth notices that in Merwin "[a]ll human projects are seen through a lens of oblivion or transcendence that renders details insignificant and turns hope into something furtive and numbing" (153). Molesworth, however, is reluctant to recognize that for Merwin, hope does not reside in human as the Other, but in what is other than human, although Merwin's poems would grow more "human-friendly" (more affirmative of human values) after the mid-1970s. The numbness of hope testifies to the need of a more radical understanding of hope, for Merwin's is another kind of hope, which is not *for* or *of* humans, but largely *without* humans. In this sense, Merwin has radicalized the (im)possibility of poetic language to signify the alternative modes of being: the encounters with the monstrous, the inanimate, and the undead.

All these characteristics of Merwin differ significantly from the nineteenth-century American Transcendentalism, which Harold Bloom espoused and used as a yardstick for contemporary poetry. Unlike Emerson or Whitman, Merwin cherishes neither patent love for fellow humans nor any optimistic view of human perfectibility.[1] Merwin's stance is more critical and deconstructive. Merwin *does* believe in "the influx of light and power, " and Merwin's work in the 1980s and afterward would override this judgment of Bloom's. This "light and power, " however, should not be equated with the Emersonian idealism that proposes an autonomous subject fully capable of absorbing the object without leaving any remainder, but with a radical revelation from the infinite Other that cannot be properly subjectivized through both theoretical and poetic discourses. For Merwin, it is presumptuous to regard ego as the Whole, the unity of the pieces of the external reality, as supposed by Emerson. Human ego cannot completely transcend itself in a mystic unity with the divine, the holy, or the infinite; it remains irreducibly distant from what draws it, despite its epiphanies and approximations — or what Cary Nelson calls the "inaccessible proximity" (107). Even though Merwin exhibits a strong tendency of transcendence, it is inaccurate to categorize Merwin as a "transcendentalist" with all its Emersonian halo of self-confidence, for in the Merwinian world approximation between self and Other, desire and object, humanity and nonhumanness produces distances almost simultaneously.

In the present study, I will argue that the bulk of Merwin's poetry from *A Mask for Janus* (1952) up to *The Shadows of Sirius* (2008), despite many transformations of poetic style, voice, and motif, manifests a desire that does not call for fulfillment but circles around the infinite. Merwin's desire for infinity largely differs from the nineteenth-century American Transcendentalism in that the lyrical subject manifests certain symptoms (anxiety, amnesia, obsession, compulsion, euphoria, hallucination, etc.) before the infinite Other. Throughout his poetic career Merwin seems to maintain a transferential relationship with the deified Other. I will narrate the Pilgrim's Progress of Merwin, who indefatigably seeks what Emmanuel Levinas calls "the holiness of the holy" (qtd. in Derrida, *Adieu* 4), in both

---

[1] For a detailed treatment of Merwin's essential disagreements with Emerson and Whitman, see Byers, *What I Cannot Say* 79-110.

sacred and secular spheres. By positing a kind of fleeting divinity, not only religious but also existential, in the infinite Other, Merwin stages an endless query that retroactively produces its own object-cause. Merwin's controversial apocalyptic vision in the 1960s, as I have reviewed above, can be read as an irruption of his psychoneurotic transgression that intensified in the '60s but was already latent in the '50s and continued onto the '70s and '80s. More importantly, the vision is accompanied by an urgent decision for separation to open new existential and ethical grounds outside the existing social order. Different from Allen Ginsberg, who howls before a spiritless civilization, Merwin not only transgresses present reality but also establishes potential / alternative realities through the medium of enchanted verbal movements, as he wrote in the 1950s: "we became / The eyes of sleep that chased receding fires / Through the bodiless exile of a dream," and "We seek a new dimension for the world" (*FF* 11). The receding, beckoning fires and the new dimension of the world would herald Merwin's lifelong pursuit of a radical alternative outside any given historical conditions.

This study will elucidate the problematics of desire and infinity in Merwin's poetry from a dialogue between psychoanalysis and post-Heideggerian philosophy. I borrow the formulation of desire / drive from the French psychoanalyst Jacques Lacan and the Lacanian theorist Slavoj Žižek. Lacan incorporates structuralism into Sigmund Freud's concept of "unconscious wish," proposing that "desire is neither the appetite for satisfaction nor the demand for love, but the difference that results from the subtraction of the first from the second, the very phenomenon of their splitting (*Spaltung*)" (*Écrits* 276). Desire (*désir*) is a product of separation, of "splitting" between instinctual need (*besoin*) that can be satisfied and unconditional demand (*demande*) that cannot. Desire points to the desire of the Other when the infant first perceives that (m)Other's desire is directed elsewhere and tries to fill in that lack by asking, "What does she desire?" Replacing the desire for mother with the Name-of-the-Father, the infant enters the Symbolic (*symbolique*) of signifiers and language (the big Other, as opposed to the imaginary / mirrored other) — "that foreign language that we are born into and must learn to speak if we want to articulate our own desire" (Homer 70). In its articulation, desire is inextricably woven into the network of words and sentences, as Lacan famously claims: "[Desire] is not so much a pure passion of the signified as a pure action of the signifier" (*Écrits* 253). Generated by the abyssal desire of the (m)Other, the subject's own desire hides and slides in the network of metaphors, metonymies, and references, seeking temporary satisfaction in the very hindrance it meets.

There is, however, something that cannot be properly symbolized by signifiers and language — the Real (*réel*), which includes the objects of desire (*das Ding, objet petit a*), unconscious fantasies, ecstatic enjoyments (*jouissance*), and libidinal drives. The relationship between the Real and reality is a reversed one: the Real is more real than reality in that it, being psychic, provides the authentic cause for human actions. The Real not only resists the erosion of symbolic reality but also constitutes the kernel of the latter, and what has been excluded from the surface of reality is what truly organizes that reality and constitutes its representational frame.

Lacan specifically develops the concept of *das Ding*, the Thing, in *Seminar VII* (1959 – 1960) as "the absolute Other of the subject, " which "one is supposed to find again ... as something missed" (52). Subject is caught up in an endless circle of *déjà vu* because "[o]ne doesn't find it, but only its pleasurable associations"; "It is in this state of wishing for it and waiting for it that, in the name of the pleasure principle, the optimum tension will be sought" (Lacan, *Seminar VII* 52). Thus the Thing, what Žižek terms " the non-sensical, pre-ideological kernel of enjoyment " (*Sublime* 124), is not a tangible entity but the traumatic void within the Symbolic, functioning as the phantasmal and inaccessible object of desire by drawing subject's libidinal cathexes around it. The subject is compelled to touch the Real without touching it; every encounter with the Real (*tuché*) is a missed encounter (*Seminar XI* 52). Lacan's theory points out the fundamental and ontological alienation in the formation of human subjectivity. In his revolutionary interpretation of Sophocles's tragedy *Antigone*, Lacan puts forward his ethics as " not to compromise one's desire" (*ne pas céder sur son désir*). To work through one's desire to the end, to disavow the mandate of the Symbolic and thus to objectify oneself as the Real, becomes a viable ethical choice under the incessant domestication of desire by educators and academies (Lacan, *Seminar VII* 324).

Merwin's poetry is exactly characterized by a devotional gesture apropos of the traumatic Thing and an uncompromised drive to surpass the Name-of-the-Father and its corollaries such as the system of signification, language, and intersubjective network. The poetic signifiers seem to point to a central void, a nondiscursive field in subjectivity, which manifests only

"pleasurable associations" of the Thing but not the sublime Thing-in-itself.①
In his obsessional "wishing" and "waiting" for the phantasmal object,
Merwin attempts to subjectivize the remnants and the traces of the absolute,
inaccessible Other through his poetic fantasies. The spirituality as well as
spectrality of Merwin's poetry, as I will reveal in the present study,
corresponds to the poet-speaker's infinite proximity to the posited object
rather than its direct attainment.

In order to fully describe the libidinal economy of Merwin's quest for
the hallowed object, I will employ the concept of "infinity" in post-
Heideggerian philosophy, which overlaps much with the Lacanian Real. In
Totality and Infinity: An Essay on Exteriority (1969), French philosopher
Emmanuel Levinas rewrites Martin Heidegger's being-there (*Dasein*) by
emphasizing both the corporeality and alterity of the existent. In the book
Levinas launches a war against totality by positing the "radical separation
between the same and the other," so that one can be "at home with
oneself," coiling in his solipsistic contentment and enjoyment (*Totality*
36, 37). But unlike other sentient beings such as the animals, this egoistic
existent uniquely harbors the Cartesian "idea of the Infinite" to the degree
that this idea "overflows the thought that thinks it," and infinity is nothing
but this dynamic process of "overflowing" (*Totality* 25).② Infinity is
"produced in the improbable feat whereby a separated being ... contains in
itself what it can neither contain nor receive by virtue of its own identity"
(*Totality* 27). For Levinas, the idea of infinity could be incarnated in the
absolute Other (*Autrui*), the Stranger, "who disturbs the being at home
with oneself" (*Totality* 39). Qua the exteriority of the Other, the infinite
overflows the interiority of the self, drawing the self out of itself by
bringing forth a traumatically inassimilable otherness. The cognizing self
cannot have an adequate notion of what infinity is, and this "non-
adequation," as Levinas expounds, would define infinity proper
(*Totality* 27). So far, we may have noticed that the Levinasian infinity
strongly correlates with the Lacanian Real in that both of them breach the

---

① As for the theoretical affinity between the Lacanian Thing and the Kantian sublime,
see Žižek, *Sublime* 203.

② We may note that René Descartes's concept of "the Infinite" is derived from the
Christian concept of God, whereas Levinas's idea of infinity refers to the absolute
otherness of the Other, who is not necessarily the biblical God. The Levinasian
notion of infinity is thus more metaphysical than theological.

totality of historicized realities and both have an incarnation in a tangible entity which, being nonidentical, carries an excess of signification over itself.

For Levinas, desire is always the desire for the invisible, the infinite, and similar to Lacan, Levinas strictly differentiates desire from need that can be well satisfied. The Levinasian desire works like a metaphysical impulse that relates to the high, the noble and the good (*Totality* 34−35), as it yearns not for symbolic recognitions but for the non-understandable Stranger, the face of the Other which can be approximated but whose meaning cannot be thoroughly decoded by the self. In fact, desire and infinity can be synonymous in Levinasian discourse. "Desire ' measures' the infinity of the infinite":

> The term we have chosen to mark the propulsion, the inflation, of this going beyond is opposed to the affectivity of love and the indigence of need. Outside of the hunger one satisfies, the thirst one quenches and the senses one allays, exists the other, absolutely other, desired beyond these satisfactions, when the body knows no gesture to slake the desire, where it is not possible to invent any new caress. This desire is unquenchable, not because it answers to an infinite hunger, but because it does not call for food. This desire without satisfaction hence takes cognizance of the alterity of the other. It situates it in the dimension of height and of the ideal, which it opens up in being. (Levinas, *Collected* 56)

Levinas therefore shares with Lacan a similar formulation of desire as desire without satisfaction: human desire can be pictured as encircling around the sublime height, the ideal, or the Lacanian Thing, the last of which is " sublime " too in that it functions as the inaccessible object of representation. The dynamism of *propulsion* and *inflation* indicates the restless movements of desire / drive in an organism, [①] as the form of desire could hardly hold its content — desire always overflows and de-centers itself. In this philosophical and psychoanalytical framework, the essence of desire / drive consists in a dynamic process of "going beyond" of the self toward the infinite Other that passes through the finite and leaves traces of

---

① Lacan translated Freud's *Trieb* (drive) as *pulsion* (*Seminar XI* 162), which comes very close to Levinas's "propulsion." The Latin root *pellere* means "to drive forward" (*Webster's*).

its withdrawal.①

What characterizes Merwin's corpus then is this symptomatic propulsion and its trace of withdrawal; Merwin's works seem to aspire for a non-categorizable Other that is ex-timate to the subject — both inside and outside it.② After reading a Merwin poem, readers may find that it has actually said nothing substantial but left a haunting sense of absent traces ringing in their ears, or, to use Charles Molesworth's words, Merwin's works "achieve a kind of exhaustion and fullness by pointing on to some yet greater emptiness" (150). Harold Bloom complains that Merwin's poetry is "bare of true content" (16), and Helen Vendler, reviewing Merwin's prose book *Miner's Pale Children* in 1970, advises Merwin to "eat something, anything, to cure his anemia" (233). Bloom and Vendler refuse to acknowledge that the task for poetry, however, is not to present a tangible and substantial content but to wrap up metaphysical silence in the minimal number of words, like Roland Barthes's "mode négatif" (*Le degré* 56). Robert von Hallberg considers Merwin's diction in *The Lice* as having "severely narrowed the range of the language: simple, concrete words took on new power when he refused the syntactic structures that elaborate complexity" (140). Poetry does not represent but *evokes*, and the Black Mountain poet Charles Olson would term it "kinetics" of the open form (1054). To describe the poetic process as kinetics (from Greek *kinēsis*: movement) reveals the psychological mechanism of the post-Romantic transcendence as Lacanian *pulsion* or Levinasian propulsion. Poetry carries with it a phantasmal inner force that constantly breaches itself.

Merwin's poetry resembles a reflexive apparatus of powerfully cathected echoes that imitate the ghostly circulation of desire and drive. Merwin writes in "On Open Form" (1969) that poetry comes from "an unduplicatable resonance, something that would be like an echo except that it is repeating no sound" (*RM* 299). Charles Altieri likewise perceives Merwin's poems from the 1960s as "an elaborate system of echoes" (178),

---

① Much of Levinas's later work is devoted to "glorification of the infinite" through the concepts of "trace," "proximity," and "obsession." See Emmanuel Levinas, *Otherwise than Being: Or Beyond Essence*, trans. Alphonso Lingis (Pittsburg: Duquesne University Press, 1998).

② "Ex-timate" is a neologism Lacan uses in describing the relationship between subject and object of desire, meaning "external intimacy" or "what is in the subject more than subject," "object in subject" (Lacan, *Seminar XI* 263–276; Žižek, *Sublime* 180–182).

and Laurence Lieberman says pretty much the same concerning *The Lice*: "It is as though the voice filters up to the reader like echoes from a very deep well" (qtd. in Folsom and Nelson 10). The resonant echoes, like narcissistic desires, endeavor to capture the silent vestiges left by the infinite after it passes / shoots through the finite poetic form. It might be, however, inadequate to describe Merwin's characteristics within the dialectic of absence and presence, as many Merwin critics are fond of doing.[①] Is not poetry itself a presence through absence, since it leaves so many blanks on the white paper? Is not the core of a poem a spectral presence, generating words while simultaneously resisting words, like the Lacanian Real or the Levinasian Stranger? Merwin banishes "true content" and substantial references out of his poems, because for him, poetry functions exactly by tour, retour and detour, by encircling, circumscribing, circumventing something invisible, untouchable, and non-understandable. This is not to repeat the cliché that poetry speaks something unspeakable, but to work through that unspeakability per se.

In his "On the Subject of Poetry" (1954), Merwin allegorizes the poetic process as desire of / for the Other. I quote the poem in full because it encapsulates Merwin's lifelong endeavor to understand alterity:

> I do not understand the world, Father.
> By the millpond at the end of the garden
> There is a man who slouches listening
> To the wheel revolving in the stream, only
> There is no wheel there to revolve.
>
> He sits in the end of March, but he sits also
> In the end of the garden; his hands are in
> His pockets. It is not expectation
> On which he is intent, nor yesterday

[①] The word "absence" has been used to describe Merwin from the 1970s to the present; it was first thematized by Charles Altieri. See Charles Altieri, "The Struggle with Absence: Robert Creeley and W. S. Merwin," *Enlarging the Temple: New Directions in American Poetry during the 1960s* (Lewisburg: Bucknell University Press, 1979) 170–224. (The section on Merwin was later revised and included in *W. S. Merwin: Essays on the Poetry* edited by Cary Nelson and Ed Folsom.) Also see Sean Joseph McDonnell, " I with No Voice: Absence, Presence, and Intersubjectivity in the Poetry of W. S. Merwin," diss., University of California, Davis, 2003.

To which he listens. It is a wheel turning.

When I speak, Father, it is the world
That I must mention. He does not move
His feet nor so much as raise his head
For fear he should disturb the sound he hears
Like a pain without a cry, where he listens.

I do not think I am fond, Father,
Of the way in which always before he listens
He prepares himself by listening. It is
Unequal, Father, like the reason
For which the wheel turns, though there is no wheel.

I speak of him, Father, because he is
There with his hands in his pockets, in the end
Of the garden listening to the turning
Wheel that is not there, but it is the world,
Father, that I do not understand. (*FF* 109)

This poem from Merwin's early phase serves as an entrance into the labyrinth of the poet's longtime hysteria in relation to the inherent otherness of world and reality. The dialectic of desire is laid out on several levels. First, the concept of "the world," qua the infinite Other on a metaphysical level, forever eludes the grasp of the Cartesian cogito of the speaker. In many of his poems, Merwin has been consistently confessing a kind of Socratic ignorance in the face of external reality, or, as he said in a 1981 interview, "humility before phenomenal things" (*RM* 336). His poetics is that of "not knowing" (unconscious): "I think a real poem comes out of what you don't know. You write it with what you know, but finally its source is what you don't know" (*RM* 335). The essence of the phenomenal world is infinitely withdrawn from the poet's perspective, and what poetry can do is capture the traces of the fleeting alterity. Poetry "must mention" the "world" it fails to *understand* (to withstand and withhold), to *com*prehend or en*com*pass, because poetry is nothing but this roundabout astonishment before the order of things. Second, the "man" in the poem, the mirrored other, is a "psychotic" poet par excellence. He excessively ponders on the turning of a nonexistent / phantasmal wheel that functions as the Lacanian Thing by organizing his and Merwin's libidinal economy of observation, which is realized in the poem as the cathected movement of words without definite references. Lastly, the speaker can be seen as entering into a transferential relationship with the "Father," acting out his symptomatic confusion before this enigmatic Other. The whole poem thus can be read as a staging of an anxiously repetitious confession of a guilty ego before an omniscient God-Other. It presents no solid content but a dreamlike movement of desire around an invisible kernel.

In *A History of Modern Poetry: Modernism and After* (1987), David Perkins subsumes Merwin, together with Robert Bly, James Wright, Galway Kinnell, and Gary Snyder, under the chapter title "Against Civilization," admitting that "[Merwin] is included in this chapter partly because he would be less appropriate in any other" (556). Perkins's reluctance reveals that Merwin's style is largely *sui generis*. Early Merwin was more vague than Wright and Bly and more ultra-phenomenal, more "apocalyptically fantastic" (Zhang 713), although all of them were heavily influenced by European surrealism. Perkins comments that after 1970 the "haunting cadences" of Merwin continued into "quasi-philosophical lyrics of a vague, musing, moody description" (582). Although sharing the same melancholic moodiness with Bly and Wright in many of his poems, Merwin's personae are nevertheless more disoriented and more anonymous. According to Christopher Beach, among the Deep Imagists, Merwin comes closer to Mark Strand and Charles Simic, both of whom work toward a "surrealist mode," while Bly, Wright, Kinnell, and Snyder remain committed to a "realist or descriptive aesthetic" (179−180). Simplistic as it is, Beach's classification at least pulls Merwin away from the "descriptive aesthetic" for the Merwinesque elusiveness — that "harvest pallor" (*SF* 103).

Due to the influences of European surrealism and Asian Zen poetry, Merwin distrusts and therefore tries to avoid conscious control over the poetic process. He aims at the free play of creative forces without claiming any aim, achieving a sort of Kantian purposefulness without purpose. Merwin's poems are therefore not a conglomerate of related or disparate details, like the imagistic / objectivistic works since Ezra Pound and W. C. Williams, but an animated, haunting movement of "naked" words that strives for the infinite realm. Details in "On the Subject of Poetry" contain such nonidentity that the readers are tempted to ask: What is the relationship between the man listening to the "wheel" and the "world" that the speaker tries in vain to understand but "must mention"? The conjunctions ("but," "because") fail to function on the semantic level, appearing fortuitous and nonsensical, as they confusingly explode the infinite distances between self and Other, poetry and world. Other textual details of the poem also fail to give readers substantial information concerning the topoi of self and world; instead, they weave out an enigma in their incessant *versus*: turning, returning, circumscribing, and circumventing.

Merwin's sustained inner urgency, his dreamlike encounter with psychic realities, and his quest for the traces of the Other have already drawn full critical attentions. In *Poetry as Labor and Privilege: The Writings of W. S. Merwin* (1991), Edward Brunner comes several times to the theme of desire and infinity in Merwin's works; commenting on Merwin's early poems of the bestiary, he says, "To delight in its mystery is a strength Merwin associates with describing creatures that escape his understanding. Even as it sets a limit to our knowledge, it compels us to imagine its infinity" (*Poetry* 44). To read Merwin from the sole perspective of mythology, as Mark Christhilf does in *W. S. Merwin the Mythmaker*, is to neglect the deeper psychological and philosophical suppositions underlining Merwin's project, who stages the myth of origin in such an obsessional manner that invites both a Lacanian and a Levinasian reading. The unknown dimension of the world at once magnetizes, energizes, and paralyzes Merwin. As we shall see in this book, this circulation concerning infinity in fact corresponds to a pathological compulsion mixed with anxiety, disorientation, and even horror rather than pure delight. Brunner continues to say, "[The sea poems] reveal that we are all brushed by the unknown and that we all guard ourselves against a direct encounter with it by rehearsing details that deflect our attention" (*Poetry* 63). The necessary guarding, deflecting, and rehearsing before the Real initiate the dialectical circulations of desire that manifest by tour, retour, and detour of poetic energy. In the epilogue of the book Brunner theorizes that Merwin actually interacts with two worlds: the "orderly" world of institution and its opposite, "which cannot have a single name, which unfolds equidistantly through time and space and seems riddled with exceptions" (*Poetry* 287). For Merwin, the second world might be taken as an infinite One, since it has not been defined / confined by human language and intention: it is *exceptional*.

If early Merwin criticisms revolved upon deconstructive stylistics (absence, silence, alienation, disembodied voice, etc.), ① myth and mythology, apocalyptic vision, Heideggerian disclosure, ② and Merwin's ambivalent relation with the United States, ③ recent studies have recognized Merwin as an early pioneer of ecopoetry. Much of the ecocriticism on Merwin appeared in the late 1990s. While keeping an eye on *The Lice* (1967), *The Carrier of Ladders* (1970), and *Writings to an Unfinished Accompaniment* (1973), in which environmental concern lurks behind a fragmented syntax, ecocritics mainly focus on Merwin's works after he moved to Hawaii in the late 1970s: *The Compass Flower* (1977), *The Rain in the Trees* (1988), *Travels* (1993), and *The Vixen* (1996), in which Merwin writes luxuriously about fauna and flora, pleading for the ultimate infinity of nature.

For example, in *From Origin to Ecology: Nature and the Poetry of W. S. Merwin* (1999), Jane Frazier identifies Merwin's experimentation of free verse in 1963 with his first ecological "awakening": "As a result and as a reason for this move to freer form, Merwin has discovered a poetic place for himself — the wandering, alienated poet of the modern age has found a 'home' within the ecosystem and a tangible entity whose cause he can espouse for global betterment" (15). Whether Merwin, the "alienated poet of the modern age," really found a "home" in this ecosystem or whether this "home" is an imaginary construction is still open to question. According to Sean Joseph McDonnell, Merwin might have turned to nature in order to "escape the narcissistic / omnipotent position that has dominated his work" (7). Nature writing embodies an attempt to break what Levinas calls the "coiling of self," to reach out to the infinite Other that cannot be reduced to any homogeneity. In a book published in the same year, *Sustainable Poetry: Four American Ecopoets* (1999), Leonard Scigaj considers Merwin's final settlement in Maui, Hawaii, as the "event" leading to Merwin's "new environmental esthetic" (178). The author painstakingly narrates Merwin's deep involvements in Hawaiian history and its ecosystem in texts such as *The Rain in the Trees*, *Travels*, and *The Vixen*, arguing

---

① The most conspicuous are Altieri 159–197; Lieberman 96–105; Nelson 78–121; Byers, *What I Cannot Say* 79–110.

② For instance, see Altieri 159–197; Hoeppner, "A Nest of Bones" 262–284.

③ See Folsom, "Strange Country" 224–249. The essay presents Merwin's criticism of American expansionism and his endorsement of Thoreauvian humility before the natural world.

that Merwin's poetic language "refreshes the essential relation of human consciousness to the other of nature" (Scigaj 182). Reading Merwin in the double lines of Martin Heidegger's philosophy of language and Maurice Merleau-Ponty's phenomenology of perception, Scigaj seeks to locate Merwin's ecologism within the dialectics of words and things, separation and identification, body and world. Scigaj opposes Charles Altieri's "poetics of absence" (and also Marjorie Perloff's "antireferential" stance) by developing a poetics of what he calls "*référance*" (35 −81). Scigaj's phenomenological-historicist reading of Merwin's later works, however, leaves uninvestigated Merwin's psychic fantasies in those historical narratives.

Other ecocriticism of Merwin includes Carl Clifton Toliver's "W. S. Merwin and the Postmodern Environment" (dissertation, University of Texas, Austin, 1997); Jeanie S. Dean's "Re-seeding the Burnt Wasteland: W. S. Merwin's *The Rain in the Trees*" in *Passions of the Earth in Human Existence, Creativity, and Literature* edited by Anna-Teresa Tymieniecka (2001); and J. Scott Bryson's "Between the Earth and Silence" in *The West Side of Any Mountain: Place, Space, and Ecopoetry* (2005). These studies accentuate Merwin's critique of anthropocentrism, his humility before what is "other-than-human beings" (Toliver 3), his "concern about the destruction of nature" (Dean 81), and his depiction of "the world as a community founded on reciprocity between human and nonhuman nature" (Bryson 100). Plausible as they are, these comments reflect a constant misconception of ecocriticism to prioritize an impossible balance between nature and man, ecology and social development. Timothy Morton's provocative book, *Ecology without Nature: Rethinking Environmental Aesthetics* (2007), punctures this fantasy by pointing out that "[e]cological forms of subjectivity inevitably involve ideas and decisions about group identity and behavior" (17). Man could not possibly confer on "other-than-human beings" (animals, plants, organisms) the equal ontic status of man's because this very gesture of conferring already betrays a human interest / priority. That the ecological subjects form anthropic institutions and groups to fight enthusiastically for rights of animals and plants discloses the fundamental ideological fantasy of man's omnipotence: the earth *needs* us to protect her. Ecocriticism starts subverting anthropocentrism but ends perpetuating it. Following the critique of Timothy Morton, Žižek detonates the inner contradiction of ecological identification: "[T]he paradox of Deep Ecology is that, in its very rejection of anthropocentrism, it charges man with the duty of subordinating the narrow interests of the human species to the interests of all other forms of life and the entire biosphere" (*Reader* 304). Submitting to the higher / holy order of ecologism becomes another version of the quest for the Holy Grail, for a self-posited alterity before whom the subject acts out his unconscious desire.

Reading Merwin's later works as the desire for a more balanced ecosystem, ecocriticism actually weakens Merwin's deconstructive potential in those nature poems. These texts deserve a more reflective as well as speculative treatment than mere ecocriticism. Merwin's infatuation with waters, trees, and animals in *The Compass Flower*, *The Rain in the Trees*, *Travels*, and *The Vixen* evinces a fixation of libido that, as Freud concludes in numerous case studies, has its source in the infantile experience. According to Freud, the unsatisfied and unsublimated libido would regress to "early phases of the organization and of the finding of objects" (*Introductory* 346). What Merwin yearns for in his nature poems are the lost love objects that are not really lost but function as "the return of the repressed" — the desire for the inaccessible Other. Through an almost neurotic repetition of the gestures of waiting, searching, turning, and returning, Merwin has staged what Roland Barthes felicitously calls "appearance-as-disappearance" (*Pleasure* 10). For Merwin, nature as the object / Other is categorically heterogeneous; every meeting with her is also a non-meeting, an encounter that comprises separation. Nature contains in herself a radical alterity that violently refuses "reciprocity between human and nonhuman nature," as J. Scott Bryson and other good-intentioned ecocritics have failed or hesitated to admit.

What Merwin does in his nature poems, as I will argue in Chapter 3, both confirms and subverts ecologism by positing nature as the Master Signifier, "the quilting point" of other floating signifiers and memory traces.① Nature provides a matrix for Merwin to act out his unconscious desire for the "absolute Other" (Lacan, *Seminar VII* 52). Whereas P. B. Shelley conceives of soaring skylarks and wandering clouds as his own imago, Merwin finds in nature the ever-receding vestiges of what is other than self / ego. Merwin seldom describes nature without repetitively resorting to an impersonal origin where his libidinal fixation would seek its

---

① "Quilting point" (*point de capiton*) is the term Lacan uses to refer to the stopping point in the slide of the signified, the point "at which the signified and the signifier are knotted together" (*Seminar III* 268).

optimum satisfaction. In this sense, Merwin has pushed ecologism to an impossible extreme by eroticizing nature as the alien love object "caught in the throat" of the subject. For Merwin, nature becomes both the stage and protagonist of semi-sexual fantasies in which the self's obsessional devotions to the infinite are fully unleashed.

Theoretically, the extant ecocriticism of Merwin overlooks the critiques and reformulations of existential humanism from such thinkers as Jacques Derrida and Gilles Deleuze, who regard structural difference, not group identification, as constitutive of subjectivity, [1] and also Emmanuel Levinas, who indefatigably elicits the non-reciprocity and non-thematizability of the infinite Other. Merwin's encounter with the powerful water image during his infanthood, as this study will reveal, constitutes the first psychic event and becomes the nodal point to which he would constantly return. His early fascination with fluidity, amorphousness, and phantasmagoria would develop into a sustained urge to break through the socio-symbolic order toward the non-thematizable / non-subjectivizable Other — nature qua anonymous exteriority. The manifest spiritual aura in Merwin's nature poems consists exactly in this poetic excess that goes beyond the limitations of one's biological life and one's *jouissance*.

My discussion on Merwin's desire for the infinite largely follows a chronological order, together with Merwin's evolving sense of poetry as a vehicle of desire and drive. The first chapter of this book presents an analysis of Merwin's early texts with an emphasis on the sea poems and animal poems within a Freudian-Lacanian framework. In *A Mask for Janus* (1952) and *The Dancing Bears* (1954), Merwin frequently assumes a psychotic ballad-tone that informs a libidinal urge to transgress the limitations of the Symbolic. The pathological symptoms continue in *Green with Beasts* (1956) and *The Drunk in the Furnace* (1960), in which Merwin records his entry into the traumatic core of the Symbolic: the Lacanian Real. Merwin's imagination is largely directed toward the Other,

---

① For example, Derrida develops the concept of *différance* to refer to both the intrinsic difference and deferral in the formation of meaning, demoting the "center" of traditional metaphysics to "a sort of nonlocus in which an infinite number of sign-substitutions came into play" (*Writing* 353 – 354). Deleuze proposes ontological "internal difference" which "relate[s] different to different without any mediation whatsoever by the identical, the similar, the analogous or the opposed" (qtd. in Smith 51).

which is horribly fascinating. The sea monsters Merwin evokes incarnate the object-cause of desire: a massive, direful, and spectral presence outside the socio-historical order. The domestic animals that Merwin portrays — dogs, rams, goats, horses, cockerels, etc. — all share the same characteristic of inscrutability and symbolize what precedes and escapes human utterance.

The second chapter goes on to explore the substitution of the anonymous Other for the Judeo-Christian Other in Merwin's early and middle periods. Abandoning the univocal salvation theme in Christian theology after the onset of the Vietnam War, Merwin has come to envision redemption in a vast, anonymous wilderness. The urge of apocalypse paves the way for new existential and ethical grounds outside the existing social order. The poet's spirit disavows the Symbolic for an exodus into the ultra-phenomenal. This spirit is not only Hegelian / negative but also Levinasian / alternative; foreclosing the existing social order, it attempts to open a new dimension in the interval between humanity and divinity. Although the dark, sparse poems of Merwin in the 1960s were partly the products of the historical process, what Merwin sought then was an alterity beyond historicity. Merwin's poems of the 1960s also attest to a decisive change in style and voice; he now strengthened the anti-rhetorical, anti-ornamental strain that had been only latent in his earlier work. The elliptical style disrupts the smooth functioning of language, revealing Merwin's anxious desire to capture the object of divinity that eludes Judeo-Christian thematization.

The third chapter treats Merwin's transformation from severity to corporeality in *The Compass Flower* (1977) and *The Rain in the Trees* (1988), both of which witness Merwin's immersion in the life-world as a being of enjoyment. Blending the sensual, the natural, and the spiritual, Merwin's love poetry successfully conjures up what Lacan terms the "Other *jouissance*" in order to circumscribe the paternal function and its limitation of the loving subject. This chapter traces Merwin's erotic mode back to *The Dancing Bears* (1954) and then reads its full outburst in *The Compass Flower* and *Finding the Islands* (1982) in light of psychoanalytical and philosophical formulations of alterity. Merwin's love poetry follows the tradition of the troubadours in the Middle Ages in its conventional portrait of the female Other as elusive and enigmatic. In the fantasy of love, the male speaker seems able to enjoy union with the beloved woman, although in most cases she appears distant and heterogeneous, sublimated as the Lacanian object or the Levinasian Stranger. Merwin's later works are

Introduction

19

increasingly characterized by the problematic combination of nature and Eros and the subsequent eroticization of flora in *The Rain in the Trees* (1988) and *Travels* (1993): the poet fantasizes about nature and women, confusing them so as to diffuse Eros into infinite cosmos. In a counter-ecological reading, Merwin's love / nature poetry is revealed as a testimony of the structural difference or non-adequation between man and nature rather than their harmonious co-existence.

The last chapter examines the recurrent and polysemic image of the sunlight and its underside darkness in Merwin's later writings such as *Opening the Hands* (1983), *The Rain in the Trees*, *The Vixen* (1996), *Present Company* (2005), and *The Shadow of Sirius* (2008). Sunlight represents the transient object that prompts Merwin to contemplate time, origin, grief, and death. Merwin's father-complex, as I will argue, plays a crucial role in the formation of sunlight imagery in his recent poetry, as the sun, according to Freud's study on psychosis, symbolizes paternal authority. Largely foreclosing the Lacanian Name-of-the-Father in search of fluid and infinite realizations, Merwin has incurred a strong sense of guilt through the years, which finally erupts into a poetry of endless mourning after his father's death. To overcome grief, Merwin evokes ancestral origins and memory traces from childhood; his yearning for anonymous origins to surpass the paternal function summarizes his lifelong pursuit of the infinite Other outside the socio-symbolic order.

Chapter 1

"All the Uncovenanted Terror of Becoming": Merwin's Early Encounter with the Real

From the very beginning of his poetic career Merwin was obsessed with what W. B. Yeats calls the "horrible splendour of desire" (1928: 196). In *A Mask for Janus* (1952) and *The Dancing Bears* (1954) we witness Merwin's struggle with the fixed poetic form in order to articulate, as well as imitate, the truth and movement of desire. In *Green with Beasts* (1956) and *The Drunk in the Furnace* (1960), however, we wonder at Merwin's close-up delineations of the objects of desire, the biblical and domestic animals that simultaneously embody and resist human signification, the foghorn and iceberg that warn sailors of the imminent danger and fascinate them by its false look. One conspicuous feature of these early texts is the lack of specific reference to outer socio-historical facts, as if Merwin, being concerned with the landscapes of human mind, were writing completely from his intricate psyche, where reality and fantasy intermix. Merwin's traveling poems during this period therefore do not give the impression of a certain locale but register a diffused allegorical purport. The sailings, long and short, resemble the Odyssean journey loaded with temptations and hardships, and the sea poems evoke the traumatic unrealness of the kernel of the Symbolic, an all-engulfing void. Merwin the eternal traveler of mind went into the heart of wilderness and was saved there by some mysterious power testified by faith alone: "For from the very hunger to look, we feed / Unawares, as at the beaks of ravens" (*FF* 156). Many of Merwin's poems from the first three books share the Dantean trilogy of *Inferno*, *Purgatorio*, and *Paradiso*; like the biblical Job, Merwin's speaker must go through the maddening ordeal of symbolic death before he can see the light of Providence and be thus redeemed or reborn.

While Sean Joseph McDonnell sees the tension between "a rejection of the social realm and a need for the kind of stability society may offer" as the motif of Merwin's first three books (9), I would argue that the "stability" Merwin finds in the 1950s does not reside in "society" or community, but in fluidity and transgression, which have been deeply implanted in Merwin since childhood. Merwin was at home when he was largely out of home; his métier lies exactly in portraying the inner- and ultra-phenomena before which the subject is magnetized and paralyzed. These early texts present a developing pattern from high-toned, half-mad ballads to calmer meditations on desire and disaster, language and signification. Merwin dallies with an impossible combination of delicacy and violence, probing psychic realities that escape the existent socio-historical order.

The first cleavage and its concussions

To start with, I will present a biographical reading in order to sketch out the constitutive elements of Merwin's early mythic style, which has been elaborated upon by critics.[①] Indeed, Merwin's curiosity for the phenomenal world and his desire to explore the distant and the transcendent can be traced back to his early childhood. Growing up in a Presbyterian minister's family with a reticent mother and a "prohibitive" father, Merwin in his early years assumed a bohemian and rebellious posture, less fiery than Arthur Rimbaud perhaps but equally conspicuous (Merwin was later to write "Rimbaud's Piano" to show his sympathy[②]). Merwin was born in 1927, when the family lived in Union City, New Jersey, where the Hudson River was busy with traffic. While his father wrote his sermons in his study, Merwin the small boy "knelt on the blue velvet cushion on the window seat,

---

① For example, see Mark Christhilf, *W. S. Merwin the Mythmaker* (Columbia, MO: University of Missouri Press, 1986).

② In "Rimbaud's Piano," a poem in *Travels* (1993), Merwin narrates Rimbaud's youth rebellion against home and his "penniless" wanderings in Europe (*T* 17), which reflect Merwin's own experiences in his twenties.

gazing out through the leaded panes, or through the open casements ...
watching the river, without a word, utterly rapt in the vast scene in front of
[him]": the vast scene of roaring trains, busy ferries, "puffs of steam,"
"whistles and horns," "the distant sounds," and as a child he "was seeing
something that [he] could not reach and that would never go away" (*SD* 28).
Merwin in his childhood was thus seduced by the fleeting image of water
and what it symbolizes: immersion and fluidity. In spite of, or rather
because of, his parents' severe warning, Merwin was tempted to get close
to the spellbinding water, the symbol of flux, fluidity, travels, and
phantasmagoria. At the age of fourteen, Merwin strategically researched the
public library of Scranton, Pennsylvania, and built his first boat with his
ten-cents-a-week allowance, naming it "Zephyr" (*SD* 30−33).

Merwin's libidinal attachment to fluidity in early childhood persists into
his young adulthood, only in a slightly varied form. Setting Rimbaud and
Shelley as his ideal ego, the imaginary other he attempts to identify with,
Merwin in college adopted the posture of the wandering artist, occupying
himself with random reading, sailing and horse-riding. His nonconformist
behavior had incurred bad feelings from some of the faculty at Princeton, as
he later admitted, "I read far outside the assignments themselves, and often
on wild tangents, forgetting the assignments themselves. ... I must have
been exasperating to most of my professors" (*SD* 36). Merwin reminisces
that some of the Princeton faculty could not tolerate his Thoreauvian
disobedience and wanted to dismiss him when he was "busy being Shelley"
(*RM* 190). Merwin stayed at Princeton, however, largely due to the efforts
of his mentor, Richard Blackmur, who appreciated his talent and
irregularity. Blackmur himself was exemplary of a bohemian artist: a self-
made critic who did not have a degree and whose presence at Princeton was
suspected by his colleagues. Indeed, Blackmur held "an ethic of fierce
devotion to an art in a philistine society" (*RM* 190) and defined, much to
Merwin's own exhilaration, the basic characteristic of a critic and a reader
as a "house waiting to be haunted" (*SD* 45). This *fierce* and *haunting* sense
of art and poetry is perhaps what influenced Merwin most in subsequent
years.

If Blackmur struck Merwin as a paradigm of the wandering scholar,
the confessional poet John Berryman, Blackmur's assistant at the time,
came to influence Merwin for his highly emotive use of poetry. Berryman
worked like a poetic mentor for Merwin at Princeton, constantly offering
him "a cluster of new names in [his] head to be tracked down" and

spurring him to "find the fire in them," as Merwin later assimilated much of Berryman's own "intense, unremitting, and fierce" poetic language into his first book of poems, *A Mask for Janus* (*SD* 45). Berryman's unconditional devotion to poetry also stunned young Merwin: for him, poetry was "a matter of life and death" and he "cared about it more than he did about anyone's ego, including his own" (*SD* 44). In a belated poem to Berryman from the 1980s, Merwin celebrates his credo of passion:

> He said the great presence
> That permitted everything and transmuted it
> In poetry was passion
> Passion was genius (*FH* 156)

Passion, derived from the Latin *passio*, first means divine suffering, and secondly it denotes an ecstatic libidinal fixation on an object. Passion by definition is a combination of pleasure and pain. For Berryman and Merwin, passion enters poetry as the highly cathected movement of words; the poetical activity is initiated and sustained by passion — an inner urgency that dictates what is to be written. The transformative power of poetry does not come from deliberate design of the poetic form (e.g., irony, tension, balance, rhythm, as New Criticism emphasized), but from a sustaining and haunting undercurrent of desire for incantations, invocations, and enchantments. Berryman's own work *The Dream Songs* (1969) bears it out, whereas in Merwin, the "great presence" of "passion" takes a more devious and spectral path.

Merwin's spiritual growth in early years clearly follows a centrifugal pattern: things he came into contact with broadened his mind and strengthened his devotion to art and poetry, until he could no longer endure the symbolic restrictions from family and institution. In 1948, at the age of twenty-one, Merwin quit his graduate study in Romance language at Princeton and sailed for Europe with an utterly unknown future, with his "youth and inexperience" and a "vertiginous sensation" due to "complete lack of money" (*SD* 3). Like most idealistic young poets influenced by Shelleyan Romanticism, in his early twenties Merwin avowed that "I did not know what I would do for a living, and even more strangely I took it for granted that I would not know, for a while" (*RM* 194–195). Sailing for a new world seems all that matters. The first breach of one's socio-symbolic framework proves permanent, and all Merwin's later works would endlessly rehearse that first act of de-cision, of cutting off from that which preexists the individual.

The desire for fluidity, bohemianism, and poetic passion (suffering) suffuses many of Merwin's early works, which exhibit a strong urge to break off the socio-familial relationship and reach into the domain of contingency and pure ecstasy / *ekstasis*. From *A Mask for Janus* to *The Drunk in the Furnace*, despite their conspicuous formalism, Merwin constantly resorts to the emotive, irregular, and pathological trends in poetry. The efforts are impersonated in some half-insane figures as Merwin dramatizes the traumatic calling of the Other in the vein of Keats's "La Belle Dame sans Merci" and Tennyson's "The Lady of Shalott." In "Ballad of John Cable and Three Gentlemen, " the first ballad in *A Mask for Janus*, the protagonist John, spellbound by some vague calling, came all the way to "a gray river / Wide as the sea" and received an anti-Althusserian interpellation from the mysterious Other incarnated in " three dark gentlemen" who were already waiting for him (*FF* 18). The three men invited John to board the boat, but John hesitated out of consideration for his sister, wife, and mother, to whom his familial duty was bound. Under the devilish persuasion that his service to family is not indispensable and his departure not insufferable, John was finally "carried / On the dark river; / Not even a shadow / Followed him over. // On the wide river / Gray as the sea / Flags of white water / Are his company" (*FF* 21). Abandoning his family, John, similar to John the Baptist, was baptized by the magic water that had completely erased his personal history. Mark Christhilf reads the ballad as the destined calling of an artist: "[T]he gentlemen represent the Muse, for they want Cable to accompany them to a place that is clearly Byzantium" (4). This Yeatsian, symbolic reading, however, overlooks the biographical allusion to Merwin's grandfather John Otto, who had worked on the Allegheny River as a pilot for years, and his family could hardly understand this irregular profession (Hix, *Understanding* 109). This is perhaps why the three gentlemen in the poem exhorted John Cable to "follow the feet ... / Of your family, / Of your old father / That came already this way" (*FF* 18).

Though the temptation is strong to read John's unreasonable departure as the physical, real death that his paternal ancestors had all succumbed to, the ballad lays bare another type of death: the symbolic death that places the subject in the limbo between the living and the dead — what Slavoj Žižek calls "the undead" (*Reader* 279). Cutting off his ties with fellow humans, John the Prodigal Son enters the "far side" without a "shadow" (*FF* 21), exactly going through the "subjective destitution" formulated by

Lacanian psychoanalysis.[①] John, if not dead, becomes a living ghost, "the ash that walk[s]" ("Blind William's Song," *FF* 24), a subject without corporeality in a posthuman landscape of the "gray" river and "white water" (*FF* 21). The three gentlemen, in contradistinction to T. S. Eliot's three magi heralding the birth of Christ, represent the Mephistophelean Other who brings destruction to one's personal past qua a consistent story. They seem to uncannily possess that omniscient knowledge of the subject's (John Cable's) desire but stand in utter mystery themselves, refusing to be known. The whole poem thus stages John's / Merwin's desire to break away from the tender fetters of family ties by a violent separation toward an unknown future.

John did not struggle so much with Devil's temptation as with himself, with his own imagined, paranoiac socio-symbolic status. Moonstruck by an unnamable urge to welcome this Other who came over "seven hills" and "the last tree" (*FF* 18), John suddenly realized that his role-playing in the family was but a pure fantasy, which he later traversed by deciding to leave "his poorly mother," "his wife at grieving" and "his sister's fallow" (*FF* 21). This is John's psychic one-man war. In this reading, John Cable could be readily identified with one of the three gentlemen, just as Doctor Faust is already part of Mephistopheles. Shedding one's paranoiac fantasy of a stable, fully constituted self, the mythic "dark river" that John felt drawn to works as the object of man's unsatisfiable desire for, not the Beckettian, absent Other, but the Goethean, devilish Other — the "guide in the journey toward the mythic consciousness," as said by one commentator (Guy 420).

This poem is highly autobiographical in that Merwin himself has come to be the Prodigal Son who left his family for an utterly unknown future and who, as Rainer Maria Rilke says, "was learning to love, learning so laboriously and with so much pain" (113). In order to grow into a bohemian bard like Rimbaud and Baudelaire, Merwin could do no better than renounce the city of his birth, New York, as "Ruin / My city," and proclaim, "I would never have thought I would be born here" (*SF* 52). Contrary to Whitman who, in Ed Folsom's reading, embodies "the absorptive and appropriating American attitude," Merwin holds a more critical attitude toward "things American" (231). Unlike Whitman, Merwin incorporates radical self-alienation into the construction of his own identity, but the effect of "breaking up" with the U.S. and all its symbolic ties proves

---

① For an elaboration on "subjective destitution," see Žižek, *Metastases* 167–172.

definitely double: it enables the poet to explore the exotic while permanently altering his consciousness of what home is. While Merwin exhibits a strong sense of wandering and the resultant yearning for home, home itself has became more and more abstract, fictive, and even metaphysical. In 1958, Merwin wrote in the essay "Flight Home" about what he felt when he first came back to the States after seven years in Europe: "[T]he first shock of maturity: a realization that home, where you grew up and belonged — belonged with and without your own volition — no longer exists" (*RM* 179). What Merwin returned to each time was not his physical home, his origin, or ancestors, which he thought were already lost, but this symptomatic act of returning itself. It is exactly because home and origins were lost in the first place that Merwin feels compelled to evoke them again and again in his writings. Edward Brunner, who is among the most sympathetic critics of Merwin, likewise observes that "[t]he only genuine home is this aura of homelessness within which we live" (*Poetry* 65).

Despite similar motivations, this scenario should not be reduced to another version of "on the road, " of the restless rebellion of the U.S. youth during the 1960s, as if traveling away were panacea for all personal and social ills. The compulsion to split away, to leave, to travel elsewhere like troubadours in the Middle Ages, has a more ontological and constitutive significance for Merwin as well as for the modernists like T. S. Eliot and Ezra Pound. Apart from the desire to experience exotic landscapes and cultures, poets, compared with others, have a more astute awareness of the abyss of subjectivity, the void lying at the heart of human endeavor. All their works are an attempt to give a voice to the otherwise mute emptiness qua the Real, a visible contour to the chimera of human desire that hides in the network of language.

In "The Prodigal Son, " Merwin details the traumatic event, or the "primal scene" in Freudian terms, of the son's home-leaving in a haunting and somewhat psychotic vision. The poem begins with an observation on the semblance / emptiness of time and space:

> ... the semblance of afternoon
> Was all the surface that shimmered there, even
> The dust shining and hanging still, the dusty
> Carob trees and olives gleaming, all hung
> Untouchable and perfect, as in its own
> Mirage. (*FF* 158)

The luminous setting corresponds, not to Heidegger's disclosure of being (*Being* 171), but to a peculiar psychic state when the subject has crossed over the border of signification to confront the heart of the nonmeaningful. Under the quiet, shiny surface of things lies a death of all signifieds: "And between / There and the ruled shade of this white wall / There is nothing" (*FF* 158). The tabula rasa of the world qua the embedded Real is the emptiness of ego suffered by a mourning subject. In "Mourning and Melancholia" (1917), Freud asserts that "[m]ourning is commonly the reaction to the loss of a beloved person," and while "people are reluctant to abandon a libido position," they keep "holding on to the object through a hallucinatory wish-psychosis" (*Reader* 310 – 311). "Follow[ing] / The departing image of a son beyond / Distance into emptiness" (*FF* 159), the old man in the poem has unknowingly replaced the loss of the love object with the loss of the world itself, which procedure would engender endless hallucinations:

> For emptiness is lord of his hollow house,
> Sits at his side at table, devouring,
> Shows him from room to room, for all faces
> Of loss ... (*FF* 160)

Under such unbearable lightness of nonbeing, the father suffers severely perceptual disorders — he simply projects inner loss to outside reality, producing symptom-formations that would alleviate anxiety. In the poem, Merwin's persona who has lost the son seems to derive traumatic *jouissance* from the very loss.

The poet's determination to get away from home and the subsequent melancholia are truly symptomatic. No matter how difficult it is to live through the cleavage, the Prodigal Son must leave for a totally unpredictable future in order to truly return to himself. The act of decision brings a traumatic ecstasy, though the resultant journey may not be a felicitous one. The son, who has severed his ties with his father and family in pursuit of some unknown otherness, in a twist of irony, suffers from that otherness himself. Unable to integrate the meanings of the radical Other, the son in the distant land curiously beholds the same hallucinatory emptiness his father at home has gone through:

> ... a mirage
> Merely in which he had no part, a strange
> Vista made of familiar pieces caught

In an odd light in a mirror, an image
Of emptiness out of a restive daydream
Gone wrong at home; unreal, if he could turn
The mirror, open his eyes. (*FF* 161)

Through this much-commented lavish play of the mirror image, ① Merwin creates an echolalic maze that destabilizes both reality and self-identity, placing his readers in the uncanny zone between homeliness and foreignness, the Symbolic and the Real.

The paradox of radical alterity is that the self can never fully absorb it, no matter how ardently one follows and approaches it. If cleavage leaves a permanent concussion in the old father's psyche, it does the same in the son's, perhaps more deeply and traumatically. The alien landscape may be delightful at first but soon turns out to be depressive and finally, horrifying. In another poem "Anabasis (I) , " the travelers left their homes and marched into a nonsite, as it were, that was both internal and external, physical and psychic, familiar and strange:

Exhausted leaves, suspended, through

The distant autumn do not fall,
Or, fallen, fired, are unconsumed,
The flame perduring, the still
Smoke eternal in the mind. (*FF* 5)

Suffering the "perduring" consumption of desire for the new world, the speaker enumerates one after another the disastrous effects of this compulsive journey:

We fled a saeculum what sick repose
But woke at morning where the fever burned
… … … … … … … … … … … …

We have half-waked to hear the minute die
And heard our minds that, waiting toward the east,
Embraced the seed and thought of day, and we
Were by the pool of dark the crouched beast. (*FF* 9—11)

In a rather Conradian stroke, the speaker travels deep into the self till meeting its alien kernel to find that we are indeed the animal of dark, uncontrollable desire — "the crouched beast, " which is manifestly modeled

----

① For instance, see Hoeppner, "Shadows and Glass" 323—330.

on the Leviathan in the Book of Revelation and Yeats's "rough beast" in "The Second Coming" (187). Such a revelation on the truth of desire is unavailable to those who stay complacently at home: "[T]he other sons asleep / With their wives in complacent dreams / Wait in emptiness and do not know / That it is emptiness, that they are waiting" (*FF* 162), for it comes only as the reward to the displaced explorer who "became / The eyes of sleep that chased receding fires / Through the bodiless exile of a dream" (*FF* 11). Instead of repeating the Shakespearian lament that we are such stuff as dreams are made on, Merwin has radicalized the nonsensical, hysterical, and dreamlike devotion of the self to what remains forever other and unknown.

Although chasing the receding fires would leave a subject burnt out, a subject of debris and ashes — "the still / Smoke eternal in the mind" (*FF* 5) — Merwin's speaker in the 1950s seems implausibly undaunted since the first cleavage has become an irrevocable fact. In a post-Romantic manner, the poet-speaker, sick as he often is in these early volumes, attempts to give full leash to his desire for the unknown, wading through the weariness of both body and mind towards a supposedly brave new world. At the end of "Anabasis (II)," the speaker declares triumphantly, "In fear of the swift bird that shouts and sees / In these tides and dark entrails the curled / Augurs of unreasonable seas / We seek a new dimension for the world" (*FF* 11). No one can accomplish these journeys without seriously scathing himself since these anabases embody the terrible, posthumous death-drive itself that insists on the impossibility of its own satisfaction. Nausea and ecstasy surely follow those who dare to explore and confront the alien, objective world.

Welcome to the sea of the Real

Merwin's early poetry, as Charles Molesworth and a number of other critics have noticed, clearly follows "the structures of quest-romance" (145) that postulate the transcendence of truth and subjectivity. Escaping the restrictive socio-symbolic order through both land journeys and sea voyages, Merwin's early work seeks to evoke a series of phantoms with a mixture of joy and terror, yearning and avoidance. The sea, as the reservoir of uncanny simulacra and *déjà vu* — "it harbors monsters in its depth" as exclaimed by Cheri Davis (64) — opens up dimensions of the unknown which disrupts the continuum of normally perceived time and space. Commenting on the sea poems of Merwin, Brunner points out that "the poems center on moments when we are confronted with extraordinary situations, when disorientation is the norm" (*Poetry* 54). The "extraordinary situations" Brunner wonders at are in fact both outward realities and the poet's own projection. The things and beasts Merwin evokes carry such multiple allusions that any univocal interpretation would seem restrictive. Merging familiarity and otherworldliness, vulnerability and violence, detour and exigency, Merwin in his traveling poems creates a horribly fantastic situation in which the inhuman Thing will repeatedly capture the subject's desire. As said by Cheri Davis, again, "Navigating deep into the psyche, Merwin finds a place full of horror" (66).

The new dimension for the world Merwin so eagerly pursued in the 1950s did not turn out an illusion as the prodigal son had discovered but had its edifying effect: it taught the "unreasonable" danger of the radical otherness, by which Merwin seemed at once chilled and fascinated. Water, the most tender element on earth, is at the same time the most perilous, for beneath the calm surface of the sea lurks the most unexpected disaster. Some sea poems cast a glimpse at "so fearsome a destroyer" (*FF* 222), while others treat the subject with almost photographic meticulousness. For instance, in "Two Paintings by Alfred Wallis, I. Voyage to Labrador," Merwin imagines the invisible danger in crossing Labrador: "[T]here dog-hunched will the high / Street of hugging bergs have come / To lean huge and hidden as women, / Untouched as smoke and, at our passing, pleased / Down to the private sinks of their cold" (*FF* 210).[1] Such light-hearted comicalness and false familiarity will soon disappear: "Then we will be white, all white, as clothes sheening, / Stiff as teeth, white as the sticks / And eyes of the blind" (*FF* 210). As in a horror film, instead of presenting a close-up of the monster, the deadly iceberg, Merwin portrays its effects on the passengers / viewers, whose white faces indicate that they just had a very close call. This traumatic, nightmarish encounter only lasted for a short time, and when morning came, the passengers, "mindless / And uncaring

---

[1] It is no accident that the new edition of Merwin's *First Four Books of Poems* (Copper Canyon Press, 2000) adopts the painting *Floating Iceberg* by Frederic E. Church as its cover. On the picture the fatal iceberg appears as harmless as a drifting cloud, still and white, against the gray sky. Leaning slightly to one side, the iceberg is exactly "dog-hunched" as Merwin describes in the poem.

as Jesus, will find nothing / In that same place but an empty sea /
Colorless, see, as a glass of water" (*FF* 210). The homonym of *sea / see*
invites the human gaze to penetrate, to see through, the surface of the sea
and its treacherous reflectivity. The recurrent sibilant *s* also makes audible
the seething undercurrents that will prove quite dangerous if the ship hits the
iceberg, which, like the ghost of Hamlet's father, stages its mysterious
appearance and disappearance in the nightly mirage. The dreaminess of the
scene suggests that the iceberg might have been an optical illusion, a
displaced and condensed (two main mechanisms of dream-work)
"representative" of the passengers' desire for "a new dimension for the
world" (*FF* 11).

The Greek name for this missed encounter is *tuché*, as we learn from
Lacan: "We have translated [*tuché*] as the encounter with the real. The real
is beyond the automaton, the return, the coming-back, the insistence of the
signs, by which we see ourselves governed by the pleasure principle. The
real is that which always lies behind the automaton" (*Seminar XI* 53−54).
Human beings are governed by the repetitive use of symbols and signs,
which facilitates our communication but at the same time turns us into
agents who do not question the automatic exchange of meaning based on the
inherent (manmade) arbitrariness of signs and symbols. The " chance
work, " however, interrupts this automatizing of signs and redeems us from
symbolic repetitions, conferring certain subjectivity on us — "this real
brings it the subject" (Lacan, *Seminar XI* 54).

What enthralls Merwin then comes close to this *tuché*, the irruption of
the Real in the boundless sea that causes the subject to be other than its
symbolic determination. It is in the unreal sea that the Real preponderates
over reality and acquires its positive embodiment. In another exemplary
poem "The Iceberg, " Merwin would present a frontal portrait of the deadly
Thing and his spectacular enthrallment:

> It is not its air but our own awe
> That freezes us. Hardest of all to believe
> That so fearsome a destroyer can be
> Dead, with those lights moving in it,
> With the sea all around it charged
> With its influence. (*FF* 222)

Unlike the Labrador poem, the iceberg here does not even appear falsely
homely but totally inanimate, deprived of any deceptive anthropomorphism.
The astounding enjambment of *be / Dead* creates a strong psychological

suspension combined with a prolonged amazement. Also, the "fearsome" "destroyer" is not without its moment of sublimation as the "lights moving in it" also make present a certain mysterious and unknowable entity. Merwin's iceberg seems to disrupt as well as organize the apparent reality of the sea, "charging" the sea with its constitutive "influence."

Before encountering the fatal Thing, the poet-speaker could not realize the abyss in the seemingly homogeneous sea: "It seems that only now / We realize the depth of waters, the / Abyss over which we float among such / Clouds" (*FF* 222). The allegory of the poem becomes clearer when it reveals the terrible, traumatic abyss in the heart of our falsely secure realities. Lacan would say that most of the time, the abyss of subjectivity is covered from our view to make reality function smoothly; only occasionally do we get a glimpse of the Real, the phantasmal core of our symbolically constructed social reality. In Merwin's narration, we are simultaneously terrified and magnetized by such an alien and sublime (unrepresentable) occurrence: "And still not understanding / The coldness of most elegance, even / With so vast and heartless a splendor / Before us, stare, caught in the magnetism / Of great silence ..." (*FF* 222). In another prose poem, "The Songs of the Icebergs" in *The Miner's Pale Children* (1970), Merwin tells of the uncanny splendor of those destructive nonentities viewed in a distance: "They have taken the form of illuminations rising from within, toward the surfaces of the leprous cliffs, like the northern lights themselves still searching for them, or like arms and faces drowned in slow rivers, appearing and then sinking again, to reappear farther along" (*BF* 101). Entering what T. S. Elliot calls "death's other kingdom" (80), the poet seems to be spellbound by such inhuman "elegance," such "heartless" "splendor" emanating from the traumatic Thing. Echoing Odysseus, who likewise "had coursed a strange ocean" ("Cape Dread," *FF* 232), the speaker claims the iceberg to be "the terror / That cannot be charted," the unexpected event that comes to meet the subject as *tuché*, the encounter.

If Melville in *Moby-Dick* and Hemingway in *The Old Man and the Sea* present man's encounter with the Thing as a struggle of life and death, Merwin treats the same topos with ominous nonchalance. Unlike Captain Ahab or Santiago, who fought and bled for the fierce Other incarnated either in the white whale or in the marlin, Merwin's speaker, when faced with destruction, takes no direct action due to the stultification of the senses before the monstrous. Merwin's forte lies not in mighty opposition but in roundabout, suggestive description; his method is therefore phenomenological *epoché* rather than direct involvement. The poet would start a narrative about nautical experiences using a sort of Hemingwayesque understatement, but soon a vague feeling of anxiety surfaces to disturb the reader. Lacking both Hemingway's stoicism and Melville's audacity, Merwin aligns with a poetics of indeterminate anxiety that fits more with the postmodern simultaneous deferral of and yearning for meaning.

In another pertinent example "The Portland Going Out," Merwin chronicles the sinking of a ship with the silent intimation that some unknown disaster may have touched all of us — passengers on the ship of "fate." "Going out" carries the antithetical meanings of "going out of home (to explore the new world)" and "going down," "coming to an end" (*Webster's*), so the title already exposes the inherent instability of the structure of the poem. As is customarily seen in Merwin's sea poems, things start smoothly and easily, as the speaker and his friends are on another ship, watching with much glee the launching ceremony of the Portland: "[P]assing so close over our stern that we / Caught the red glow of her port light for / A moment on our faces" (*FF* 230). The intimacy and liveliness conveyed by "red glow" and "our faces" would stand in appalling contrast with the coming destruction. The speaker goes on to record the change of weather with a distant, journalistic flavor: "Only / When she was gone did we notice / That it was starting to snow" (*FF* 229). And at the climax of the narrative we do not have a panic-stricken Titanic but a Merwinesque profile of disaster — distant, nonchalant, third-personal. As every encounter with the Real is a missed one, so Merwin's *tuché*, via the sinking of the Portland, produces not so much a direct blow as retroactive concussions and ruminations. After the event, the speaker realized that disaster was "a gulf / Beyond reckoning," an abyss which opens repeatedly yet unexpectedly — "It begins where we are" (*FF* 230). This gaping gulf, as Cheri Davis locates correctly, "is lodged within ourselves" and "emanates out from us, precluding all other intimacy" (66).

This is more than the aestheticization of destruction but an elevation of an object to the status of the Thing — the traumatic kernel of symbolic reality.[①] Since subjectivity is established on the ground of such *tuché*, one would risk one's life for a glimpse of that "inhuman" beauty: "[F]oresails and clouds hiding / Such threat and beauty as we may never see" (*FF* 210).

---

① This is exactly how Lacan defines "sublimation": "[I]t raises an object ... to the dignity of the Thing" (*Seminar VII* 112).

In "Cape Dread, " fear and exhilaration are curiously mixed when Merwin encountered *l'homme fatale* in the sea when "we sighted / The shape of what we knew we would not pass" (*FF* 232). Unlike the unfortunate crew on the Portland, our eagle-eyed poet made out the shape quickly: "You cannot mistake it: the dun headland / Like a dreaming Dutchman, dough-faced, staring / Seaward to the side we did not penetrate" (*FF* 232). After describing the treacherous water around what he called "Cape Delight" or "Dutchman's Point, " the speaker savored the cove he found there: "In / The south corner of the cove there is / An inlet flowing with sweet water, / And there are fruits in abundance, small / But delectable, at least at that season" (*FF* 233). Edenic, the cove symbolizes the far reaches of human reality and the final object of the sea journey.

Most of Merwin's sea poems are ambiguous in that they cast a veil over invisible dangers while at the same time try to tear that veil, to probe into the infinite abyss of the sea. Sometimes, Merwin would even go down to the ocean floor, assuming the tone of the mythically drowned sailors to tell their story. In "The Bones of Palinurus Pray to the North Star, " Merwin adopts an Eliotic combination of mythology and religiosity:

> Console us. The wind chooses among us.
> Our whiteness is a night wake disordered.
> Lone candor, be constant over
> Us desolate who gleam no direction. (*FF* 45)

In Roman mythology, Palinurus was the helmsman of Aeneas' fleet. It is told in Virgil's *Aeneid* that the god Neptune had enchanted Palinurus into sleep to let him fall overboard into "the limpid waters" (V. 1135). After Palinurus got onshore, the native tribe killed him and left his body to the sea waves. Embodying the Eliotic posthumous yearning, Merwin's poem invokes the timelessness of the Real vis-à-vis the temporality of desire. The speaker still feels discontented and grievous ("Console us") after death, his bones crying for a certain order or direction from the North Star. "The wind choos[ing] among us" suggests that man's desire, projected as gods' desire, is basically metonymic, just like the wind seizing and choosing its objects. Palinurus fell into the sea out of the pure wind / will / whim of Neptune, who thought that one mortal must be sacrificed to save many. The bones are the remnants, the ashes, of gods' desire; possessed by a libidinal drive to obtain consistency, the bones stay in the limbo between life and death and become what Žižek terms the "organs without body" (*Organs* 30), the scattered, blind life-force that demands for eternity.

The drowned sailors in Merwin's poems find little peace in death but keep feeling, cognizing, and even philosophizing. In "The Eyes of the Drowned Watch Keels Going Over," the dead would "shift and turn over slightly" as if sunbathing under the sea; their scopic drive is hardly less salient: "[L]ooking / Upward through the leaves that turned over and back / like hands, through the birds, the fathomless light, / Upward" (*FF* 216). Shooting through various obstacles ("leaves," "birds"), the gaze of the dead persistently follows the sunlight "upward" like the eyes of the living; moreover, the dead begin to reconsider the purpose of following the stars, since they find the keels that they watch actually "follow nothing." Gradually the dead realize that "our eyes fastened upon stars" simply because "we traced / in their remote courses not their own fates but ours" (*FF* 216). In this way, Merwin reveals that our spiritual quest for eternity ("upward," "star") is largely a human presupposition, a psychic movement producing its own goal — what the New Critics term the "pathetic fallacy." The persistent drive to see the stars is reversed into making oneself recognized and thus guided by the stars ("be constant over / Us"). Giving voice to the dead, the poem exposes the rationale behind all myths: it is actually the human drive that is pulling the string of fate. The undead not only lie deep down the sea but exist in human subjectivity, taking the form of a powerful, insatiable propulsion for the self-reflexive gaze, as Merwin laments that the dead are unable to die:

> The darkened dead have no peace,
> World-without-end shifting;
> All, all are there, and no resting. (*FF* 217)

The survivors who have made it to land do not fare better; a sailor on shore at best resembles a fish out of water. Accustomed to the hallucinatory instability of the sea, sailors find it difficult to readapt to the stable worldly reality. Their perception of the world is irreversibly transformed because they have lived on the sea for too long. Reentering the human world, they would only stumble and stagger. In "Sailor Ashore," Merwin tells us what happens when a sailor steps ashore: "What unsteady ways the solid earth has / After all. The lamps are dead on their feet / Blinking and swaying above the wet cobbles" (*FF* 228). Like drunkards, they lose a firm hold on reality, mixing illusion with reality: "[T]he sleeping houses / Reel and almost fall but never wake; / And the echo of feet goes round and round / Like a buffeted gull" (*FF* 228). Merwin's sailor fully captures Einsteinian relativity of movement: "If you / Put your foot down the spot moves: the waters are / Under the earth" (*FF* 228). And as in Alfred Hitchcock's *Rebecca*, the sea has become a returning ghost, a specter that haunts the sailor's five senses: "Gull shriek, boozy guffaw, woman / Laughing — turn your back on each in turn / And you hear the waters' laughter" (*FF* 228).

In this reading, the sailors have become obsessional neurotics whose libido is excessively fixated on the water image, on its instability and lack of signification. At the end of the poem, Merwin commands the sailor to "get back to the bare-faced original / Bitch-sea. Which is what they gave you legs for" (*FF* 228). The grim humor here subverts the common preference for equilibrium in an organism by presenting the sailor's pathological attachment to alternative or displaced reality. The oxymoron points out the ambiguous charm of the sea — it is the origin of meaning ("original") due to its utter lack of meaning ("bare-faced"). For the poet, seas and rivers both reveal and cover the void of subjectivity; in a folkloric style Merwin sings that "for so long / It will be the seethe and drag of the river / That I will hear longer than any mortal song" (*FF* 190). This looks like more than nostalgia for the transient object; it is an outburst about the retroactive effects of the first scene of leaving. Seas and rivers have become the non-understandable objects stuck in the throat of the enunciating subject: the poet and his sailor can neither swallow it (subjectivize it) nor spit it out (reject it or fully articulate it). This is perhaps why the speaker anathematizes it as the "Bitch-sea, " the sticky object that one has to enjoy with such anguish.

All the uncovenanted terror of becoming

Merwin's impassioned sea journey is largely a mental excursion full of imaginary projections from the human psyche. The icebergs, capes, shipwreck, and sailors dead and living are not so much mythological as pathological: they repeatedly evoke scenes of destruction with a mixed feeling of horror and exhilaration, anxiety and release. From very early on, Merwin has indulged himself in the interplay of psychic and physical realities to explore a radical otherness in selfsameness, a nonhumanness in humanity, a death in the very center of life. It seems hard for Merwin to get rid of this "fierce devotion" (Merwin's term for Richard Blackmur) to *tuché*, in which the poetic language burns "intensely, unremittingly, and fiercely, " to use his comment on the poetry of John Berryman (*SD* 45) .

Apart from the sea, the legendary sea monsters and creatures provide one more important fantasy-frame for Merwin to stage his poetic cathexes, his encounter with the unknown dimension of the world. In *Green with Beasts* (1956), Merwin paints several "sublime" animals with a highly intensified poetic language. Critics are quick to point out that almost all of these animal poems are linked with the sea. For example, Edward Brunner has noted that "the sea is a presence to which the [creature] poems compulsively return, " because both the sea and the creature "escape his understanding, " and "[e]ven as [the creature] sets a limit to our knowledge, it compels us to imagine its infinity" (*Poetry* 43, 44). Brunner traces Merwin's "Physiologus" back to the twelfth-century tabulations of biblical animals, characterizing them as "objects of endless speculation that can never be resolved into simplifying categories" (*Poetry* 39). What preoccupies Merwin then is the mystery of signification because the sublime / monstrous animals simultaneously absorb and subvert the descriptive power of words, functioning as the extimate object of man's epistemological, metaphysical desire.

In "Proteus, " the earliest poem manifestly dealing with a sea monster in *The Dancing Bear* (1954), Merwin dramatizes man's struggle with his own radical otherness embodied in the beast-god who can assume various shapes as he wishes. Such a struggle is not only comical: by dispersing man's blindness to his absurd existence, it also endows him with a kind of tragic courage to face up the fundamental *Spaltung* in his earthly existence. The poem starts as the outcome of an Odyssean quest: "By the splashed cave I found him" (*FF* 110). The legendary sea monster did not appear to terrify the speaker at all: "[H]is face flicked with a wisp / Of senile beard, a frail somnolent old man" (*FF* 110). The deceptively amiable portrait only sets the stage for the drama of drastic metamorphosis later. Dallying with the fateful encounter, the speaker gratifies himself temporally in hearsays or what Edward Brunner calls "extravagant digressions" and "lavish allusions" (*Poetry* 46) :

> I had heard in seven wise cities
> Of the last shape of his wisdom: when he,
> Giver of winds, father as some said
> Of the triple nightmare, from the mouth of a man
> Would loose the much-whistled wind of prophecy. (*FF* 110)

Wind is synonymous with desire for its insubstantiality and mobility. In the

Homeric tradition, Odysseus' return was delayed because Poseidon had simply changed the wind, that is, changed his will, his desire. Like the amorphous water, wind stands between something and nothing; it comes from a void, a crack, an opening but can be extremely propelling. Lacan points out that "[t]he question of das Ding is still attached to whatever is open, lacking, or gaping at the center of our desire" (*Seminar VII* 84); Merwin in his own context also traces out the etiology of desire: "[t]he nothing into which a man leans forward / Is mother of all restiveness, drawing / The body prone to falling into no / Repose at last but the repose of falling" (*FF* 110).

The real battle begins when the pilgrim-speaker "seized" Proteus — the Other as the posited locus of knowledge — "by sleeping throat and heel" and remained deaf to the beast-god's "pleadings," "arguments," and "threats," forcing him to divulge the prophecy. At this moment, the wonderful metamorphosis occurred:

> When he leapt in a bull's rage
> By horn and tail I held him; I became
> A mad bull's shadow, and would not leave him;
> As a battling ram he rose in my hands;
> My arms were locked horns that would not leave his horns;
> I was the cleft stick and the claws of birds
> When he was a serpent between my fingers. (*FF* 111)

Mingling the temptation scene in the biblical Eden with the sacrifice story of Isaac, Merwin consciously blurs the boundary between self and other, protagonist and antagonist, to intimate that this struggle is largely self-reflexive — all the surreal transformations happen in the domain of human psyche. The ego seemed to prevail its double when the speaker "felt the beast's sinews / Fail, the beast's bristles fall smooth / Again to the skin of a man," and not surprisingly, the speaker came to find that "[t]he head he turned toward me wore a face of mine" (*FF* 111).

These lines dramatize Merwin's vehement desire to access the otherness of the Other: both imaginary and real.[1] Proteus is at once Merwin's ideal

---

[1] Žižek usefully summarizes three types of Other: imaginary, symbolic, and real. The imaginary Other are "my fellow human beings with whom I am engaged in the mirror-like relationships of competition, mutual recognition, and so on," while the real Other refers to "the impossible Thing, the 'inhuman partner,' the Other with whom no symmetrical dialogue ... is possible" (Žižek, *Totalitarianism* 163).

ego — man of sinews, visions, changeability (since then, Merwin's style has changed so much that Harold Bloom has to call him "the Protean Merwin" [11]) — and his own non-understandable yet commanding otherness. Here Merwin seems to agree with Lacan that "[t]he ego is this master the subject finds in an other, whose function of mastery he establishes in his own heart" (*Seminar III* 93). The mastering ego has to constantly battle the surging otherness in the id. At the end of the struggle, Merwin's narrator was disillusioned and enlightened, accepting that "[h] ere was no wisdom but my own silence / Echoed as from a mirror; no marine / Oracular stare but my own eyes / Blinded and drowned in their reflections" (*FF* 112). Hearing his own voice saying, "You prevail always, but, deathly, I am with you / Always, " the narrator does acquire a certain truth of desire by the end of this pantomime: "I am he, by grace of no wisdom, / Who to no end battles the foolish shapes / Of his own death by the insatiate sea" (*FF* 112). Pushing the scene from the desire for truth to repetitions of a senseless struggle marks the poet's resolution to work through the problem of self-alienation by recognizing it as constitutive of human subjectivity.[①]

If in "Proteus" Merwin battles with his own mirror image, in another epic poem "Leviathan, " he would encounter the ghostly object of desire and transmit his otherwise narcissistic cathexes onto the object. Manifestly, the apocalyptic sea monster from the book of Revelation inspires much of Merwin's imagery, but he has added more savory details to invest the monster with an aura of psychic reality. As in the iceberg poems, the sea here unmistakably figures as the vast reservoir of id in which the core of the Real hides and from which it occasionally emerges. This beast is truly sublime in the Kantian sense in that its dynamism and dimension surpass human imagination, holding the viewers in fear and trembling, exposing their helplessness before the raw, dangerous nature (Zhang 711). In order to introduce this gigantic beast that overwhelms any adjectival approximation of words, Merwin employs a particular syntax that permits the gradual laying-out of subordinating clauses and adverbials. The heavy, wavelike enjambments also contribute to the unusual proportion of the

---

① Alice Benston clearly saw Merwin's painstaking effort to solve "the problem of solipsism, " but her dismissal of "all change" as an "illusion" seems only too hasty (186), for this epic poem on self-transformation has radicalized the constitutive otherness of subjectivity and clearly transcends solipsism conceived as the question or denial of the existence of the Other.

subject, as if the describer's imagination is trying hard to catch up with the movement of such a "Leviathan":

> This is the black sea-brute bulling through wave-wrack,
> Ancient as ocean's shifting hills, who in sea-toils
> Travelling, who furrows the salt acres
> Heavily, his wake hoary behind him ... (*FF* 141)

Through alliterations of the explosive *b* in the first line of the quotation, the monster seems to jump out of the deep sea, "bursting the bounds of the poetic form" (Andersen 280), when the dynamism of raw life-energy is conveyed by the successive motion of *bulling, shifting,* and *traveling.* The metaphor of plowing ("who furrows the salt acres / Heavily") intimates that the whale is existentially at home in its environment; it has its own life-world, which radically differs from man's but shares the same characteristic of being an *Umwelt.* With much authenticity, majesty, and masterliness, the sea monster marches undaunted: "[R]avening the rank flood, wave-marshaling, / Overmastering the dark sea-marches, finds home / And harvest" (*FF* 141).

In this fantastical scene, the poetic signifiers are saturated with *jouissance,* as an autonomous aestheticism prevails over historicity. As Mark Christhilf finds, Merwin's animals "exist in human's preconscious depths and are prior to historical life and the domesticating consciousness in which humans conduct their lives" (57). Evoking the prehistoric creature in its horrifying dynamism, Merwin would get even closer, presenting us a frontal snapshot of the Real: "The hulk of him is like hills heaving, / Dark, yet as crags of drift-ice, crowns cracking in thunder, / Like land's self by night black-looming, surf churning and trailing / Along his shores' rushing, shoal-water boding / About the dark of his jaws" (*FF* 141). The present participles here, as in the famous opening in T. S. Eliot's *The Waste Land* ("April is the cruelest month, breeding / ... mixing / ... stirring / ... covering / ... feeding"), create not only a sense of rhythm and motion as critics are quick to point out (Andersen 280), but also a deferral of ultimate confrontation with "the dark of his jaws," the abyss of the Real. The movement of signifiers via multiple similes reveals Merwin's, as well as any poet's, inability to accurately render the traumatic Thing through the verbal form. (It is in this domain of impossibility that poets toil and compete.) The excessive use of similes does not testify to Merwin's poetic eloquence; contrarily, it lays bare a certain linguistic disorder in contiguity. It seems that Merwin was stunned by the presence of this ultra-phenomenon and could not find the right word for it, doing what Lacan says about a delusional subject who "employs enormous, extraordinarily articulate bla-bla-bla" and "can never get to the heart of what he has to communicate" (*Seminar III* 220). Anyone who stumbles upon this Leviathan "would find gates of no gardens, / But the hill of dark underfoot diving, / Closing overhead, the cold deep, and drowning" (*FF* 141). Merwin is again engaged in a self-defeating enterprise to name "the nameable beyond the name, the unnameable nameable" (Derrida, *On the Name* 58). Facing the phantasmal, infinite nonentity, what can the poet do but plunge into these vertiginous as well as orgasmic alliterations of "wave-marshaling," "hills heaving," "crowns cracking," "black-looming," and "hill of dark ... diving ... Closing ... drowning"? Merwin's naming procedure thus happily founders and flounders.

This confrontation with the Real involves what Gilles Deleuze and Felix Guattari formulate as "anomalous":

> The anomalous is neither an individual nor a species; it has only affects, it has neither familiar or subjectified feelings, nor specific or significant characteristics. Human tenderness is as foreign to it as human classifications. Lovecraft applies the term "Outsider" to this thing or entity, the Thing, which arrives and passes at the edge, which is linear yet multiple, "teething, seething, swelling, foaming, spreading like an infectious disease, this nameless horror." (*Thousand* 244-245)

Deleuze and Guattari read Melville's Moby Dick as "the borderline" which "represents a power of another order," claiming that Ahab "has an irresistible becoming-whale," as if the captain has made "a monstrous alliance with the Unique, the Leviathan, Moby-Dick," "a pact with demon" (*Thousand* 245, 243).

It seems that Merwin has made a similar "pact with demon," if more inwardly. For Merwin, the beast is the first creation of God: "the curling serpent," "the shadow under the earth," "a lost angel" (*FF* 141). It beholds the empty, unpopulated world: "[W]ith one eye he watches / Dark of night sinking last, with one eye dayrise / As at first over foaming pastures" (*FF* 142). Before long, we will have the whole story of paradise lost and original sin, but at this moment we only witness a world that is still in the process of becoming. As Edward Brunner points out, "[T]he leviathan is only a beginning, a prototype. He is not crude, only incomplete .... The ocean too remains incomplete, the mark of 'the hand

not yet contented / Of the Creator,' still in the process of being shaped"
(*Poetry* 44 - 45). Language, signification, and subjectification have not
entered this primordial world and have not alienated the Leviathan from its
Umwelt. The beast is not only a Jungian archetype, as Brunner suggests,
but also the Lacanian Thing, or the Deleuzean simulacrum that "implies
huge dimensions, depths, and distances that the observer cannot master"
("Simulacrum" 258). Unlike Adam and his descendants, the beast lives
without what Deleuze calls the "structure-Other," without the differentiation
between animal consciousness and the object. Swelling perpetually in the
undifferentiated real order, the Leviathan is directly identified with its
environment. Merwin's similes and metaphors ("ocean's shifting hills,"
"crags of drift-ice," "surf churning and trailing / Along his shores'
rushing," etc.) definitely register a merging of the beast's self with the
ocean. Unlike the Leviathan in the book of Revelation, the beast here can
hardly be described as "evil," since the dichotomy of good and evil is not
formed yet; it is monstrous without being evil, "await[ing] as emblem of
all possibilities, the conditions of the world that wait for man" (Benston
190).

In fact, Merwin admits that he has never seen a sea monster. In a
memoir about George Kirstein, former publisher of *The Nation*, Merwin
recollects his experiences with the sea and the conception of the sea
monster:

> It was a subject that had occupied my imagination since childhood. ...
> But my actual experience of the sea, apart from a couple of Atlantic
> crossings, was limited almost entirely to some sailing in summer with
> friends almost as inept as I was, on an old Dutch fishing boat off the
> south coast of England. (*EE* 3)

When George, who was passionate about sea voyages himself, wrote to
Merwin inquiring after his poem on the sea monster, Merwin admitted, "I
need hardly say that I had never beheld a sea monster, and my piece was a
complete fiction" (*EE* 4). In retrospection, Merwin attributes the
conception of the monster to possible optical illusions due to "cold rains and
fogs" and "the complicated tides and currents" (*EE* 3-4). These situations,
as Merwin explains, "were not extensive but they were, and they
remained, immediate, and they came to focus years of reading and
daydreaming about the sea into the writing of the poems that occasioned
George's letter," so the fantasy of the sea monster serves not so much to
excite sensation as to blur "the distinction between the waking world and the

world of sleep" (*EE* 4). From Freud and Lacan we have learned that it is in dreams that the unconscious and the Real could be released, so Merwin's sailing experience provides him a good chance to stage imaginary yet *real* meetings with what is other than the socio-historically determined self and reality — a rendezvous with the "elusive semblance" (Žižek, *Ticklish* 197).

The terror of becoming the Other, becoming the sea monster that symbolizes the object of desire, culminates in "Sea Monster." The poem is more about the hallucinatory aftermath of the encounter than the encounter itself, which only makes it more haunting. Calling into question the boundary between facticity and fantasy, Merwin's mise-en-scène of the inner fantasy reverses the usual relationship between subject and object and thus summons up the whole philosophical problematic of human perception. The poem begins with the bright day, the shining sea, and all seem felicitous, but then "after / The noon watch, it was, that it slid / Into our sight: a darkness under / The surface, between us and the land, twisting / Like a snake swimming or a line of birds / In the air. Then breached, big as a church, / Right there beside us" (*FF* 231). These lines do not endeavor to encapsulate and represent the phantom but largely work through similes to create an ominous, amorphous, and unnamable presence. The proximity of danger ("Right there beside us") spellbinds the beholders, echoing "The Portland Going Out" and "The Shipwreck," in which destruction wears a deceptively homely mask. The strange thing, however, is that "None of us will / Agree what it was then, but / None of us showed the least surprise, and truly / I felt none" (*FF* 231). Merwin may have familiarized himself with the sea monster through "years of reading and daydreaming," yet the lack of surprise nevertheless invites a deeper psychological explanation.

In effect, this non-surprise betrays the internal exteriority of psychic fantasy: the sea monster is not merely a psychic projection but an incarnation of the nonhuman core or object-cause of desire, and that is perhaps why Merwin deprives the monster of all human features, rendering it an empty husk of the Lacanian Thing or Deleuzean simulacrum, a pure appearance: "I would say its eyes / Were like the sea when the thick snow falls / Onto it with a whisper and slides heaving / On the gray water" (*FF* 231). The beast's eyes open up an abyss of non-meaning that silently absorbs the natural process, the "snow." More uncannily, the beast "looked at us / For a long time, as though it knew us, but / Did not harm us that time, sinking at last, / The waters closing like a rush of breath" (*FF* 231). It hardly matters whether Merwin has invented the whole epiphanic scene or not; the crucial point is that the poet portrays the beast as looking at us, the human subjects. This reversed gaze immediately reduces the onlookers to humiliation: "We were all ashamed at what we had seen, / Said it was only a sea-trick or / A dream we had all had together" (*FF* 231). The beholders felt "ashamed" because their object of desire had been externalized and substantiated. Under normal situations, the object is repressed into the unconscious while at that moment it emerged to the surface of the conscious, confronting the subject with its monstrosity. Also, the viewers feel ashamed because their secret *jouissance* has been exposed before each other, and it is this exposure from the reflexive gaze that constitutes their *jouissance* proper. *Jouissance* comes from being watched by the third eye, the impersonal gaze, the gaze that belongs more to the object than to the subject (Lacan, *Seminar XI* 83).

This kind of impersonal gaze has been one of the topoi in Merwin's early "Physiologus." Urged by a curiosity to understand nonhuman existence, Merwin would probe the creature's consciousness through its very eyes, expanding the domain of poetry into the gray zone — the zone between the Symbolic and the Real, desire and drive, signification and asignification. For instance, in "Dog," Merwin reports that the dog's "glazed eyes / Fixed heavily ahead stare beyond you / Noticing nothing; he does not see you" (*FF* 148). This, however, does not mean that the dog sees nothing. Merwin continues: "But wrong: / Look again: it is through you / That he looks, and the danger of his eyes / Is that in them you are not there" (*FF* 148). Animals have this nearly "psychotic" vision that instantly annihilates human pride: "[Y]ou are not there." In a mixture of superstition and humor, Merwin reminds us that there might be eyes that can look through us and our painstakingly constructed civilization of signs, meanings, and intentions, reducing us to "that punctiform object, that point of vanishing being" (Lacan, *Seminar XI* 83). The dog's eyes are Cerberus' eyes, piercing us with infinitely melancholic *jouissance*: "[F]or he guards all that is gone" (*FF* 148). The dog's gaze also exposes the hubris of our human intelligence as we are invited to question the validity of the built-in notion of the self as the observer and object as the observed. These two poles are exactly reversed in this disquieting play of gazes.

Standing for what escapes symbolization, Merwin's animals all share certain characteristics of the Real, and in this way the poet has conjured up a whole spectral world by defamiliarizing and enigmatizing the creatures that seem too common in daily life to arouse amazement. Edward Brunner

46 considers one of the themes in Merwin's "Physiologus" to be "a virtue to proceed without fear of hesitation into unpredictable areas — areas inherently unstable or on the margins of the comprehensible" (*Poetry* 48). Such an unpredictable effort would lead to tragic outcomes in the coming epic "Two Horses, " in which the poet fantasizes about the glory emanating from the two mythical horses-in-themselves. Waking up in an artificially idyllic garden consisting of "grove, " "bees, " "fountain, " "gold light, " and "olives, " the narrator found "wild horses tethered improbably / To the withes of a young quince" (*FF* 145). Similar to the description of the Leviathan, rhetorical maneuvers are lavished here to bring out a sense of mighty motion and stasis: "[T]heir flexed tails like flags float, " "their brows down like bulls, " "the broken arches / Of their necks in the dim air are silent / As the doorways of ruins" (*FF* 145). In this *ekphrasis*, the archetypal horses have been sublimated into the stand-ins of the object of desire: "[D]awn would be eastward / Over the dark neck, a red mane tossed high / Like flame, " and, echoing the steeds in the Homeric tradition, the beasts dragged a long trail of war and destruction: "[A]ll dust was of their making; and passion / Under their hooves puffed into flight like a sparrow / And died down when they departed" (*FF* 145).

The moral of the poem soon becomes clear: the coming and going of the two horses (agents of war) inspire artistic creations but could also cause irremediable damages to the world. The dialectic of desire and disaster is set in motion by the intrusion of this agency of fate, this inexorable Other, when "the blood of beasts herald morning" (*FF* 146). After evoking wars, ruins, and vicissitude of dynasties in a Shelleyan vein ("chariots are broken, " "wailing at sundown, " "mourning for kings, " "Weeping of widows, " "columns have fallen like shadows, " "fires drifting in darkness like the tails / Of jackals flaring, " etc.), [1] the poet brings us to the atemporal core of all temporality and historicity:

> Beyond the terraces the misted sea
> Swirls endless, hooves of the gray wind forever
> Thundering, churning the ragged spume-dusk
> High that there be no horizons nor stars, and there
> Are white islands riding, ghost-guarded, twisted waves flashing,

---

[1] We may compare Merwin's lines with Shelley's famous "Ozymandias." Whereas Shelley only mocks the vanity of kings, Merwin is more concerned with the inherent traumatic ahistoricity of the "vain" historical processes.

Porpoises plunging like the necks of horses. (*FF* 146)

Only by the end of the poem do we catch the full import of the "two horses": they are pre-creaturely animals, as the "porpoises" here also recall an earlier poem "Proteus, " in which Merwin classifies both "porpoises" and "horses" as Proteus' "daughters" (*FF* 110). If Ted Hughes has written about the quiet dignity and stoic endurance of the animal in his well-known poem "The Horses, " Merwin goes further in mystification by transposing the animal into a Deleuzean simulacrum and placing it in the "anomalous" zone ("the misted sea") that resembles chaos prior to the biblical Genesis. Like the Leviathan, the fiery horses " become exotic sea creatures, uncontained and uncontainable" (Davis 55), incarnating the id-devil that resists symbolization and socialization.

"Two Horses" embodies the full Merwinian paradigm of the minimal and elemental (gold, flame, passion, summer, sea, rain, wave, whiteness, silence, departure), and this chiaroscurism has remained largely unchanged throughout his poetic career. The contrapuntal employment of fire and water epitomizes Merwin's *ars poetica* as a tender subversion — to withdraw from the social-symbolic system towards amorphous nature, and to invoke destruction, not in its manifest horror and cruelty, but in its theatrical anamorphosis: destruction viewed from the tender side. What concerns Merwin then is not just animal characteristics in humans but how this rawness operates unconsciously. Unlike Shelley, who is emphatic and univocal, Merwin transposes violence and destruction to what Freud called "the other scene, " and this is perhaps where he parts from Shelleyan Romanticism although Shelley has been an important influence. In other words, Merwin's displacement renders the poem more indeterminate, for we could always read the epilogue in a " spectral" way: it is neither presence nor absence; thematically, it is neither inside nor outside the poem. Merwin might have used this epilogue to signify the closure of human history, conjuring the unrepresentability of the horses qua death-drive, and as Alice Benston perceives the situation: " destruction accompanies creation, which seems to be Merwin's point" (192).

The question of the animals' participation in human desire and signification culminates in "White Goat, White Ram, " the last long poem in Merwin's "Physiologus." In this single poem Merwin deals with the entire theo-philosophical problem of representation: how animals become the objects of desire, how they simultaneously submit to human signification and resist it. The poem differs from "Two Horses" in that

Merwin here employs a meditative mode, instead of a descriptive one — the speaker is incessantly reasoning with himself. The tone of the poem is lighthearted at first but soon turns serious and finally becomes pious, paralleling the three stages of phenomenon, essence, and transcendence of the text. H. L. Hix's comment that "[a]s he had done with the leviathan, Merwin uses the goat and the ram as points of reference for understanding ourselves" only seem to catch part of the story (*Understanding* 27), because Merwin also attempts to fathom the nonhuman creatures themselves instead of merely "using" them "as points of reference for understanding ourselves." Cheri Davis's analysis seems more justified. Davis claims that the goat "has spiritual powers beyond human scope or comprehension," though she accedes that the animals are "language-blind," lacking "mental constructs" and "cognitive memory" (44). The interception of transcendence by immanence, of infinity by finitude, of "beyond" by "below," is the textual axis around which "White Goat, White Ram" endlessly weaves.

Desiring a certain spirituality that carries throughout his entire work, Merwin resorts to Christianity and scatters divine signs here and there to set up a quasi-biblical backdrop. Again, we enter a landscape that resembles more a psychic projection than normally perceived reality: "The gaiety of three winds is a game of green / Shining, of gray-and-gold play in the holly bush / Among the rocks on the hillside, and if ever / The earth was shaken, say a moment ago / Or whenever it came to be, only the leaves and the spread / Sea still betray it, trembling" (*FF* 150). Merwin then introduces the goat as "stand[ing] at the side / Nearer the sea, not far from the brink" and "her back and belly / Slung like a camp of hammocks" and her "[e]yes wide apart like the two moons of Mars / At their opposing" (*FF* 150). Treated as a lesser version of the Heideggerian Dasein, Merwin's goat finds herself thrown into the world, unable to account for her own "uncanny" existence. Like the dog with its empty eyes abhorred by the poet-speaker, the goat here is deprived of any orientation towards *the* meaning in this flood of meanings: "So broadly is she blind / Who has no names to see with: over her shoulder / She sees not summer, not the idea of summer, / But green meanings, shadows, the gold light of now ..." (*FF* 150).

Merwin, not without a twist of irony, laments that the goat and the ram have been mercilessly used by us humans as signifiers of our own desire. We unjustly equate the animals' "whiteness" with a loss of memory and a radical innocence that could have been exploited by our own "gracelessness," which recalls the biblical story of Abraham's sacrifice of "the thicket-snared ram" "instead of the son" to propitiate the Jewish God. As if to counter any possible abuse of animals under the name of religion, Merwin reflects that these beasts need not be gentle "for us to use them / To signify gentleness, for us to lift them as a sign / Invoking gentleness" (*FF* 150). We humans just need metonymies for the articulation of *our* desire, and that is why we need the animals:

> ... conjuring by their shapes
> The shape of our desire, which without them would remain
> Without a form and nameless. (*FF* 151)

Human desire is nameless because ontologically it is no-thing, merely a *Spaltung*, an abyss between need and demand, "a pure action of the signifier" (Lacan, *Écrits* 253). It has no shape, for it is in the constant process of becoming another desire — of transformation, transmutation, and transgression, bringing what Merwin calls "the uncovenanted terror of becoming" (*FF* 152). Sacrifice is directly related to the desire of this posited big Other, since the purpose of any sacrifice, as Žižek surmises, is to "conceal the Other's lack, inconsistency, 'inexistence,' that transpires in this desire" (*Enjoy* 64). With a mixed tone of satire and lament, Merwin's speaker peers into the abyss of desire qua the split between need and demand, exclaiming that "our uses / Also are a dumbness, a mystery, / Which like a habit stretches ahead of us / And was here before us" (*FF* 151). Human desire is inexplicable in that it is at once familiar ("a habit") and alien ("a mystery"). Facing the unknown subjective becoming, as Merwin foretells, we are prone to use the beasts to "designate what was before us, since we cannot / See it in itself" (*FF* 151). Therefore, the beasts conveniently function as ideal figures of human desire in their following of "their own preference": the animals' desire is not and could not be alienated by language, signification, subjectification, and thus is freer. Merwin further insists on the alterity or infinity of the beasts by claiming that they choose "routes through no convenience / And world of ours, but through their own sense / And mystery" (*FF* 152). Very soon the poet uncovers the cause of man's desire as the unbridgeable gap between signifier and signified:

> ... yet the mystery they stand in
> Is still as far from what they signify
> As from the mystery we stand in. (*FF* 152)

A double difference appears: first, between animals as signs and animals in themselves; second, between humans as socio-linguistic subjects and animals as pre-symbolic, pre-linguistic creatures. For Merwin, these antipodes cannot be facilely sublated into a certain version of humanism that exercises hegemony over nonhuman kingdoms. Instead, Merwin perceives the limit of representation faced with "mystery", as he recounts later in the poem, "There in the thin grass / A few feet away they browse beyond words; for a mystery / Is that for which we have not yet received / Or made the name, the terms, that may enclose / And call it" (*FF* 152). To "enclose" and "call" by a name implies the human endeavor to comprehend the incomprehensible, to treat the Other as an object and type of epistemology. This paradoxical desire is what elevates us above worldly beings or what Merwin calls the "small voice":

> And by virtue of such we stand beyond
> Earthquake and wind and burning, and all the uncovenanted
> Terror of becoming, and beyond the small voice; and on
> Another hand, as it were, a little above us
> There are angels. (*FF* 152)

Here we may pause for the English preposition *beyond*, as it is composed of *be* and *yond* (yonder, there), which exactly corresponds to Heidegger's concept of Dasein (being-there). The word *beyond* has several meanings, all associated with transcendence: "out of the reach or sphere, " "surpass, " "in addition to" (*Webster's*). This word orientates us toward the direction of being's yearning for the infinite in Merwin's creature poems. Far from meaning *having nothing to do with* or *spectating indifferently*, to "stand beyond" here means to surpass by having worked through. Standing by the angels might entail the most painful, most ecstatic transformation imaginable, as readers readily recall Rainer Maria Rilke's famous cry in *Duino Elegies* that "Ein jeder Engel ist schrecklich" (150).

What can humans know about angels and their desire? "We know only the whisper of an elusive sense, / Infrequent meanings and shadows, analogies / with light and the beating of wings" (*FF* 152−153). "Wait[ing] / Beyond our words, " the angels are *above* and *in addition to* words, speeches, and logos, standing "beyond earthquake, whirlwind, fire" and "all the uncovenanted terror of becoming" (*FF* 153). A glimpse of the legendary war between Satan's army and the archangels in paradise, as narrated by John Milton in the beginning of *Paradise Lost*, tempts us to read Merwin's *beyond* as working through. There are indeed "whirlwind" and "fire" in paradise, and this apparent contradiction discloses the poet's desire to plunge into the unforeseeable and unshielded process of becoming *beyond (in and out of) any religious discourse. Towards the end of the poem, the narrator finds himself caught in the purifying fire, desire, wind, will,* and whim of God:

> ... Listen: more than the sea's thunder
> Forgathers in the gray cliffs; the roots of our hair
> Stir like the leaves of the holly bush where now
> Not games the wind ponders but impatient
> Glories, fire: and we go stricken suddenly
> Humble, and the covering of our feet
> Offends, for the ground where we find we stand is holy. (*FF* 153)

Cary Nelson questions the authenticity of the poem; he thinks that Merwin "tries unsuccessfully to draw an organizing symbolism from Christ's story by adapting it ironically to fit our situation" (85). Setting aside Merwin's "real" intention of the poem, which is unfathomable as well as largely indeterminate since New Criticism, what strikes readers most is not how Merwin simply "adapts" the antiquated sacrifice story from the Bible and "fits" it to "our situation," supposedly the postwar U.S. society, but the poet's meditation on the perennial questions of perception, signification, and transformation, which brings the poem, tonally and thematically, close to Hölderlin's *Hexameters and Elegies* (1800) and Rilke's *Duino Elegies* (1923). Nelson's historicization might have missed the inherent unrealness of Merwin's poem; Merwin's irony does not usually carry throughout the whole poem, and most of the time he treats the imagined subjects rather seriously.

Merwin's bestiaries are thus more real than normally perceived reality in that they incarnate our unconscious projections and objects of desire that refuse to be named, to be represented by words. Although we use the beasts as signifiers, they ultimately elude symbolization by being *pure* symbols that erode the binary opposition of signifier / signified as we learn that "the mystery they stand in / Is still as far from what they signify" (*FF* 152). This aporia of signification could be pushed even further: "Oh, we cannot know and we are not / What we signify" (*FF* 153). As Lacanian psychoanalysis reveals, there is always some alien object (fragmenting otherness) stuck in the very heart of the subject; all our efforts to articulate, represent, and signify this traumatic Thing are doomed to fail. And it is exactly this glorious failure that constitutes the flesh and bone of Merwin's writings. At the end of an earlier poem, "Anabasis (II)," after a long, hard journey the disembodied speaker comes to the same limit of naming and signification: "Fixed to bone only, foreign as we came / We float leeward till mind and body lose / The uncertain continent of a name" (*FF* 12).

Continuously, Merwin's speakers are losing their names, escaping a name and thus being made anonymous, desubjectivized, working at the "dissolution of self in the chaos of sea reality," as Stephen Stepanchev comments on the above lines (110). The poet would go on to become the Nobody that Odysseus once proclaimed to be, not in the cunning or ironic sense, but in an excessively devotional gesture. The poet would go on to confront the void of subjectivity, that is, the abyss of freedom, to suffer the irruption of the Real, to welcome "the Stranger who disturbs the being at home with oneself" (Levinas, *Totality* 39) and to suspend the hegemony of signification by conjuring "anomalous" simulacra — all these concerns thus distinguish Merwin's project of the 1950s from those of his contemporaries. As the following chapters will explore, Merwin's poetics is that of "not knowing," of ecstatic *tuché* with the infinitely holy Thing; a poetics of primordial loss and (re)finding, of conjuring and confronting the anonymous holiness.

This obsession with psychic processes and incessant becoming, which invalidates any stable naming, could imbue Merwin's early poetry with a unique liberating potential, which came to prominence later in his anti-Vietnam War poems in *The Moving Target* (1963) and *The Lice* (1967). Incessantly undermining the bedrock of ideology — the subjection to sameness — Merwin, from his early stages on, has compelled readers to imagine the beyond-of-the-signified that keeps sliding away from their perceptual apparatus. Contemporary life, marked by the quantifiable (market) and daily shadowed by the terrible (military mobilization), may begin to investigate the limit of its own totalizing logic. As we have discussed so far, Merwin would rather locate the nature of the terror of becoming, not in any pre-established national, global, ethnical, or religious agenda, but in what remains massively unrealized or utterly unrealizable.

Chapter 2

Spirit in Flame: Merwin's Dallying with Anonymous Holiness

The dance around the holy, around what the French philosopher Emmanuel Levinas mysteriously calls "the holiness of the holy" (qtd. in Derrida, *Adieu* 4), has mesmerized Merwin since the early 1950s.[①] Merwin has remained concerned with the realm of the holy, even when postwar thought tends to discredit all established belief systems, including the Judeo-Christian notion of the holy, which has preoccupied him for quite a long time. In Merwin's early work, the urge to suspend the existing symbolic order in favor of a "higher reality," what Jacques Lacan formulates as the *Real*, finds its convenient outlet in religious and spiritual motifs. "Wild as heaven erupting into a child" ("Proteus," *FF* 11), the spiritual revelation that affords ecstasy would ever haunt Merwin and become a major form of divine contact which brings mystical *jouissance* at the moment of separation. As I will argue in this chapter, Merwin's poetry evokes a kind of fleeting holiness, not only in religious but also in existential spheres, that prompts the self to follow the traces of the posited holy Other. In his obsessional pursuit of the phantasmal object, Merwin attempts to subjectivize the traces of the immeasurable object through poetic fantasies in order to become the authentic cause of his own poetic career. The spirituality of Merwin's poetry

---

① In Judaism, "the holiness of the holy" refers to the most holy in the sanctuary, separated from the holy by a veil or a curtain, see Exod. 26. 31, 33. Derrida explains that Levinas's phrase can be read both theologically and ethically, as it may mean holiness of the sanctuary and holiness of the other person, see Derrida, *Adieu* 4.

54 is produced by the poet-speaker's proximity — forever diminishing yet remaining distance — to the posited sublime object rather than its direct attainment.

While commentators emphasize silence, absence, lack, void, alienation, self-depletion, fragmentation, asceticism, and generally, *via negativa* in Merwin's poetry in the 1960s, I tend to read Merwin's poems from that period and later as a Derridean *supplément*, a substitutive supplementation, to his earlier Christian poems. Merwin's divine comedy does not end with the intrusion of apocalyptical events (the Vietnam War) in the 1960s but persists in a more devious and spectral mode in his later work. Critics have noticed the continuous medievalism in Merwin's early and middle period. Victor Contoski, finding that "[n]ecessary pilgrimages of discovery permeate his work," places Merwin among "anonymous craftsmen of the Middle Ages, artists whose vision was so fixed on the spiritual world and our journey thither" (319−320). In a more comprehensive study, Reed Daniel Wilson defines Merwin's corpus as deeply religious, elaborating how Merwin "has journeyed toward an affirmative vision founded on and grounded in an experience of the dark night."

These studies proposed the existence of a religious consciousness, or what Reed Daniel Wilson calls the "animistic visionary root of all religions" in Merwin's poetry, but since they tend to align that consciousness with either a known spiritual tradition or a univocal devotion to nature which can be traced back to American Transcendentalism, ① the existing criticisms on Merwin may not be sufficient to fully address the poet's longtime engagement with the aftereffects of the divine contact and his uninterrupted play with the holy and its traumatic self-distancing. The poet's spiritual journey is not only a "search for a meaningful life in a world apparently devoid of meaning" (Contoski 310) based on the binary opposition of meaning / void; more importantly, this journey is accompanied by highly cathected acts to capture and (re)find the traces of the holy Other as posited by the poet's imagination. The spiritual aura of Merwin's work in the 1950s and onward consists of a poetic surplus that stands in contrast to the

① For example, from an ecocritical point of view, Jane Frazier reports that Merwin's poetic vision, like that of Thoreau, is firmly grounded in nature and its representations. See Jane Frazier, *From Origin to Ecology: Nature and the Poetry of W. S. Merwin* (Cranbury: Associated University Press, 1999).

limitations of ordinary human life, especially of American life during the booming 1950s and the restless 1960s. Just as artists who "construct a place in which people can ecstatically perceive the traumatic excess around which their life turns" (Žižek, *On Belief* 96), Merwin presents various epiphanic states to enunciate the surplus object of Christian theology in order to work through that theology and its ideological corollaries. If in the 1950s Merwin was chiefly concerned with the "enigmatic" desire of the Judeo-Christian deity — if we can attribute this quality to a holy entity with the understanding of its anthropomorphism — and the death-drive of the saints, in the 1960s and afterwards Merwin's speakers seemed to directly adopt the status of *objet a* — "the non-symbolizable surplus" (Žižek, *Metastases* 179).

The unbearable holiness of being

Orthodox Christianity had played a structuring role in Merwin's early texts such as "Rime of the Palmers," "Dictum: For a Masque of Deluge," "Carol of Three Kings," "The Passion," "Saint Sebastian," "The Annunciation," "White Goat, White Ram," but in 1960, when *The Drunk in the Furnace* was published, Merwin rejected Protestantism for its primness and narrow-mindedness, calling Martin Luther "that old slider, the Prince of Falsehood" who "took the pulpit," "mocking me with a scholar's prim tone" ("Luther," *FF* 268). Consequently, he would rather identify with his drunken grandfather the boat pilot than with his Protestant grandmother, who believed in "the strait gate and the needle's eye" (*FF* 270). In his later work, Merwin seldom wrote about Christianity at full length, as he did in the 1950s. It seems that Merwin grew more cautious about religious intentions, rituals, and sacrifices, maintaining a distance from it. In 1967, stunned by US military actions in Vietnam, Merwin declared the total lack of divinity in humans, refusing any gnostic spark: "The Gods are what has failed to become of us // Now it is over we do not speak / Now the moment has gone it is dark / What is man that he should be infinite" (*SF* 100). Had the "receding fires" ("Anabasis (II)," *FF* 11) Merwin chased in the early 1950s died when the real, mass-destructive fire broke out in Vietnam? Was the gesture of closure the only thing left for the poet, when the atrocity of history had so repeatedly intruded upon the poet's imagination, that the idea of the holy itself was reduced to nothing but a failure of divinity to account for the limited state of human beings? After the War, man's resemblance to God, upheld in the Judeo-Christian tradition, seemed to disappear due to the common failure of both men and God, the failure of the holy.

In his seminal work *Das Heilige* (1917), which was translated as *The Idea of the Holy*, Rudolf Otto wrote that, different from the good, the holy or holiness "contains a quite specific element or ' moment, ' which sets it apart from ' the Rational, '" because it "remains inexpressible — an ἄρρητον or *ineffable* — in the sense that it completely eludes apprehension in terms of concepts" (5). Alien to the order of the good and the useful, the holy initiates what Otto coined as the "numinous" experience — creature-feelings and mystical tremor, for example, which cannot be "taught" but has to be "awakened" (7). Otto also placed religious experience in the category of the "wholly other" (26). This designation, together with the formulation of the numinous, has exercised a tremendous influence on contemporary theological, philosophical, and psychoanalytical discourses on the radical status of the other.

Merwin in his poetic praxis similarly espouses such a notion of the holy beyond conceptual realization, but unlike Otto, who analyzed the holy within a theistic framework, Merwin does not locate holiness in any established religion with its respective Holy Scriptures — be it Judaism, Christianity, or Zen Buddhism, the last of which he studied in the 1970s. Merwin's stance seems more equivocal and elusive. Instead of associating the holy with an orthodox belief that involves rituals, practices, norms, prohibitions, and sometimes even schisms, Merwin, like any post-Romantic poet, understands it as manifested in the essential freedom of human spirit embodied in the poetic process. For Merwin, holiness does not interpellate a person into a religious subject but secretly incubates an umbilical connection with the numinous inside the person.① In "Notes for a Preface" (1966), Merwin puts forward his rather "Judaic" view on poetry:

> The encouragement of poetry itself is a labor and a privilege like that
> of living. It requires, I imagine, among other startlingly simple
> things, a love of poetry, and possibly a recurring despair of finding it

---

① We may note that Merwin's skepticism on the matter of the holy, due to his unwillingness to assign the holy a name, contrasts with Allen Ginsberg's sarcastic numerations of the "holy" objects and sanctification of human parts in the footnote to *Howl* (1956).

again, an indelible awareness of its parentage with that biblical waif, ill at ease with time, the spirit. No one has any claims on it, no one deserves it, no one knows where it goes. (*RM* 295)

Like the Prodigal Son, the biblical waif is the one who is not at home, out of home, unhomely (*unheimisch*) and uncanny (*unheimliche*), whereas the *spirit,* qua the biblical waif, may refer to the elemental wind, fire, passion, desire, specter that animates and inhabits a poem as a chain of words. The waif incarnates the spirit and is driven forward by it. Merwin suggests that to find poetry again means to release historically conditioned subjectivity into an alienation that alienates the very cause of its own genesis, which further leads to the paradoxical position of being an heir without any property, for the biblical waif, as Merwin says, is the dispossessed yet the *inviolable* one. When Merwin states that "[n]o one has any claims on" the spirit, he is asserting its essential freedom to wander wherever it wants, a freedom born of inner necessity and outward struggle against "man-made circumstances" (*RM* 295).[1] Seen from a postmodern perspective, what Merwin regards as the spiritual may correspond to a phantasmal, indestructible surplus over mechanic, material life.

The unforeseeable terror of becoming God's chosen is rehearsed in such rapturous and symptomal poems as "The Passion" in *The Dancing Bears* (1954), and "Saint Sebastian" and "The Annunciation" in *Green with Beasts* (1956). These poems palpably convey a sense of pain combined with elation, as if Merwin, with an unusual capacity for empathy, took up the role of divine suffering himself. These poems also seize upon what Merwin calls "presence": "Presence is inescapable and at the same time it's something that we cannot express, we cannot hold, and yet cannot escape. And that's why one of the main forms in which presence comes to us is through suffering, and sometimes through moments of great joy, too" (Irwin 48). We are caught in a strange situation: the present can only come to us in the form of either euphoria or anguish, as Merwin's perception of presence normalizes psychic trauma as constitutive of the poetic process. The poets are those who maintain a constant vigilance before the flux of phenomena and a compulsive proximity toward the traumatic present.

---

[1] Edward Brunner likewise regards Merwin's "Notes for a Preface" from the 1960s as an analysis of "the limitations of contemporary culture" even though it "explores the connection between a cultural crisis and the rediscovery of the essentially poetic" (*Poetry* 137).

As if to practice John Berryman's dictum that "great presence / That permitted everything and transmuted it / In poetry was passion" (*FH* 156), Merwin's "The Passion" centers on the double meaning of "passion" (*passio*) as both divine suffering and ardent human desire / drive. These two levels are so libidinally interwoven that readers cannot tell whether Merwin was narrating the Crucifixion of Jesus or lamenting the two lovers who were persecuted by the public. For Edward Brunner, "The Passion" simply "compares the public exposure of a love affair to the Crucifixion" (*Poetry* 33). The poem, however, is not so much about the consecration of a secular love affair as about the explosion of the inner split of Christ himself between divinity and mortality. Shifting between the first-person singular *I* and a collective *we*, the narrator's role ranges from Merwin himself to Jesus, Christian martyrs (St. Peter or St. Paul) and the two thieves who, according to the Gospels, were nailed up together with Christ. To push the textual indeterminacy to an extreme, the whole speech addressed by the speaker to the unspecified *you* can be read as an internal anguished dialogue between Jesus's mortality and divinity.

Critics, Cary Nelson for example, who treat Merwin's religious poems as ironic seem to neglect the elegiac tone in them (85). Consider this stanza:

> We heard the nails scream
> In the wood as they were drawn
> Out from the last time,
> And felt their pain; the cry
> You swore was old affection
> And smiled upon the sound
> Not woodenly, but I turned
> My wooden face away. (*FF* 84)

The pathos, terror, and *jouissance* of the situation derive from the fact that *you*, the all-powerful deity, "swore" my death-cry as an "old affection" and "smiled upon" the sound of the nails that were driven into my flesh. Here the "wooden" face indicates that the divine suffering was so excruciating even for Jesus himself that his flesh could hardly endure it.

Apparently, Jesus here is presented as a hysteric torn between bodily pain and spiritual faith in a God who inflicted this pain as his divine side reassures his weaker side that all this drama of death has to be lived through: "The earth shook; and, although / You said it was not real, / The dark was ours ... / Doubt not, love, though the first / Death is original"

(*FF* 84). It is only through this "original," gratuitous, and nonsensical sacrifice — a sacrifice eluding symbolic exchange of words and intentions — that the "logic of sin and punishment" would be "suspend[ed]," as Žižek suggests, and that a new ethical order as Christian love could be established (*Totalitarianism* 49). What attracts Merwin, however, is not Christian theology per se but how this theology is inscribed on human body, or to apply the words of Levinas, how "the Infinite passes the finite," leaving a holy subject hystericized, decentered, and eventually devastated: "This being torn up from oneself in the core of one's unity, this absolute non-coinciding, this diachrony of the instant, signifies in the form of one-penetrated-by-the-other. The pain, this underside of skin, is a nudity more naked than all destitution" (*Otherwise* 49).

Confronting the desire of the God-Other, Merwin's disoriented speaker in the poem seems to oscillate between, or rather combine, Levinasian obsession and Lacanian fantasy: "Che vuoi?" ("What do you want from me?") Is all this suffering staged for the sole purpose of fulfilling what is prophesied in the Scripture? Will this pain, "this underside of skin," be healed by divine love when this tragi-comedy of holy suffering is over? Merwin offers a rather ambiguous ending:

> They led us away
> To this place we were to harrow
> And rise from, the third day,
> And how so scripture be truthful,
> Yet this pain we pass through,
> Though shared, consumes us by
> Dividing infinitely,
> Is at all times eternal. (*FF* 85)

Instead of obtaining mystic unity with the Christian God, the speaker finally realizes that the holy oneness is unattainable. The subject is enabled to approach the transcendental holiness through human sacrifice, only to find himself caught again in an endless separation from that holiness. For Levinas as well as for Merwin, the holy encounter has already presupposed separation, or put more directly, the encounter *is* the separation: "[I]n order that the desire beyond being not be an absorption, the desirable (or God) must remain separated within desire: near, yet different — which is, moreover, the very meaning of the word 'holy'" (Levinas, *God* 223).

Merwin's *spirit* and saints answer the interpellation of God while remaining helplessly distant from Him, and the war between one's corporeality and spirituality produces a voice that is internally split. In "Saint Sebastian" for example, we witness the speaker's inability to integrate / contain his traumatic desire for God; as Merwin uses the first-person narrative to present a varied version of the Passion, the scene would come more acutely alive. St. Sebastian died a martyr: he was tied to a post and shot with arrows. In "St. Sebastian," painted by Giovanni Antonio Bazzi (1477-1549), the saint is shown tied to a withered tree, three arrows shooting through his neck, rib, and leg, his head turning upward with a terrible agony on his face, and above him an angel visibly hovers and shines. Merwin might have had this picture in mind when he wrote the poem. What strikes readers first is a painful admittance that welcomes death as the absolute unknown Other, as the final moment of ecstasy / *ekstasis*, what Heidegger in *Being and Time* famously formulates as "the possibility of the absolute impossibility of Dasein" (294). The poem begins:

> So many times I have felt them come, Lord,
> The arrows (a coward dies often), so many times,
> And worse, oh worse often than this. Neither breeze nor bird
> Stirring the hazed peace through which the day climbs. (*FF* 176)

The repeated conjunctions of sibilant *s* with long vowels (*ai*, *i:*, *ə:* in *arrows*, *worse*, *stirring*, *peace*, *times*, *climes*) set up certain Latinate heaviness characteristic of sacred occasions, as if the impending death were all but solemnly silent with each breath prolonged and then fading away.[①] The speaker here, watchful of the "hazed peace through which the day climbs," epitomizes what Levinas says about awakening and insomnia as "an exigency or demand," "a more within the less," "a piercing or a fission" in the subject (*God* 209-210). In this seemingly peaceful opening, Merwin introduces the violence of the holy Other done to the self, a recurrent topos in Christian spiritual writings as can be found in the works of St. John of the Cross and St. Teresa of Avila. Discourses, poetic or prosaic, on holy afflictions (wounds) abound in church history; Merwin,

---

① In Latin, conjunctions of sibilance and long vowels (diphthongs) are common because of the particular morphology and the declensions of the language. In St. Fortunatus' well-known hymn "Lingua Gloriosi Proelium Certaminis," we witness the divine triumph over human weakness similar to Merwin's poem, delivered in an intricate sound system containing sibilant fricatives and vowels that could be read with much emphasis: "Pange lingua gloriosi prœlium certaminis / Et super crucis tropæo dic triumphum nobilem, / Qualiter Redemptor orbis immolatus vicerit."

however, seems to play with the idea of it without truly committing himself, for the poetic mask always invites the possibility of a double reading.

Merwin reports that, like Jesus in "The Passion," who observed that "virgins darkly / Coming with their lamps untrimmed" (*FF* 84), St. Sebastian in his own moment of death keenly observed what was happening around him. He heard "few sounds that come / Falling" and doubted whether "the noise of angels, // The beat and whirring between Thy kingdoms" could possibly "Be even by such cropped feathers raised." Here Merwin intimates that St. Sebastian in his dying moment might have mistaken the sound of the flying birds for "the noise of angels." The saint's final fear is surely not death but the possibility that God might have abandoned him in death to death with nonaction, recalling Jesus's agonized death cry: "Eli, Eli, lama sabachthani? that is to say, My God, my God, why hast thou forsaken me?" (*King James Version*, Matt. 27. 46). What if the noise of angels is nothing but the sound effect of the birds in the air? This could be one of the final questions flashing through St. Sebastian's mind. The speaker was further hystericized when he stunningly found that he was unable to "fly *from* Thee," "for it is / Thy kingdom where ... I stand in pain" (*FF* 176; emphasis added). The anticipated passage from the secular world where "the archers move" to the holy kingdom, in its Christian context, appears not liberating but restrictively ominous. The mystical *jouissance* is engendered exactly in the final cry that initiates the believer into the holy — there seems no other choice — through the crack of wounds: "entered with pain as always, / Thy kingdom that on these erring shafts comes" (*FF* 176).

The tone of the poem is far from univocal, since Merwin frequently engages his speakers in an unironic, or sympathetic, religious narrative in which the subject goes through various symptoms before the enigmatic demand of the Judeo-Christian God. The most epic treatment of this divine affliction is found in "The Annunciation," a long poem dealing with Gabriel's annunciation to Mary about the birth of Jesus the holy child. Like "Saint Sebastian," the poem records the fantastic inner process of divine penetration. H. L. Hix has observed that the poem "appears to focus not on the annunciation but on the immaculate conception, the event in which the Holy Spirit causes Mary to conceive a child," attributing Mary's mental confusion to her failure of language and weakness of memory (*Understanding* 30). Consider the following lines:

Chapter 2 Spirit in Flame : Merwin's Dallying with Anonymous Holiness

> ... And I thought, Lord, Lord, and thought
> How if I had not gone out on the light
> And been hidden away on the vanished light
> So that myself I was empty and nothing
> I would surely have died, because *the thing*
> That the darkness was, and the wings and the shaking,
> That there was no word for it, was *a thing that in myself*
> *I could not have borne and lived.* (*FF* 166; emphasis added)

As in "Saint Sebastian," here we witness a hystericized subject before the desire of the God-Other when Mary asked: "what am I / That He should be mindful of?" (*FF* 169−170). What is this recurrent thing that Mary saw? Is it the Lacanian Thing caught in the throat of the believing subject, the Thing as the void-kernel of subjectivity ("myself I was empty and nothing") placed by the Christian God in her own body? It is impossible for Mary, a mortal woman, to bear — that is, to conceive and to endure — Christ the divine, infinite Thing in her body without some kind of miraculous intervention. Mary tries to articulate this intervention, but her speech at best resembles the discourse of a "psychotic" subject for her verbal hallucinations and confusions of syntax, preposition, and conjunction. Merwin's transformation of this failure of language into the triumph of poetry is worth considering, for poetry (*parole*) may proceed, or succeed, where language (*langue*) blunders.

The linguistic dysfunction resulting from cognitive dissonance is surely a sign of panic in this dazzling play of light and darkness in which the Thing, the embodied Word, emerges. Mary's breathless repetition of "the thing ... / was a thing" discloses a tremendous fear that can only be found in nightmares or horror films. In a Dantean stroke, Mary's cry that "there was no word for it" names the Christ-Thing as the postmodern sublime: "[T]here was suddenly / A great burning under the darkness, a fire / Like fighting up into the wings' lash and the beating / Blackness, and flames like the tearing of teeth, / With noise like rocks rending ..."(*FF* 166−167). Such an ultra-phenomenon has penetrated Mary's perception-conscious apparatus and left memory traces, which she tries in vain to integrate. Randall Stiffler's comment on Mary that "her memory cannot grasp nor her language reproduce the breadth, depth, and intensity that her experience of the body of God possessed" conveniently summarizes the situation (qtd. in Hix, *Understanding* 32).

The most intriguing thing in "The Annunciation," however, may not be the failure of language and weakness of memory but the paradoxical notion of encounter as separation. Mary's meeting with the holy is already a separation, a deferred action, since she could not locate the vital break from pre-creational chaos (*apeiron*) to origin (*arche*), from "there was no word for it" (*FF* 166) to "If I could only remember / The word" (*FF* 171). For Mary, the "word," God's logos, is that ghostly Thing that has disappeared before it can appear, or, the logos appears exactly by fading away. It never appears as such. Merwin's Mary becomes a melancholic subject whose libido is excessively fixated on the loss of the "word," for "the subject possesses [the lost object] in the very mode of loss" (Žižek, *Plague* 195). Hence Mary's endless sense of guilt and self-recrimination: "Only / If I could remember, if I could only remember / The way that word was, and the sound of it. Because / There is that in me still draws all that I am / Backward, as weeds are drawn down when the water / Flows away; and if I could only shape / And hear again that word and the way of it" (*FF* 171).

What is "the way of the word"? Did Mary ever grasp it in a certain, univocal way? Contrary to standard Christian theology, which regards the "word" as the Logos or Christ himself, Merwin's Mary understood it as a plenitude, an undivided One: "It was a word for / The way the light and the things in the light / Were looking into the darkness, and the darkness / And the things of the darkness were looking into the light / In the fullness" (*FF* 167). Although she believed that she had grasped the "word": "I knew it, and held it and knew / The way of it, " she soon conceded that "Or almost, Or believed I knew it, believed, like an echo" (*FF* 168). Mary's contact with the divine word is based on an infinite withdrawal of the word which is forever to come ("the coming of it, " "when it comes"), and this coming and going, this non-present trace of the holy, would haunt her till the end of the poem, and as James McCorkle said perceptively, "The poem is itself a recounting or remembering — thus a supplementation — of the loss of the vision, rather than a re-creation of the vision" (*Still* 135). The ultimate pathos of the poem comes from the fact that after the divine visitation Mary lost her former self and was caught in the predicament of having to articulate that which would constitute her new identify as Mother of Christ, a "terrible" gift. In a compulsive repetition she laments her infinite (non) separation from the divine thing (Christ, word, logos, revelation) that was once part of her own soul and breath:

> If I could only remember
> The word, if I could make it with my breath

> It would be with me forever as it was
> Then in the beginning … if I could remember
> And make the word with my breath. (*FF* 171)

Distance is where we were

The Christian poems in the 1950s, as Merwin's first stage, laid down a matrix of poetic cathexes that Merwin would employ later in non-Christian modes. The "passion of signifiers" around the holy Other produces a spiritual discourse that does not consist in one's mystical union with this Other, as some critics have conceived. For instance, Anthony Libby concludes his long essay on Merwin's 1960s poems: "In Merwin's world, human union with animals and gods can come only through an acceptance of otherness so complete that it obliterates the doomed human self, now unable to hear the messages that might save it" ("W. S. Merwin": 40). Libby's observation of the "complete" "otherness" is accurate, but the "human union with animals and gods" seems too simple a formula to explain away Merwin's encounter with the holy entity. Instead of a wishful "union," what happens to Merwin and his speakers comes closer to an anticipated or missed encounter as witnessed by his representations of St. Sebastian and the Virgin Mary.

This provides a new paradigm in locating Merwin's continuity; although entering a new phase of writing in the early '70s, Merwin would frequently return to the earlier Christian motifs, with a less recognizable form but an equally conspicuous signature. Those critics who see personal pessimism and cultural dissolution in *The Moving Target* (1963), *The Lice* (1967), and *The Carrier of Ladders* (1970) as definitive are reluctant to acknowledge Merwin's longtime transferential relationship with the deified Other.[1] This reluctance, not surprisingly, reveals that some critics in the 1970s were not ready to credit Merwin's dallying with an uncanny God in place of urgent national and political agendas. But if we have really probed into Merwin's noncommittal gesture, we could see what occupied Merwin in the late 1960s and early 1970s was not merely the merging of historical closure with an inner emptiness, but his continuing exploration of what he elsewhere calls "the other side of despair," the exterior to the fallen socio-

---

[1] For instance, see Libby, "W. S. Merwin" 19-40; Lazer 262-284.

symbolic order. The non-despairing side manifests itself in the indefatigable demand for a more fragmented, therefore more truthful, self who keeps its integrity by staying with wilderness.

One of the opening poems in *The Moving Target*, "Lemuel's Blessing," focuses on the relationship between spirit and wilderness, subject and object, the Same and the Other; again, Merwin inhabits the consciousness of a biblical figure, conflating author and persona. The poem heralds the dramatic turn of the biblical Lemuel into the Lacanian object and his experience of becoming "one-penetrated-by-the-other," or being taken as hostage, as it were, by this extimate Other (Levinas, *Otherwise* 49). Cheri Davis points out that "Merwin creates a Lemuel who *is* the wolf who begs his Spirit to give him purity and strength in his independence and solitary exile" (52; emphasis original). H. L. Hix likewise notices that "the identification with the wolf becomes so thorough that the subject and object are hard to distinguish" ("Thematic" 69). The confusion of identity is already implied in the epigraph Merwin quotes from the English poet Christopher Smart (1722−1771): "Let Lemuel bless with the wolf, which is a dog without a master, but the Lord hears his cries and feeds him in the desert" (*SF* 12). Readers do not know for certain whether the pronoun "which" refers to Lemuel or the wolf; we can read it either way: the wolf is a dog without a master, or, Lemuel is a dog without a master. Both readings suit Merwin's purpose of portraying a dislocated subject who has abandoned the symbolic community by forming a non-reciprocal relationship with the wolf-spirit qua the heterogeneous Stranger. As Paul Carroll says aptly, what Lemuel prays for "is to become free of the human community, its traditional values, and its definition of who or what he is or should be" (146).

The poem begins with a Hölderlinian apostrophe: "You that know the way, / Spirit, / I bless your ears which are like cypresses on a mountain / With their roots in wisdom. Let me approach" (*SF* 12). This opening makes explicit Merwin's preference for the psalmist tone throughout his writing career. Unlike other postmodern poets who adopt irony as the governing principle (John Ashbery, Frank O'Hara, Ginsberg), Merwin sticks to a tone that joins elegists with psalmists, which may sound familiar or even outmoded to modern ears. Yet the *poesis* of spiritual matters (saints, angels, Godhead) seems to require a pietistic procedure to stage the enthrallment of the finite by the infinite. Before the wild wolf-spirit, Lemuel willingly surrenders all his egoity; he was desubjectivized on the

Symbolic level — got rid of his social ties — while resubjectivized on the Real level — tied to a Thing he could not quite understand. The nominative address ("You that know the way, / Spirit") places the Other into the Same, establishing the "exceptional" notion of infinity with "its ideatum surpass[ing] its idea" (Levinas, *Totality* 49). This mysterious *you*, as Bin Ramke remarks, is "assumed to have insight or answers unavailable to the poet" (135). From Lemuel's pleading for proximity ("Let me approach") readers can extrapolate that the spirit qua the desirable still remains remote, just as Lemuel's desire is directed "toward an absolute, unanticipatable alterity, as one goes forth unto death" (Levinas, *Totality* 34).

Lemuel's unconditional devotion to the wolf-spirit reverses the normal relationship between subject and object: "[F]or without you / I am nothing but a dog lost and hungry, / Ill-natured, untrustworthy, useless" (*SF* 12). The deprecation of the self before the Other originates from the superegoic function of the divine as creating a primordial sense of guilt, which is also seen in Mary's lament over the lost "word." Like St. Sebastian's ecstatic cry of "Thy kingdom ... comes," Lemuel anticipates that which is not exactly anticipatable: to be led by the spirit into the wilderness in order to escape his community: "Deliver me // From the ruth of the lair, which clings to me in the morning, / Painful when I move, like a trap" (*SF* 13). "Ruth" is an archaic word for "grief," yet Merwin may have chosen it out of its similar sound to "ruse," "trick." Lemuel's long litany provides an intriguing case of Merwin's medievalism that denounces worldly symbolic exchange as vanity or trick: "From the ruth of kindness, with its licked hands; I have sniffed baited fingers and followed / Toward necessities which were not my own: it would make me / An habitué of back steps, faithful custodian of fat sheep; // From the ruth of prepared comforts, with its / Habitual dishes sporting my name and its collars and leashes of vanity" (*SF* 13). Lemuel therefore becomes a Christian saint who adamantly refuses false necessities in order to realize a higher, capitalized Necessity: "May I bow to Necessity not / To her hirelings" (*SF* 97).

Reading the poem along with other biblical psalms, Paul Carroll finds that "here the Psalm is used to petition a spirit who seems to embody characteristics which are anti-communal" (145). Actually, Lemuel has gone much further to transform himself into a Christian counterpart of Antigone who, in a psychoanalytical interpretation, might have equated "her particular / determinate decision with the Other's (Thing's) injunction / call" (Žižek, *Totalitarianism* 163). Seduced by the spirit qua the infinite Other,

Lemuel becomes the death-drive that endures triumphantly, ignoring all worldly hindrances: "Let my nails pour out a torrent of aces like grain from a threshing machine; / Let fatigue, weather, habitation, the old bones, finally, / Be nothing to me, / Let all lights but yours be nothing to me. / Let the memory of tongues not unnerve me so that I stumble or quake" (*SF* 13-14). With such iron fortitude, Lemuel equates himself with the *spirit*, the non-symbolizable excess over material life that takes care of its well-being, "a pure impersonal Willing ... that wills nothing" (Žižek, *Abyss* 15).

Since "Lemuel's Blessing" Merwin has preferred a merciless and even antihuman evocation of sainthood, fostering what Paul Carroll characterizes as "lonely austerity" (148). Through a psychological identification with the holy, Merwin's saints are those who have replaced desire (spiritual yearning) *for* the holy with their own drive (repetitive gestures) *as* holy. Such a Merwinesque reversal is best seen in "The Saint of the Uplands," which supplements "Saint Sebastian" by continuing what was left unsaid about entering "Thy kingdom." Customarily, Merwin himself dwells in the consciousness of the saint, exploding the inner nonidentity of the holiness of the holy: "Their prayers still swarm on me like lost bees. / I have no sweetness. I am dust / Twice over" (*SF* 20). The repetition of sibilant sound coupled with long vowels, like a long strain of sighs, introduces an elegiac tone, and the decreasing length of each line adds finality to the declaration of a burnt-out holy subject: "dust twice over," because the saint, unlike ordinary people, assumes the lack not only of humanity but also of "divinity." It may seem paradoxical that the saint, as the poem tells us, does not possess divine knowledge (a higher value) but disavows it. Furthermore, the following lines exhibit a kind of non-Christian holiness that seems to associate Christian sainthood with a simulacrum, an appearance that refuses or is unable to offer gnosis or salvation:

> In the high barrens
> The light loved us.
> Their faces were hard crusts like their farms
> And the eyes empty, where vision
> Might not come otherwise
> Than as water.
>
> They were born to stones; I gave them
> Nothing but what was theirs.
> I taught them to gather the dew of their nights

> Into mirrors. I hung them
> Between heavens. (*SF* 20)

These lines are unusual for their exhibition of the saint's problematical, surreal denial of a higher vision concerning spiritual redemption. This is not the only place where readers are left with a non-operative deity, and it is easy to conclude that in the 1960s Merwin's deities were alien to mankind: "irreducibly alien" (Libby, "Merwin's planet" 37), or empty: "the nothing behind everything" (Bowers 252), or simply nonexistent: "Merwin is a symbolist emptied of God" (Gross 105). These comments might have overlooked the fact that there is an uncanny, shimmering, and transparent *something* in Merwin's God, gods, and saints. In this poem, the saint was both alien and intimate, a mirror reflecting the believers' own images: "I gave them / Nothing but what was theirs. / I taught them to gather the dew of their nights / Into mirrors. I hung them / Between heavens" (*SF* 20). In a Socratic manner, the saint of the uplands confessed his own lack and mocked the believers' blind desire for revelation:

> I took a single twig from the tree of my ignorance
> And divined the living streams under
> Their very houses. I showed them
> The same tree growing in their dooryards.
> You have ignorance of your own, I said.
> They have ignorance of their own. (*SF* 20)

By presupposing a sort of non-understandable holiness, the believers in the poem confer their asymmetrical, non-dialogical trust in the saint, who ironically exposes his own emptiness as foundational of religious discourse: "I taught them nothing. / Every where / The eyes are returning under the stone. And over / My dry bones they build their churches like wells" (*SF* 20).

"The Saint of the Uplands" deviates from traditional Christian poetry if we take that to mean carols, hymns, and psalms, and more generally, poetry that centers on God's supreme powers of redemption and damnation (George Herbert, John Donne, T. S. Eliot). Merwin's poem is not simply a recasting of biblical themes but an ironic — bordering on "heretical" — treatment of Christian sainthood that overshoots the canonical denotations of the holy as shown in the Old and New Testament. The poem stretches readers' expectation toward a more primitivistic, anonymous, and fragmentary holiness, laying bare the inner contradiction in sainthood. Like the elements of water and light, divinities are phantasmagorical entities showing no concern for humans. In a poem titled "Divinities" Merwin writes: "The air itself is their memory / A domain they cannot inhabit / But from which they are never absent // *What are you* they say *that simply exist /* And the heavens and the earth bow to them / Looking up from their choices / Perishing" (*SF* 116; emphasis original). Instead of denying the existence of gods, Merwin exposes gods' own inanities and the false necessities imposed by them, and this redefinition of divinity perhaps constitutes Merwin's "critical move" typical of his generation — disillusioned Americans in a postwar, postindustrial era.

The exploration of the divine simulacra is relentlessly launched in a later poem "Words from a Totem Animal," where Merwin abandons the Christian narrative and lives in the voice of a pagan totem. Similar to Robert Bly who can feel the "nomad bands" under his own skin (*Selected* 94), Merwin would inhabit the soul of a nomadic animal, entering, as it were, the sacred spirit to see what happens there and report it to readers. Consistent with his Christian poems, Merwin would make the divine Thing talk about itself: "Distance / is where we were" (*SF* 141), echoing an earlier line that "remoteness is its own secret" ("The Wilderness," *FF* 156). Fleeing from the socio-symbolic order into the undefined wilderness seems to establish an extimate aura through which the poetic subject is speciously immortalized: "When you think of the distances / you recall / that we are immortal" (*SF* 230). The immortal totem goes on to confess "its own secret," its own *Spaltung*: "I would rather the wind came from outside ... / ghost of mine passing / through me" (*SF* 141). The "wind" inside the totem animal, like Rilke's "der Wind voller Weltraum" (150), maddens even divinity itself for the vast, wild, and excessive emptiness, as H. L. Hix puts it aptly, "this wholly disembodied voice speaks from nowhere, to no one, and a propos of nothing" ("Thematic" 73). To explore the inwardness of poetry is a shared concern among American deep-imagists such as Robert Bly, James Wright, and Charles Simic, who endeavor to do what Bly urges as the "journey into dark place," "leap to spirit" and "solitary wildness" (*American Poetry* 48). But Merwin's strategy here is even more radical in that it debunks the unicity not only of the lyric subject but also of the deified object, which are one in "Words from a Totem Animal." Merwin has pushed Bly's program of an unconscious poetics toward the great purge of authorial control, dallying with the alien spirit to create an undead, uncontainable state in which we —

readers situated exactly in *nowhere*, only hear "the repetition / like that of a word in the ear of death / teaching itself / itself" (*SF* 141).

Although exclaiming the totem as the "god of beginnings / immortal, " Merwin insists on a heterogeneity that resists any anthropocentric categorization: "Caught again and held again / again I am not a blessing / they bring me / names / that would fit anything" (*SF* 142). The poet criticizes man's presumptuous act of reducing animals to a "name, " a holy signifier which substitutes and erases its own being.① In fact, Merwin has been very cautious about the double use of naming, as he said in a 1988 interview: "[Naming] sets up a concept between you and what you are looking at. The cat doesn't know it's a cat until you teach it that it is a cat" (Elliott 18). The naming process, as Derrida would say, is indeed a violent imprint of human signification on innocent nature. What Merwin strives at here is crossing the manmade border of *les mots* to get into the heart of *les choses*: "[T]here is an *evocation of the thing* that is there before there's a name, before there's a concept of it" (Elliott 19; emphasis added). This would involve the paradoxical procedure of having to enunciate the phantasmal Thing *in words*, as Merwin did in "The Annunciation, " before it is subsumed under a fixed identity and to expose its constant flux without resorting to any fixed concept. Looking back at Merwin's " wild " imagination in the early 1960s, Richard Howard finds that "the generally unpunctuated poems look as though they had been exploded, not written down, the images arranged so that the lines never enclose but instead *expose* them" (436; emphasis original). Through evoking and exposing the desire of / for the holy, Merwin's images send readers on a strange, vacuum-driven, minimalistic journey few US poets have embarked upon: "My eyes are waiting for me / in the dusk / they are still closed / they have been waiting a long time / and I am feeling my way toward them" (*SF* 142). Embodying the lack in the chain of signification, the totem is caught in the eternal flux of becoming, entering a domain where "there are no stars / there is no grief / I will never arrive / I stumble when I remember how it was / with one foot / one foot still in a name" (*SF* 142). Such exposure is not readily available in a postindustrial world where the *spirit* is daily threatened by machines or produced by them, nor is it a representation of

① For Jacques Derrida, any naming process necessarily involves "originary violence of language" (*Grammatology* 112); here Merwin agrees with Derrida in cautioning us against the ethnocentric / anthropologic use of the proper name.

the wilderness that one may simply escape into. It offers a picture of the uninhabitable, the otherwise unseen interval between mortality and immortality as laid down in all theology and philosophy.

Climbing the holy mountain

Throughout his poetical career, Merwin longs for the redeeming spirit that can elevate one above a life that is all too human, although the nature of that spirit remains unknown and unclear. As in many extant spiritual writings, the ascension takes the form of mountain climbing. The approach to the infinite seems to necessitate a distance from the maddening crowd, so the mountain felicitously serves as a spiritual elevator for its auratic proximity to posited divinity. In fact, Merwin's 1960s poems are conspicuously marked by the climbing gesture: "The heavy limbs climb into the moonlight bearing feathers"; "Climbing northward / At dusk when the horizon rose like a hand I would turn aside"; "I have climbed a long way / there are my shoes"; "and once more it climbs / trying to cast again" (*SF* 108, 114, 188, 254). "Climbing northward, " Merwin would "once more celebrate our distance from men" (*SF* 114). Merwin's endeavor, however, is directed at diluting the Judeo-Christian connotation of the mountain image while maintaining its rapport with spiritual quest. Even in the most manifestly Christian poems we find a landscape quite different from what Dante or Eliot, in his late work, have portrayed. Instead of preaching Christian values, Merwin explores the speaker's consciousness when it is confronted with the divine. The poet associates the ascent of mountains not only with spiritual advancement of *Homo sapiens* but also with an eager attempt to explore the division between mortality and divinity, temporality and eternity.

The mountain was a mysterious subject as early as *Green with Beasts* (1956), which contains a long discursive poem, "The Mountain, " which records the searing power of the divine on high. The mountain, like Mount Sinai, the site of the Judeo-Christian God, remains inaccessible to mortals, except for those like Moses, enwrapped in a shining aura. "Only on rarest occasions, when the blue air, / Though clear, is not too blinding / ... can one trace the rising / Slopes high enough to call them contours" (*FF* 172). Allegorizing the mountain in the vein of Dante, Merwin conjectures that "the slope, to be so elusive / And yet so inescapable, must be nothing / But ourselves." If the "elusive" yet "inescapable" presence of the holy corresponds to an uncontainable longing in the human psyche, then the mountain as the site of the infinite Other would help to release that desire for its intimate strangeness: "its / Strangeness composed of our own intimacy" and "our necessary / Ignorance of its limits." The sublimity of the mountain escapes common observation, so instead of portraying the mountain from a tourist's point of view, Merwin approaches it with a folklorist's curiosity and awe: "No one, / From whatever distance, has ever so much as seen / The summit, or even anywhere near it." He further compares the mountain to "Mecca / For fanatics and madmen" and calls any attempt to approach it "a kind of holy maelstrom," "a mode of ritual / And profane suicide." Manifestly echoing an earlier poem "White Goat, White Ram" while foretelling "Words from a Totem Animal," Merwin's holy mountain is again full of "ceaseless wind / With a noise like thunder and the beating of wings" (*FF* 173), a familiar representation of divinity in the Christian tradition.

There are those who try to approach the inapproachable, and as Merwin reports in fear and trembling, "Very few / Who set out at all seriously have / Come back." The poet invests the mountain with what Walter Benjamin calls the "divine violence," which strikes "without vanity, without threat, and does not stop short of annihilation" (*Reflections* 297). The blinding force on top of the mountain, if not totally annihilating the climbers, at least maims them for their lifetime: "For of those / Who attained any distance and returned, most / Were deafened, some permanently; some were blind, / And these also often incurably; all / Without exception were dazzled, as by a great light" (*FF* 174). The symptoms resulting from the *tuché* (encounter) with the holy consummate in the dysfunction of the signifying chain, as the farthest climbers, when they came back, "completely lost the use of our language" and only "babbled incoherently / Of silence bursting beyond that clamor" (*FF* 174). The climbers suffered from an infinite vision that could not be contained by their forms of life and speech.

Like a gigantic magnet, the mountain draws the psychic energy of the climbers and pilgrims, functioning as the object of man's infinite desire. Levinas asks: "Does not the desiring one derive from the desirable a satisfaction in desiring, as if he had already seized the desirable?" (*God* 222). Similarly the desirable, the holy mountain, the Promised Land, still remains distant, which only makes the spirit torture itself in its incessant pursuit. In the prose poem "Hunger Mountain" in *Houses and Travellers* (1977), Merwin shows the possibility of redemption after a long, hard pilgrimage, yet with such indeterminacy that we may divest it of any Christian intention and read it as a manifesto of one's metaphysical desire — "a bursting of the Same, whom the Other disturbs or tears out of his repose" (Levinas, *God* 195):

> Who has been to the top of Hunger Mountain and seen what can be seen from there, and returned? The view of The Promised Land. Most who have come to tell went only part way. Many have died part way. And even they have seen things that no one else ever saw, things they could not describe, too hard for the words, and then too hard for them, the witnesses. But certain ones who never forget and who never sleep gave us their words to eat. They buried their words in us and went away, leaving us hungry, part way. (*BF* 263)

The paragraph is full of allusions to the Bible: the historical exodus of the Israelites, their wandering in the wilderness, Joshua and Caleb, together with ten others, "spy[ing] out" Canaan, the Promised Land, from the top of a mountain in the Old Testament, and anachronistically, the virgins in the New Testament who "slumbered and slept" while waiting for the resurrection of Christ (*King James Version*, Num. 13.16; Matt. 25.5). In this paragraph Merwin reveals the presencing absence of the mysterious "things" and their inexplicable hold on travelers' psyches. In its exigent desire for the Land, provoked by what Derrida calls "the irruption of a speech or a promise," the *spirit* shatters the repose of the self, "leaving us hungry, part way," undermining the divine speech that made the very promise. If, as Derrida says elsewhere, "language, the word — in a way, the life of the word — is in essence spectral" (*Sovereignties* 103), then we may regard Merwin's account as a picture of how desire is exactly maintained on the level of the revealing "words." Merwin's climbers are always on the way toward the holy without arriving; it is this immeasurable mirage of the holy that affords unmistakable *jouissance* and directs the projection of the self, which only continues to exist by eating words left by the "witnesses."

"His is not a poetry of rhetoric, but of spirit," Amy Newman says of Merwin (127), but we know how much suffering without knowledge, as organized through speech, could inhere in this kind of spiritual recording. If in the 1950s Merwin was still an apprentice of spiritual writing, honing his talent on traditional carols, hymns, psalms, in the late 1960s the time was ripe to launch a less ornamental, perhaps more authentic, even bare-knuckled spiritual discourse. The desire to transcend the mundane permeates Merwin's most "pessimistic" book in the 1960s, *The Lice*, as a defense mechanism against historical impasse. Reading *The Lice*, William Rueckert finds, as a few other critics also have, that "it is one of Merwin's attempts to understand the other, nonhuman world — not to find reasons to explain it away, but to understand it and himself in relation to it" (61). Merwin's "relation" with the Other is simultaneously a diachronic nonrelation because for him hope comes from a radical heterogeneity. In the preface to the 1960s poems Merwin writes: "Wild aspiration and vertiginous despair existed not alternately but at once, and at times we may have clung to visionary hopes ... because we felt it would be not only mean-spirited but fatal to abandon them" (*SF* 1–2). The "wild aspiration" and "visionary hopes" presuppose an omnipotent Other who is capable of redeeming the believers from their specific historical conditions. Read together with earlier Christian poems, *The Lice* is not so much a book of desperation as of anticipation. Although different from the sea poems of the 1950s in detail and treatment, Merwin's pilgrimage poems of the 1960s largely continue the search for the "sublime object" — the mysterious aura outlined but not contained by language and speech.

"December Night," a poem about climbing, typifies Merwin's approach to the non-Christian holy in the 1960s and in his later period. Presently he drops biblical figures, experimenting with a sort of anonymous holiness. The poem begins with what he elsewhere calls "a description of darkness" (*SF* 99): "The cold slope is standing in darkness / But the south of the trees is dry to touch" (*SF* 108). The landscape stands in a time devoid of human meanings and intentions, a dark, strange domain: "The heavy limbs climb into the moonlight bearing feathers / I came to watch these / White plants older at night / The oldest / Come first to the ruins" (*SF* 108). Merwin might use *feathers* to suggest the vestige of divinity, partly fulfilling the responsibility of a poet in a "destitute" time: "to attend, singing, to the trace of the fugitive gods" (Heidegger, *Poetry* 94). But in Merwin's stanza the situation is more equivocal for the oxymoronic coupling of "heavy limbs" with "feathers"; Merwin seems to emphasize the interrelation between mortality and divinity, which both Rilke and Heidegger have thought of as constitutive of humanity, while at the same time Merwin intimates that such a relation may be intrinsically ironic and even violent. Though the climbing gesture recalls Dante's ascent in

Purgatorio, it still remains undefined for its mergence into the anonymous "moonlight."

The speaker came to the slope to watch the old trees that were struggling through the hard winter. The "ruins" may hint at historical closure, but they might as well indicate the cycle of nature that begins a new life on the debris of the "oldest" ones. The next stanza continues in its otherworldliness, rendering the speaker "I" a mere spectator in the nightly mountain-view:

> And I hear magpies kept awake by the moon
> The water flows through its
> Own fingers without end (*SF* 108)

Merwin's pilgrimage, although conducted in the month of Christ's birth, proclaims not the birth of a personified savior but an anonymous purification in the wilderness. Merwin ends the poem with lines that Dante would never have written: "Tonight once more / I find a single prayer and it is not for men" (*SF* 108). The lesson the speaker gleans on the desolate mountain slope substitutes cosmology for theology, as the prayer is directed toward the unknown force that operates through animate and inanimate worlds.[①] But we should not hasten to crown Merwin "a poet of animism," as some critics do (Hix, "Thematic" 68); Merwin's climbing spirit desires a holiness that seems to transcend any known formulation or thematization, recalling Zen Buddhism — which Merwin has practiced since the 1970s — which similarly cancels the ontological status of ego to reach a numinous whole. It is on the mountain that Merwin beholds the origin of life and death — the holy water. In another poem, "The Herds," Merwin also witnesses the hushed baptism of the dead on the mountain:

> Sleeping by the glass mountain
> I would watch the flocks of light grazing
> And the water preparing its descent
> To the first dead (*SF* 114)

The mountain represents the primitive site where the dead, as American Indians, receive a natural and mystical ceremony that welcomes their return to Mother Earth. On this "magic mountain," life and death are not socio-

---

① In an alternative reading, the poem might suggest Christ's own "journey into the wilderness" in the Bible, though the naturalistic, impersonal tendency of the poem seems to contradict Christ's prayer to God the Father.

76

historical processes but natural mutations, subjected to a higher necessity than intersubjective norms. The juxtaposition of the grazing flocks and "the first dead" has diluted the intensity of personal mourning when the water descending from the high mountain prepares the dead for the netherworld.

The surreal image of the "glass mountain" strikes us as luminous and evasive, producing an auratic shimmer or what Mark Christhilf calls "the creative, celestial dimension" on the height (50). Climbing the mountain, the speaker discovers an ultra-world where historical time is foreclosed and where light and darkness, life and death, mysteriously interpenetrate. In "The Dream Again," for instance, the speaker gradually merges himself in the glory on the height:

> I take the road that bears leaves in the mountains
> I grow hard to see then I vanish entirely
> On the peaks it is summer (*SF* 113)

Manifestly echoing Goethe's famous lines "Über allen Gipfeln / ist Ruh" (58), this Zenic tercet visualizes the author's spiritual ascendance toward an anonymous, luminous, and overwhelming presence that felicitously obliterates the individual self, if only temporarily. The poetic aura is completed in the convergence of temporal and spatial altitudes: "On the peak it is summer."

The title of the poem "The Dream Again" suggests the realness of the epiphany, just as the repeated dream makes known Merwin's uncompromised drive toward wholeness, even at the expense of completely erasing the self.[①] That the union with the anonymous presence happens in the season of summer, which is highly transient as Merwin records in his memoir *Summer Doorways* (2005), exposes the very momentariness of that union. As Edward Brunner has noted, the other unfragmented world sought by Merwin is itself an ephemeral one: "The silent world of immanent origins is viewed, if at all, as a matter of fleeting impressions, flashing glimpses, for that is the only way we can perceive its unimaginable

---

① In the preface to his translation of the French poet Jean Follain (1903 – 1971), Merwin notes that Follain's works all share a "suspended regard," and it is the "evocation of this 'impersonal,' receptive, but essentially unchanging gaze [that] often occupies, in Follain's work, the place of the first person"("Preface," xii). In "The Dream Again" and other Zenic poems, Merwin's lyric self, as can be found in various mystical practices, is not only *erased* but also *replaced* by an unchanging, divine, vantage.

wholeness" (*Poetry* 287).

Merwin's imagination thus rests on the present that looks so much like death, on the wild anticipation that the old self is dying, making room for the new one. In *The Lice* Merwin often combines the spatial climbing with a temporal one, standing on the threshold of both space and time: "I desire / To kneel in a doorway empty except for the song" (*SF* 111). In "How We Are Spared, " the mountain image is associated with the beginning of a new time sequence:

> At midsummer before dawn an orange light returns to the mountains
> Like a great weight and the small birds cry out
> And bear it up (*SF* 113)

The birds and magpies have replaced the saints and angels in the 1950s as the anonymous messengers of the divine, bringing the speaker undecipherable news which nevertheless concerns him. Climbing the mountain of time, the poetic self is able to evolve with the constant renewal of the days, seasons, and years.

The "orange light" on the mountain, like the "receding fires" Merwin's travelers chased in the early 1950s, animates the poet's spirit and sets it in "conflagration" — to urge him toward a transcendence of imagined origins. In the discussion of Georg Trakl's poem "Grodek, " Heidegger explores the motif of spirit as flaming: "The spirit is flaming. ... Flame is glowing lumination. What flame is the *ek-stasis* which lightens and calls forth radiance. ... The spirit chases, drives the soul to get underway to where it leads the way" (*On the Way* 179 – 180). Derrida explains that "Heidegger can claim to de-Christianize Trakl's *Gedicht*"; Heidegger ventures to locate in Trakl's poetry "an *other* birth and an *other* essence, origin-heterogeneous ... to all the testaments, all the promises, all the events, all the laws and assignments which are our very memory" (*Of Spirit* 108, 107; emphasis original). The suspension of personal history before the "origin-heterogeneous, " infinite Other who ignites the destructive flame of spirituality prepares the rapturous re-temporization of Dasein by burning away false necessities — historical closure, limitations of ideology and habit, etc. For Merwin, as well as for Trakl and Heidegger, the commencing and ending of years, the destruction and rebirth of time, claims the status of being "spiritual" and "revolutionary" and thus *historic* (Derrida, *Of Spirit* 89). Merwin's poems in the 1960s, in this reading, are conspicuously marked by a quest for what Otto, Heidegger, Levinas,

Derrida, Lacan, Žižek have all thought about in their own different ways —
an otherness that constantly dislodges one's socio-historical identity by
returning the subject to an origin that ceaselessly auto-affects its inscriptions.

The initiation of a new temporal-symbolic relation affords a basic
pattern for Merwin to stage his search for what is other than the historically
determined being. The circle of time brings not sameness but difference; the
metamorphosis of the self into the other happens within time and through
time. Just as Merwin asks his French neighbor in the early 1970s: "[S]hall
we set out for the great days / and never be the same / never" (*SF* 149),
every decision to break with the personal past automatically opens a new
horizon for projection, though this opening can be quite indefinite. Merwin
is in fact highly aware of, and even obsessed by, the passage of time,
which can be glimpsed from the titles of poems such as "New Moon in
November," "December Night," "After Solstice," "Midnight in Early
Spring," "Late Night in Autumn" and so on. In "Early January" for
instance, the speaker recognizes the New Year as the heterogonous stranger
who has "arrived from an unknown distance / From beyond the visions of
the old" (*SF* 110). The desire to supersede history ("the visions of the
old") toward an unknown futurity would even take the poet himself by
surprise, since "[e]veryone waited for it by the wrong roads ... / A stranger
to nothing / In our hiding places." Surely there is pain in suffering
existential nothingness, but there is also joy in anticipating that the new
beginning may bring an unexpected change. In a later poem, "End of
Summer," Merwin envisions a new self which, though arising from the old
one, is different from it: "High above us a chain of white buckets / full of
old light going home // now even the things that we do / reach us after long
journeys / and we have changed" (*SF* 229).

The vicissitude of time brings forth a correspondingly decisive change
of the self illuminated by an other carrying water or wine "high above us,"
yet the "old light going home" evokes not an ecclesiastical holiness but a
naturalistic one, and if we take "light" here as a metaphor of time, then time
itself becomes luminous. Although disavowing an omnipotent God in the
1960s like many of his contemporaries, Merwin does not abandon faith — he
puts it in the wandering spirit that "marched and marched on the candle
flame / hurrying / a painful road" (*SF* 182). Merwin's redeeming spirit, his
personal messiah, is always on the way, forever to come, yet to come.
This encounter-in-anticipation marks Merwin's works in the 1960s as pious
without being overtly religious or animistic. In "Midnight in Early Spring"

the speaker was wide awake and anticipating what was not exactly anticipatable:

> some alien blessing
> is on its way to us
> some prayer ignored for centuries
> is about to be granted to the prayerless (*SF* 184)

The exteriority of the blessing evokes the radical contingency of salvation in the postmodern age characterized by flux of all kinds, and the question *who* is going to "grant" the blessing remains unanswered, but it does not mean that it is forever unanswerable.

Calling from above: experiences on Mt. Athos

Merwin's contact with the divine — Christian as well as non-Christian — is a mixture of unchangingness and fleetingness, encountering and anticipating, conviction and illusion. In the early 1970s Merwin visited the Virgin's Holy Mountain of Athos several times and recorded the journeys in a long essay "Reflections of a Mountain, " which was titled "Aspects of a Mountain" when it first appeared in 1975. The essay reveals Merwin's unusual interest in holy services and the meditative tradition of the Orthodox Church. However, Merwin's identity, as the Christian monks on the mountain perceived it, was curious: occasionally he was denied entrance into the ikonostasis because he was not an orthodox Christian, while most of the time he was received cordially for his sympathy for spiritual matters. He was fascinated by church histories, buildings, murals, frescos, icons, and legends of the saints; from the text, we learn that he was already familiar with Church history and Orthodox Christian art before his visit. The Fathers also shared with him their private stories, cooking for him, trusting him as a brother (*EE* 102).

Throughout the visit, Merwin consciously adopted the posture of an outsider: he was suspicious of those monks who proclaimed themselves the owners of spiritual truths, listening to their theological arguments without truly committing himself. In one episode, a young monk lectured him "severely on the perilous folly of [his] heretical state, " as Merwin was not paying attention to the sermon but looking elsewhere to find that "[t]he courtyard was more beautiful: the smooth pallor of the stones in the open air" (*EE* 107). He seems to derive more spiritual revelations from amorphous nature, "the open air." Merwin visited the monasteries for a glimpse of the "living" holy — the Edenic landscapes on Mt. Athos, the hospitality of the monks, and their simple and pious lives. It is with a photographer's eye that Merwin captures the flashes of the holy. He describes the landscapes on the way to Karyes, a settlement on Athos: "Sounds of horsebells, finches. The road switches back and forth, climbing, heads up a wide ravine, doubles back to a point above the sea, turns inland. Holly oak, arbutus, bay trees. Bees. Large languid butterflies in the morning stillness" (*EE* 61). In this condensed, fragmented, breathless description, the author's feet could hardly follow the swift succession of scenes, which, functioning as endless metonymies for the desirable, have only left shining traces for him to pick up. The signifiers point to a vacant center that eludes thematization, for the desirable, the real — "The gods belong to the field of the real," according to Jacques Lacan (45) — presences in its transience. This transient center prods Merwin to climb higher and higher, literally and metaphorically, vertiginously yet indefatigably, till the first view of Karyes:

> The ascent continues as steeply as before. ... The sun climbs but the heights grow cooler. ... The last mists have burned off; the road winds higher and higher. Then, without warning, a sudden presence, off to the right, across a great empty space: the first view of the mountain. Once it has been seen, the sense of it remains wherever one goes on the promontory, whether or not the peak itself is visible. The road clambers on over the ridge, and the eastern sea, the Holy Sea, comes into sight through the chestnut leaves, and down through the woods the roofs of Karyes appear ... (*EE* 61).

The weavings of emergence and disappearance, visibility and invisibility, literality and metaphoricity, realism and dreaminess, make Merwin's travelogue a locus of spiritual discourse. Every natural, phenomenal object he encountered on the mountain — trees, flowers, bees, rocks, vines, stairs, gates, mists, waters, fountains, etc. — was charged with extra denotations, echoing *Psalms*, a book rich in divine metaphors. But Merwin is not a psalmist; he did not impose the Jewish or Christian God, nor would he expose his state of mind easily. Epiphany is for Merwin a hidden, anonymous, even agnostic matter. Although the openness of Merwin's text allows no univocal, theological conclusion, the inner joy of the pilgrimage cannot be mistaken: "On the way down from Koutloumousiou to the south there is a high arch over a rocky torrent ... the hidden water whispering and splashing like mice. Rags of the cloud appeared up on the ridge and vanished over it. Bright sun on the slope to the south" (*EE* 73). It is the hidden water, the vanishing cloud, the bright sun — the living manifestations of the holy — that have spellbound Merwin in his ascent on the mountain. "I had climbed through a grove with another spring ... the path growing even steeper and less probable, but the horsebells still rang from above me, in the cloud" (*EE* 83). With subtlety and grace, nature's alterity has been sublimated into signs of the infinite. Merwin's faith seems to lie in exterior intimacy with the holy, in the separation-in-encounter with the object of divinity that eludes Judeo-Christian thematization, though, bearing a conspicuously non-conclusive mark of it. At the end of the visit, when Merwin was preparing to leave, his last glimpse of the Holy Mountain revealed a shimmering landscape embodying concealment and revelation: "The mountain itself had been hidden in cloud all morning. The rain stopped. For a moment the clouds separated and a part of the peak could be seen — then the blank clouds closed over it again. I could not tell which part it had been" (*EE* 133).

The inability to locate the infinite constitutes infinity proper, and all of Merwin's poetry can be defined as the desire to capture its traces. Like Trakl who claims "Gott sprach eine sanfte Flamme zu seinem Herzen: / O Mensch!"(54), Merwin by poetry and prose has incessantly fanned the "sanfte Flamme" of the spirit which "drives the soul to get underway to where it leads the way," as Heidegger said. In 1977, ten years after *The Lice*, Merwin set out for another pilgrimage of the phantasmal fire:

> even our names are made of fire
> and we feed on night
> walking I thought of a fire
> turning around I caught sight of it
> in an opening in the wall
> in another house and another
> before and after
> in house after house that was mine to see
> the same fire the perpetual bird (*FH* 66)

In these obsessional pilgrimages toward the same nameless and sacred flame, Merwin stages the self's constant dislocation and projection, not in this historically determined, "known" world which is "death to accept" (*RT* 74) but in the fertile rupture between mortality and divinity. It is this eerie yet fundamental gap that directs Merwin's writings towards an ever-growing manifestation of spirituality.

Merwin's open form has thus approximated the diffusing lights, the shimmering sounds, and the infinitely compelling messages from the fantastic object that resists categorization. The proposition of a trace-leaving holiness as what the self cannot bring into discursive knowledge is especially meaningful in today's highly administered and systemized world where the exterior is daily encroached upon by technocracy. Instead of offering a dry "secular theology," as concluded by Thomas Byers (*What I Cannot Say* 114), Merwin offers a rather precarious deployment of desire: to desire an infinity without God or gods, an alterity without a stable Other — a desire that is problematic and vulnerable, more tenuous than humanity, yet stronger than God. Merwin's petition that "let me love what I cannot know" (*SF* 288), as if echoing what Derrida, in a critique of Levinas, calls the "transcendental violence" (*Writing* 156), exposes the inadequacy of both *techné* and *epistēmē* in confrontation with what might be other than self, logos, God, and named essence. Such a "violent" realization beyond knowledge and dialectics perhaps affords postmodern subjects a chance to obtain individual freedom by forming deeper bonds to the immanent calling for abolishing all forms of "in-the-name-of," self-legitimating theology, ideology, and religiosity.

Chapter 3

From Eros to Nature: The Impossible Partner in Merwin's Love Poetry

When W. S. Merwin wrote in *A Mask for Janus* (1952) that "Mirrors we lay wherein desire / Traded, by dark, conceits of fire" (*FF* 64), he was heralding a whole spectrum of erotic desires that would make him suffer and enjoy, lament and celebrate. Following the tradition of biblical psalmists, Merwin blends holy hymns and love poetry into a single discourse, closely knitting together the sacred and the secular. Yet unlike the psalmists, who emphatically use the secular as a vehicle of the sacred, Merwin sings of secular love alone, for love between man and woman can be divine in his eyes. Although at the beginning of his poetic career Merwin was preoccupied with ultra-phenomena and religious experiences, since he settled down in Maui, Hawaii in the mid-1970s, he has paid more and more attention to the mundane that is more than mundane. Merwin's wandering, creative spirit yearns for the distant and the infinite, yet it also dwells and lives in local, present situations. The transformation from severity to sensuality in *The Compass Flower* (1977) and *Finding the Islands* (1982) witnesses his immersion in and enjoyment of what Edmund Husserl calls the life-world, in which human beings live together and share experiences.①

Critics are divided in their assessment of *The Compass Flower*. Some condemn Merwin's turn from negation to affirmation as ontologically inconsistent with his tragic vision in the 1960s (Nelson 113) or as aesthetically tactless and naïve (Hix, *Understanding* 91; Byers, "Present Voice" 259), while others greet the turn as salutary and ground-breaking (Davis 160). On a more fundamental level, *The Compass Flower* is not so much about affirmation as about "an assertion of presence" or what is alternatively called "the moment of ecstatic presentness" (McCorkle, *Still* 162, 161). It does little justice to describe Merwin's turn to Eros in a "destitute time" as tactless, naïve, or simply a failure, as emphasized by a number of critics,② because for such a Janus-like poet as Merwin, spiritual transcendence may come from secular love that nevertheless comprises divinity as the excess of a love relationship. In this chapter, I will read Merwin's love poetry as a transference of libidinal attachment to the primal scene — the fleeting alterity, which in its very transience offers a redemptive moment for the male speaker.

Delving into Merwin's post-1960s work, particularly his love / nature poetry, this chapter will swerve from previous ontological and aesthetical controversies by offering a counterpart based on the idea of alterity. In many of Merwin's love poems, the poet-speaker seems "spellbound" by the female Other who is supposed to possess more knowledge about love than the speaker himself when the protagonist stages his indefatigable detour of desire by seeking, finding, and re-finding the lost love object.③ This

---

① Husserl's life-world refers to "the prescientific world of experience," that is, the surrounding world constituted intersubjectively where everything is said to be "given concretely, sensuously, and intuitively" (Zahavi 125, 126). This term usefully orientates us towards Merwin's adoption of a more nourishing and habitable world after his dark defeatism in the 1960s.

② See for example Byers, "Present Voice" 261, 262, and Nelson 113. Like many other critics, Byers and Nelson dismissed Merwin's employment of the erotic mode in the 1970s as inconsistent and ultimately unconvincing, ignoring the poet's early concern with violence in erotic desire.

③ The female Other also includes the natural object as far as it has been feminized and infinitized. As this chapter will recount, the dialectical relationship between the little female other (woman in a reciprocal, romantic relationship) and the big female Other (who embodies radical alterity) largely structures Merwin's love / nature poetry.

pattern seeps into Merwin's much-celebrated "ecopoetry" in the mid-1970s. His work had been increasingly characterized by the problematic combination of nature with Eros and the subsequent eroticization of flora. For Merwin, nature is basically feminine or a model of femininity: magical, sensual, fluid, and infinite. Merwin's fantasy of pan-eroticism can be reckoned as a strategy — an extension of his earlier efforts — to fend off the void left by his renunciation of the socio-symbolic order in his quest for the holy in the 1960s.

Destruction and creation: the paradox of love

The early stage of Merwin's love poetry follows the tradition of the troubadours in the Middle Ages for its conventional portrait of woman as both goddess and *femme fatale*. In *The Dancing Bears* (1954), Merwin allegorizes the incessant hindrance, torment, and enigma of love in such poems as "The Lady with the Heron," "When I Came from Colchis," "Fable," "East of the Sun and West of the Moon," "December: Of Aphrodite," and "Canso." These poems are more meditative than erotic, more imaginative than realistic as love still remains an abstract notion for the poet to explore. In some poems, the male speaker seems to derive a pleasure-in-torment from the failure to be united with the female Other, while in others he preaches unreservedly a religion of love, celebrating love in an impossibly elevated language. Knowing well the risks of sexual desire, Merwin strives to sublimate desire into love through an idealization of his partner.

The cruel tension between love and sex constitutes the motif of the highly symbolic and phantasmal poem "Fable." It recounts the story of two lovers who decided to make "one heart" between them (*FF* 80), but when the night came, the object of desire emerged as an invisible beast, teasing them and reducing the lovemaking into a comic scene. The lovers only heard "[a] noise as of a breathing beast / Swung between them; when they kissed, / All about them it raged and played / But nothing could they see"; they "sank upon knee" for having recognized "[w]hat had failed them from their creation" (*FF* 80). In the end of the poem, the lovers were humiliated by the revelation and had to accept the constitutive lack in their subjectivity, and the harmonious oneness in the sexual relationship proves to be an illusion, as if in response to Lacan who famously claims that "there is always the One and the Other, the One and the a [*objet a*], and the Other cannot in any way be taken as a One" (*Seminar XX* 49).

Lacan has also remarked that "there's no such thing as a sexual relationship, " because the male subject relates to his partner through partial objects instead of the whole person (*Seminar XX* 12, 80). The fusion of two subjects in a love relation is at best a fantasy, if not a purposeful deception, to screen off the fundamental antagonism of the two sexes. In Merwin's poem, the illusory oneness torments the two lovers beyond measure. The voyeur-poet reports that next morning when the lovers watched each other, they "saw within the other's eyes / Where they all tenderness had set, / Burning upon the day, a great / Bull-shouldered beast with horns of brass / Who cried in fury, // Who lunged between them like all pain … / In mortal rage, till brass and beast / Gored nothing but the ground at last, / And empty, where a heart had been, / Love's body lay" (*FF* 81). If Robert Lowell has spoken of the woes of marriage, then Merwin has spoken of the woes of sexual love, even more ruthlessly.[1] By alluding to the apocalyptic beast, Merwin expresses his reserve about sexual desire: frustration, monstrosity, and even destruction are waiting upon it.

To grasp the imaginary treasure in the other — *objet a*, the unobtainable object of desire as formulated by Lacan — lovers may torment each other till death, turning love into a hunting game. Since desire is inherently linked with the concept of lack / loss, the sexual act may become a crude and even desperate strategy to cover up that lack. The pleasure of the flesh worries Merwin, for it embodies the death-drive, a blind, autonomous repetition that brings excessive *jouissance*. In the poem "Song" Merwin laments thus: "But flesh, dark forest to the mind, / Took at our breaths repeated wind / And from our eyes an equal glare: / Our distance broke and burned us there. // In married dark these fevers learn / Alternate loss; the bodies, worn / Indefinite, attend together / Night's pleasure and the press of weather" (*FF* 64). The poet, however, is not a Platonist who prefers mind to body; instead, as Dinitia Smith says, "Merwin is a curious mixture of sensuality and reserve." Far from condemning man's carnal desire, Merwin fully recognizes its ambiguity, its strange mixture of

---

[1] A cursory comparison of Robert Lowell's "To Speak of Woe That is in Marriage" with Merwin's "Fable" reveals the two poets' different approaches toward sexual desire. Lowell employs a confessional mode to lament the coarseness of desire while Merwin uses allegories to reveal fantasies in desire.

tenderness and violence, its attraction and repulsion, necessity and crudity.

Biographically, these poems mark the failure of Merwin's first two marriages. Raised up in a priest's family and sexually repressed in his youth, Merwin was eager to have a girlfriend at Princeton, and as he recollects, Princeton did not admit female students in the late 1940s, so for him "[t] he idea of having a woman partner living in one's own room was a tantalizing notion" (*SD* 47). Urged by both desire and vanity, Merwin in his early twenties asked Dorothy Jeanne Ferry, a teaching assistant he met at Princeton, for marriage after knowing her for only a few months. In "a rush of impatience," young Merwin had plunged into his first marriage and fully tasted its pleasure and bitterness soon after (*SD* 47). After the young couple moved to London in the early 1950s, Merwin came to know and fell in love with Dido Milroy, a well-known English playwright who was fifteen years older than him. Merwin married Dido right after he broke up with Dorothy. The second marriage, however, was not entirely successful, though it was more dramatic and lasted longer than the first one. Unlike Dorothy, who stood utterly out of Merwin's literary world, Dido, according to Dinitia Smith, played the "devouring" mother figure who "wanted to inhabit Merwin's very existence." Dido arranged for Merwin's career in London, introduced him to literary circles, and helped him get translation jobs with the BBC. As Moira Hodgson, a one-time girlfriend of Merwin, says, Dido "had a very powerful personality" and was "a bit like the mother who says, 'Let my son bring his girlfriends home'" (qtd. in Smith). If Dorothy Ferry failed to share Merwin's literary interest, Dido Milroy had an overwhelming presence in it. What attracted Merwin about Dido was perhaps her combination of maternal tenderness and dominance, an image of the (m) Other who "introduces the phantom of Omnipotence" despite her own unperceived lack (Lacan, *Écrits* 299).

Like Ted Hughes, Robert Graves and Gary Snyder who have been exploring the mythical nature of Eros, Merwin intimates from the very beginning that the female Other, as the *infinite* object of man's desire, can be both redemptive and destructive, and the irony of Eros is that it is always under the shadow of Thanatos.[1] In his second book, *The Dancing Bears*,

---

[1] Eros the love-drive, which aims at establishing unities, and Thanatos the death-drive, which destroys organic unities, could not work independently. In Freud's formulation, the two basic drives "work against one another or combine with one another" (*Reader* 5).

dedicated to Dido Milroy, Merwin idealizes the female figure as the goddess of love who stands high above human interests, emanating an infinite aura. The paradox is that when the goddess of love descends, strife, not peace, prevails on earth. Love, as Merwin sees it, is both creative and destructive — it enchants humans exactly because of its double face. Following the Greco-Roman mythology, Merwin portrays Aphrodite and her agent, Helen, as the prototypical femme fatale. Behind Helen always lurks Dido the queen of Carthage, whose curse on Aeneas foreshadowed the three Punic Wars as recounted by Virgil. In "December: Of Aphrodite," Merwin recasts the legend of Helen / Dido in a dramatic monologue, with the poet himself inhabiting the consciousness of the heroine, telling the story from her perspective. The poem can be taken as an apology for love, and the tone of the poem calms down so that readers are induced to forgive the terrible wreckage a powerful beauty can bring to the world. Merwin's Helen acquits herself of guilt imputed to her by historians, claiming that she only acted in the name of love:

> Whatever the books may say, or the plausible
> Chroniclers intimate: that I was mad,
> That an unsettling wind that season
> Fretted my sign and fetched up violence … do not
> Believe them. In her name I acted. (*FF* 115)

Helen goes on to argue for the innocence of love / Eros: love itself is innocent; it is humans who kill in the name of love, although she confesses that

> … I in my five senses
> Cut throats of friends, burned the white harvest, waged
> Seven months' havoc even among
> Her temple; but because she waited always
> There in the elegant shell, asking for sweetness. (*FF* 115)

The terrible contrast between throat-cutting and divine sweetness indicates that the violence of love transcends the normal boundary between good and evil. The notion of love, as Slavoj Žižek puts it, belongs to *"the domain of pure violence"* (*Violence* 205; emphasis original), which categorization Merwin has exploited by understatements and paradoxes in the poem.

Hatred, strife and retribution are all inherent in love, as the Other enters into such a diachronic relationship with the Same that the result can be quite detrimental, even disastrous. Merwin revisits this karma of love —

love entwined with retribution — in "The Judgment of Paris" in *The Carrier of Ladders* (1970). As a mortal, Paris has to select the fairest woman among "the three / naked feminine deathless" (*SF* 146). The first two candidates tempt him with wisdom, power, pride, and glory, while the goddess of love, the last one, promises him a woman, but with an ironic prophecy of doom: *"Take / her / you will lose her anyway"* (*SF* 148; emphasis original). Merwin recounts with a telepathic view that when Paris

> reached out to the voice
> as though he could take the speaker
> herself ... a mason working above the gates of Troy
> in the sunlight thought he felt the stone
> shiver (*SF* 148).

The goddess of love qua the object-cause of love, as can be inferred from mythological and philosophical discourses on love, must remain partly invisible, "slipping away, " as Levinas says of the beloved (*Ethics* 67). The goddess, being divine, maintains her invisibility and infinity before the mortals, so Paris and we, the readers, witnesses of his ill fate, can only infer the event from the aftereffects of the confrontation with the divine. But strangely, what Paris really wants in the poem is not Helen but "the speaker herself, " and Helen seems to be reduced to a stand-in or an agent of love, not love per se. Even so, Paris's love for Helen could not pacify her alterity — her destructive otherness. The poem ends with a tragically beautiful picture:

> and Helen stepped from the palace to gather
> as she would do every day in that season
> from the grove the yellow ray flowers tall
> as herself
> whose roots are said to dispel pain (*SF* 148)

This ending intends not only irony but also lament. For Paris, Helen is *infinite* in that she arouses in his heart an uncontainable ideal of love detrimental to his own symbolic world, the city of Troy. Her innocence and goodness (gathering pain-dispelling flowers) only enhance her ideal image and the final irony. The momentum of this last stanza derives from a Merwinesque understatement — a dreamlike, auratic, and indeterminate description that resists any univocal interpretation and value judgment. It leaves the question of love unsettled.

The powerful alterity of love not only annuls but also creates. The paradox of love resides in the fact that it could bring forth a new temporal-symbolic relation by obliterating the old one and maintaining this renewal constantly. Love smites, soothes and heals. The speaker in "December: Of Aphrodite," after enumerating irrecoverable damages, beholds a renewed world nevertheless: "[W] here I stand / In the hazed gold of her eyes, the world is green" (*FF* 116). As the poet-speaker knows the pains of desire so well, he plunges into a praise of love, fervently expecting love to frame "the single metaphor of coherence / In the dying riot of random generation" (*FF* 118). Merwin's strategy is aimed at breaking the vicious circle of desire through an encounter with the love object so as to replace the lack / loss with plenitude, if tentatively, as he attempts to conjure up a sort of completeness from the figure of Dido, who he believes has opened a whole new dimension of existence for him. In three long poems titled "Canso," a song style used by the troubadours, Merwin praises the goddess of love passionately, deliriously, almost religiously. Following the tradition of the troubadours and its modernist revival in Ezra Pound, Merwin appeals to the notion of love and its redemptive power:

> ... yet you
> Beyond words believed me to be a gentle
> Season, and I, as from sleep returning,
> Was thence the sign and green wind of spring. (*FF* 117)

Apparently, love's fantasy has concealed the fundamental division between the lover and the beloved, as the impersonal season of spring, though promising renewal, in its abstraction cancels the particularity of any human characteristics. Echoing the book of Psalms, the poet compares love to a living breath, "the infusion of the real / Upon this dust," and credits love with an event that supposedly redeems an existent from its fallen state: "I walked incredible / As death, a gaunt preposterous ghost, until / Your creed included me among the living" (*FF* 118).

Merwin has thus produced a poetic discourse on love that recognizes pros and cons, benefits and risks. Love / Eros is worthy of praise despite the destruction it can bring; by sublimating sexual drives, love elevates humans to a spirituality that reanimates the dead sensibility. The female Other, as imagined by the poet, is more faithful and more spiritual than the male self — she brings out the better part of a man:

> It is by your faith that I believe, I am.
> Therein is genesis, as though a man,

> In love with existence, should bring to belief
> A divinity, an imagination
> ... as though a man could make
> A mirror out of his own divinity,
> Wherein he might believe himself, and be. (*FF* 119−20)

Eros here is closely related with the genesis, maternity, and conception of *la vita nuova*, as Dante once emphatically expressed.[①] Love as a sacred belief produces something out of nothing:

> ... Believing is
> Conception, is without artifice the making
> Perpetually new, is that first holy
> Aura and ordinance of creation. (*FF* 120)

In the fantasy of love, the male speaker willingly believes in the omnipotence and the oneness of the (m)Other, as he continues to confess,

> That I, perfected in your love, may be,
> Against all dissolution sovereign,
> Endlessly your litany and mirror,
> About your neck the amulet and song (*FF* 120).

In this way, Merwin has sublimated the female Other into an infinite goddess who mutely but effectively organizes his psychic energies, his object-libido, toward poetical creation. In an experience similar to mysticism, the speaker obtains what Lacan in *Seminar XX* famously calls the Other *jouissance*, "a jouissance beyond the phallus," which, as Lacan surmises, lies very close to a religious experience (74).

As already implied in many of Merwin's poems on human desire, what drives this kind of verse forward is exactly the quasi-mystical *jouissance* that goes beyond the phallic function of the symbolic social order. "The Other jouissance involves a form of sublimation through love that provides full satisfaction of the drives. The Other jouissance is a jouissance of love," as Bruce Fink summarizes regarding Lacan's formulation of *jouissance* (120). In the last "Canso," out of mere fantasy Merwin constructs an image of Dido, not as a being-toward-death, but as an immortal, life-giving sea-nymph: "She is clear amber and the heaven's face / Seen under simple

---

① Both Merwin's "Canso" and Dante's *La Vita Nuova* (1295) follow the tradition of "courtly love" in presenting the essence of love as spiritual or divine.

waters ... / Under the fish flying and the laugher of her dolphins, / First cold, final echoes, and the salt dead, she is marine" (*FF* 131). In her mythic creativity, she builds a womb-like Eden where all evils are excluded, and lovers may walk there as some primitive Adam and Eve: "Here is the gate of psalms, swordless, and the angel's country / For which we became as children ... / here will not the dark / Worm come with his sliding season, though the leaves fall / Nor the snake in the small hours / Molest the young doves and thrushes with the snare of his hands ..." (*FF* 133–134). Being a place of origin, this garden of love makes *ex nihilo* an impossible world outside the socio-historical process. Unlike the grievous tone of "Fable" and the apologetic discourse of "December: Of Aphrodite," the third "Canso" happily purges love of all crudity and violence:

> Now, now I enter the first garden and the promised moon,
> The silver of her thighs and shoulders; oh, here where the sheaves
> And shadows sway to her breath, in the caroling darkness
> We embrace at last, and the night and morning are together.

> (*FF* 134)

It is at this moment that the sea-nymph becomes a full-bodied desiring woman. As the imagined goddess has answered the call of love, she also confers subjectivity to the male speaker by giving him "answer of the Real" when "*eromenos* (the loved one) changes into *erastes* (the loving one)" (Žižek, *Metastases* 103), thus temporarily fulfilling the reciprocity of love by the dramatic turning of the words. The erotic finally joins hands with the spiritual in the poet's fantasy, and in Merwin's love poems of the 1950s this stanza seems the most felicitous compared with other anxiety-ridden pieces, though readers may find this redemption too tenuous to hold for long.

While we made love the rose opened

The combination of sensuality and spirituality, eroticism and natural symbolism, characterizes most of Merwin's love poems since the 1970s. In the preface to his translation of Pablo Neruda's *Twenty Love Poems and a Song of Despair* (1969), Merwin expresses his indebtedness to Neruda: "This volume was one of the first to open my eyes and sensibility to the possibility of poetry... . Not only did these poems deeply resonate with me, but they galvanized me, finally, into starting to write myself. They stirred me body and soul" (xvi). Merwin admires Neruda's "connect[ing] the erotic with telluric forces and the organic cycles of nature" (ix), identifying Neruda's love poetry as a "combination of the sensory and the natural, the subjective and the eternal, the instinctual and the commonly transcendent" (x). Besides the oral, limpid tradition of the troubadours, Neruda influences Merwin yet on another level: the sensuous experience and the exuberant energy of being in the life-world. Like Neruda, Merwin celebrates the female form, linking the corporeal with the "telluric forces" of mountains, islands, trees, flowers, rivers, and birds. The female body becomes the locus not only of phallic *jouissance* but also of Other *jouissance* through its infinite revelations and withdrawals. The relationship between the self and the female Other in Merwin's poetry consists of what Levinas terms " a movement unto the invisible " through touching, caressing, and lovemaking (*Totality* 258). In the late 1970s, Merwin's partner was no longer a femme fatale as in the 1950s but a "commonly transcendent" woman who, though deeply immersed in the life-world, still maintained her mysterious alterity.

The sensual power in Merwin erupts in *The Compass Flower* (1977) and *Finding the Islands* (1982). In the 1950s, his love poetry was dominated by mythologies and abstractions; in the 1960s, haunted by historical closure caused by the Vietnam War and its urgent breakthrough, Merwin seldom wrote about erotic experiences. "The Judgment of Paris" in *The Carrier of Ladders* (1970), looked at retrospectively, is focused more on the doom of love than on its experience. It was in the late 1970s that the influence of Neruda began to prevail, as Merwin tried to get rid of the emotional "anemia, " pointed out by Helen Vendler in relation to his 1960s poems, and to write more directly on sensual experiences (233). Daringly and systematically, Merwin fuses corporeal sensuality with transcendent elements to create a poetic discourse on love — at once surreal and lucid, raw and refined, earthly and otherworldly.

The female body enthralls Merwin for its structural similarity to unexplored nature and its heterogeneity to the given socio-symbolic order. In an Ovidian vein, the poet grafts impersonal and natural elements onto the female body. The following stanza exemplifies such an astounding metamorphosis:

> You were shaking and an air full of leaves
> flowed out of the dark falls of your hair
> down over the rapids of your knees

> until I touched you and you grew quiet
> and raised to me
> your hands and your eyes and showed me
> twice my face burning in amber (*FH* 36)

Echoing Neruda's "The great roots of night / grow suddenly from your soul" (5), Merwin here entangles the female body in a cluster of plants and water. The magic of this erotic poetry is that it takes readers to an open, primal space saturated with feminine *jouissance*. By caressing and engaging the parts of the body other than genitals (hair, knees, hands, eyes), lovers obtain pleasure greater than sexual intercourse. The male speaker reached orgasm when the female other, as a *quiet* mirror, reflected *twice* his "face burning in amber." Femininity exposes the true state of a man's desire by setting this desire on fire and then observing it from a certain distance; the woman disengages herself in this erotic play by engaging the man. Touch and caress, as imagined by Levinas, already presuppose separation between the self and the other, as the beloved is "at once graspable but intact in her nudity" (*Totality* 258). In Merwin's poem the woman is still invisible, enwrapped in darkness, and the man, though taking the initiative of touching and caressing, appears deliriously passive, and in that matter "obsessive" too, as again we learn from Levinas: "Obsession ... is inscribed in consciousness as something foreign, a disequilibrium, a delirium" (*Otherwise* 101).

In the naked female body Merwin sees an exuberant life form that quite enjoys itself, and this feminine autoeroticism both disquiets and fascinates the male speaker:

> What I thought I knew fall aside a thought at a time
> until I see you naked
> in your eyes the bronze ferns older than seeing
> unfurling above the dark springs (*FH* 39)

The woman's nakedness undoes the speaker's self-assured knowledge ("what I thought I knew") by substituting it with a kind of non-knowledge symbolized by the luxuriant plant. Indifferent to the male gaze, the primeval "bronze ferns" unfold themselves like flowers over "dark springs" — a dynamic imagery of feminine *jouissance*. The poet thus endows the beloved with a Nerudean "telluric force," fusing the erotic relation with a mysterious relation with nature.

What is problematic and unsettling about this Merwin's fusing procedure lies in its excessiveness, as if nature were no longer content complementing the love object but had to substitute for it. Nature and the female Other no longer stand, in Merwin's discourse, as metaphors for each other but strangely form a hybrid of a half-woman / half-nature. In a similar poem, "Islands," the rich variety of nature is laid out on the female body to maximize the enjoyment the lover-speaker can get from this fusing fantasy:

> Wherever I look you are islands
> a constellation of flowers breathing on the sea
> deep-forested islands mountainous and fragrant
> fires on a bright ocean
> at the root one fire (*FH* 45)

The female body is presented as diverse partial objects (island, flower, forest, fire) around which the poetic imagination cathects its associative energy. The poet, however, does not merely use the woman's body as a means to satisfy his erotic desire. The Lacanian object (*objet a*) causes desire and sustains it exactly through its nonsatisfaction; the object is *infinite* for its resistance to be caught in any intersubjective negotiations. Žižek once described the *objet a* in Levinasian rhetoric: "[T]he nearer you get to it, the more it eludes your grasp" (*Fragile* 24). In the poem, the male speaker disseminates signs and symbols drawn from nature without truly encapsulating the female Other or nature — the words only produce more desire / fire regarding the object.

The island, a vivid image of exteriority, recurs in many forms in Merwin's love poetry. Islands are on the outskirts of civilization; geographically remote, they become the much projected guardian place of man's spiritual freedom. Merwin had lived on the island of Majorca in Spain in the early 1950s before settling down on the island of Maui in Hawaii in late 1970s where he has lived for nearly forty years. Many of his love poems since the 1970s have been written on the island as he conveniently combines the island imagery with the description of female body: both are a mixture of intimacy and exoticness. This kind of "deep-forested" body commits Merwin's creativity to an uncontainable yearning:

> all my life I have wanted to touch your ankle
> running down to its shore
> I beach myself on you
> I listen
> I see you among still leaves

regard of rock and pool
by sun and moon and stars (*FH* 45-46)

Rather than create a romantic setting for love, Merwin compares the beloved to the setting per se: she is both the exotic background and the heroine in the act of love. Merwin thus puts Eros into a play of differentiation by introducing the "telluric force" as nature displaces and amplifies Eros to an infinite degree.

Although the poet lavishes passionate signifiers to describe the lover's body, the woman still maintains her "ex-sistence"[1] outside the socio-symbolic world; moreover, she embodies what is other than humanity: the nonhuaman world. Hence "island waterfalls and their echoes / are your voice your shoulders the whole of you standing / and you turn to me as though your feet were in mist" (*FH* 46). Rooted in mist and mystery, the woman *turns* and beckons the man to follow her into the hermetic garden of love. For Merwin, the woman and her body, like the distant call from the mountain, is what summons without summoning and appears without appearing. She is always out there, silently beckoning, always on the way, always to come, bringing infinitely blissful vision: "The shadow of my moving foot / feels your direction / you come toward me / bringing the gold through the dust / you step to me through the city of amber" (*FH* 41). Even when the male speaker seems to catch her body she would retain her rapport with infinite nature, and unlike the cold and inaccessible goddess in Merwin's earlier love poems, the female partner now seems to enjoy erotic love although she is partly above this game.

Merwin may have borrowed the fusing practice from Pablo Neruda, but there are biographical reasons as well. In 1968 Merwin separated from Dido Milroy, and in 1975 he met Dana Naone, a Hawaiian poet and a Buddhist who lived with Merwin for several years after he moved to Hawaii. She shared with Merwin similar interest in Buddhism and inspired much of the fusion of Eros, nature, and spiritualism in Merwin's love poetry in this period. If Dorothy Ferry initiated Merwin into love's first ecstasy and frustration, and Dido Milroy opened Merwin's eyes to love's creativity and violence, then Dana Naone helped shape Merwin's love

---

① Following Heidegger and Lacan, Bruce Fink explains "ex-sistence" as "'an existence which stands apart from,' which insists as it were from the outside; something not included on the inside, something which, rather than being intimate, is 'extimate'" (122).

poetry towards a simplicity based on an Eastern view of nature as epiphany. Sexual love is no longer viewed as complementary to spiritual love but remains originary on its own account. The title of *The Compass Flower* already makes it clear: woman, by virtue of her affinity with nature, offers a compass, a spiritual guidance, to man.

This pattern of infinite proximity permeates the love poems in *Finding the Islands* (1982) and the later *The Rain in the Trees* (1988) in which the poet continues to explore the uncanny connection between erotic love and nature. In "To Dana with the Gift of a Calendar," the first love poem in *Finding the Islands*, Merwin describes love in a minimalistic style: succinct, crystal, epiphanic, a mixture of Japanese haiku, Neruda, and troubadour poetry:

> In the winter in the first month of every
> year of my life I was
> looking for you (*FI* 41)

In less than twenty words Merwin opens up an infinite world that comprises the season, the lovers, and an absence haunting everything present in the poem. This tercet illustrates Merwin's concern with finality in poetry. In the foreword to *Asian Figures* (1973), Merwin emphasizes the merit of poetry as "an urge to finality of utterance," "to be irreducible and unchangeable" and "to be self-contained, to be whole" (*RM* 285). He pursues this urge of brevity throughout *Finding the Islands*, adopting the tercet form to establish vital connections between subject, object of love, and the outer world. Merwin's attempt at wholeness, however, does not contradict his desire for infinity in the erotic relationship. Though the poetic form is complete and finite, it cannot contain all significations of the female Other functioning as the addressee in many of his love poems: "[Y]ou avoid the words / about you / like a mountain goat," or, "If I were to talk of you / how would anyone know / what the words meant" (*FI* 57, 66). Essentially, human language is unable to comprehend and circumscribe this *you* — not necessarily Dana Naone, Merwin's girlfriend at the time — but any sublimated, elusive Other whom the poet has to "look for," not in order to find but to sustain the pure act of searching.

Irreducible exteriority invariably enters the erotic relationship. Merwin's is not one of those Renaissance pastorals like Christopher Marlowe's "The Passionate Shepherd to His Love," in which nature is reduced to the role of a handmaid in the love scene. In *Finding the Islands*,

Merwin relies on the revelatory power of nature, not only to sublimate the sexual drive but also to diffuse and expand eroticism, blurring the boundary between sexual love and spiritual ecstasy. The love scene can be very raw yet full of spiritual illuminations:

> we go up to a cold high lake
> and make love
> before dark (*FI* 42)

The coldness of the lake and the burning of desire form such a sharp contrast that the Romantic projection of human feelings into nature is largely suspended; instead, here we have nature as the infinite Other nonchalantly watching the lovemaking. Echoing the "dark springs," the slant rhyme of *lake / dark* implies the allurement of death, the dissolution of self in the face of mysteriously deep nature. This tercet impresses readers for its precise, Zen-like combination of reality and semblance, Eros and death, humanness and nonhumanness. In another poem, "February in the Valley," nature again enters the scene of lovemaking in a highly ambiguous way:

> It is winter still
> but this morning while
> we made love the rose opened (*FI* 65)

Instead of comparing his beloved to a rose, as Robert Burns did, Merwin synchronizes the act of lovemaking with the opening of the rose. The poet does not say that love causes the rose to open; he simply juxtaposes the two to suggest some uncanny relation between nature and erotic love. The other tercet continues to explore this link in a dreamlike setting:

> as we enter
> the tender rapids
> you look up and tell me you dreamed this (*FI* 65)

Different from Romantic poets such as William Wordsworth and Robert Burns who feel too easily an empathy with nature, Merwin treats nature as the unfathomable third agent binding and haunting the two lovers. Nature functions as a fantasy to conceal as well as reveal the distance between the finite and the infinite, the lover and the beloved. Merwin's is not such an easy empathy as *even nature feels our love*, but rather a deep endearment with nature: *because we both love nature, we can love each other*. To put it more bluntly, Merwin makes love to Mother Nature herself when he makes love to a woman.

This logic may sound strange, but it characterizes most of Merwin's love poems. With Merwin, the Nerudean "telluric / earthly" force serves to expand Eros to the degree that nature seems to replace and suture Eros: "[T]he soft rain / for seven years I have felt your skin / and the light of your fingers"; "I saw the mountains / where we were going / where you would be"; "The same sunlight on the wet / banana leaves by the window / and on your wet skin" (*FI* 42, 56, 61). Similar lines are abundant in *The Compass Flower*. In contrast with Neruda, who starts a love poem with a direct declaration of love, Merwin begins his with a description of nature (rain, mountain, sunlight) to attenuate the erotic intent so as to make it a part of heaven and earth. Merwin lets Eros participate in the symphony of the infinite cosmos, not vice versa.

The lady sitting in white

Cheri Davis notices that in Merwin's love poems "nature is experienced as it enhances the beauty of the beloved; it creates a dynamic environment for their love, while she is the inspired and inspiring center of the poem" (122). Davis may have neglected the possibility that this center could be absent; the beloved is more on the margin than at the center. If the ideal of love is as infinitely dynamic as nature, then all separations might be justified and made into love poetry with good reason. The essence of erotic love consists in the finite's contact with the *infinite*, which is paradoxically a noncontact. As Levinas puts it, "In contact itself the touching and the touched separate, as though the touched moved off, was always already other, did not have anything common with me" (*Otherwise* 86). A short poem in the early 1960s makes explicit that in the dynamics of love, the Other keeps the self in bondage or even holds it hostage:

> Your absence has gone through me
> Like thread through a needle.
> Everything I do is stitched with its color ("Separation," *SF* 15)

Robert Scholes finds this imagery of Merwin's to be irrational: "[O]ur spatial-visual sense tells us that a person cannot be visualized as a kind of needle going around stitching things with a thread the color of absence" (75). Exploiting the aporia of representation, this surreal image evokes a sense of internalized loss analogous to melancholia in which "the subject possesses [the lost object] in the very mode of loss" (Žižek, *Plague* 195).

The "thread" indicates the recognizable trace left by the beloved, who has passed through the self ("needle") both tenderly (thread and needle are intimate companions) and violently (stitching brings pain). Connected with absence, love itself forbids words, so the poet can only speak of the paraphernalia or the aftereffects of love and its colorless "color." In "St. Valentine's Eve," Merwin writes with similar wistfulness: "[H]earing you in the house / I think of the ways / you put yourself around me," and "I remember you talking / to me a long time in whispers / our early nights our late mornings" (*FI* 70, 71). The site hollowed out by the absence of the beloved is consequently filled up by acts of hearing, imagining, and remembering — all of which betray the momentariness of the love object.

Merwin broke up with Dana Naone at nearly the same time he published *Finding the Islands* in 1982. Read retrospectively, those short, intimate poems bear witness to the climax, as well as the end, of a love affair that started with *The Compass Flower* seven years earlier. In 1983, Merwin married Paula Schwartz, an editor of children's books. Merwin first met Paula in 1970 and was immediately attracted, and in 1982, Merwin finally obtained a divorce from Dido Milroy, so when he met Paula again at a dinner party the old affection was stirred up. They married in a Buddhist ceremony instead of a Christian one. As Merwin enters old age, the love poems for his third wife Paula Schwartz in *The Rain in the Trees* (1988) are not ostensibly sensuous; they rather strike readers as a man's late spiritual yearning for love — a man who, to quote John Keats, has fears that he may cease to be. The last phase of Merwin's love poems seems to combine the goddess image of Dido Milroy with the sensual-naturalistic tendency in poems about Dana Naone. Writing more simply and wistfully than ever, Merwin exhibits the virtuosity of a master reaping his final mellowness.

"Late Spring," the first poem in *The Rain in the Trees*, envisions a goddess whom the poet fantasizes to be lost yet found again. Merwin uses a vertiginous syntax to accumulate anticipations toward his third and last femme éternelle: "Coming into the high room again after years / after oceans and shadows of hills and the sounds of lies / after losses and feet on stairs" (*RT* 3). The predominant iambics and the conspicuous sibilant rhyme of *s* bring out the weariness of a pilgrim who has traveled far and wide in quest of love.[1] The poem proceeds:

---

[1] See Chapter 2 of this book for a discussion on Merwin's use of the sibilant consonant *s* to evoke a sense of holiness.

```
        after looking and mistakes and forgetting
        turning there thinking to find
        no one except those I knew
        finally I saw you
        sitting in white
        already waiting ( RT 3)
```

The lady sitting in white is both nature (late spring) impersonated, as the title suggests, and an easily recognizable reproduction of Dante's Beatrice, who famously wears white in paradise. Is she waiting for the poet to greet and take her? Merwin writes elsewhere that "all the time I love / most your own longing / drawing me" (FI 60). After so many detours of desire (*looking, forgetting, turning, thinking, waiting*), is Merwin finally able to grasp his fetishistic and infinite object of love? Besides purity, whiteness also connotes blankness, erasure, and absence. The next stanza reveals that love and redemption are still absent and yet to come. In Merwin's "evangelistic" discourse on love, love is seen as a faith in the invisible and the infinite figure, a pure anticipation for exteriority shown toward the other person: "[Y]ou of whom I had heard / with my own ears since the beginning / for whom more than once / I had opened the door / believing you were not far" (RT 3). To open the door repetitively for the other, whom one has only heard of, bespeaks all the irrationalities in a romantic relationship. Merwin suggests that it is the infinite proximity rather than self-assured understanding of the beloved that arouses this uncontained longing in the self.

    Merwin's portrait of the distant female figure largely follows the tradition of courtly love which flourished in the twelfth-century France. In his Princeton days, Merwin had developed a strong interest in Provençal troubadour poetry, so after graduation, partly influenced by Ezra Pound, he decided to go to southern France to study the poetry of Bernart de Ventadorn and chronicled the whole event in his *The Mays of Ventadorn* (2002).[1] In this book Merwin highly appreciates Bernart's love poems, in which separation, loss, and lamentation are expressed in limpid, artless diction. While he admires the "musical transparency" (MV 135) of

---

[1] Merwin gives a full account of his meeting with Pound in St. Elizabeth's Hospital in the opening pages of *The Mays of Ventadorn*. Pound advised young Merwin to translate "the Provençal" and Spanish *Romancero* and to "get as close to the original as you can" (MV 8).

Bernart's poems, Merwin is mainly attracted to the distance between self and Other in troubadour poetry:

> The recurring burden of Bernart's song is distance ... distance between the lover and the beloved ... and *amor de lonh* (far away love) became essential to the tradition of the troubadours. Distance is a measure of absence. Even in Guilhem's love poem with its candid sensuality, the beloved is out of reach, too far to hear him, there is no message from her, he remembers another time when they were together. (*MV* 124)

In a rather Levinasian formulation, the desired one, as in both Merwin and troubadour practitioners, Pound's "Cino" included, [1] is incessantly slipping away, for the norm of love poetry resides not in union but in separation. There is an infinite gap between desire and its object, since there is "no way to obtain what you desire" (*MV* 125), as Merwin quotes from Ibn Hazm's treatise on love, *The Dove's Neck-Ring.* All troubadour poetry can be reckoned as a passionate movement of signifiers to approach the enigmatic Other: "Courtly love has remained enigmatic" (Lacan, *Seminar XX* 86), partly because the love object has been divested of any identifiable or determinate particularities and thus becomes an object-in-itself.

In *The Rain in the Trees* (1988), Merwin often associates woman with the cycle of seasons and years, identifying her with the origin of temporality. In "The Sound of the Light," Merwin chants such a haunting litany of time and age:

> it is the year in which you are sitting there as you are
> in the morning speaking to me and I hear
> you through the burning day and I touch you
> to be sure and there is time there is still time (*RT* 32)

The contact (touching, hearing) engenders a projection of the self, an *ekstasis* that throws the speaker into the expectation of becoming, although he realizes that there is not much time left for that becoming. Echoing "Late Spring," "you" here remains indefinite: Merwin seems to refer to both the spring light as the title suggests and the beloved person, Paula Schwartz,

---

[1] "Cino" opens with "Bah! I have sung women in three cities, / But it is all the same; / And I will sing of the sun"; in a dramatic monologue, the poem goes on to mourn the lost "lips," "words," "dreams," and "nights" when Cino the Italian Don Juan raves along the open road (Pound 6).

his third wife, to whom the book is dedicated. The poet's desire for the Other is literally "blind," in that he does not describe her particularities, nor can he see her (the transparent light). In the poem, all communications are unilateral as the poet only receives silent signals from the woman / light and has to interpret them by his own efforts. The radical asymmetry between self and Other, who initiates a new sequence of time, produces such an obsession that the poet would repeatedly cross over the threshold of time together with this Other whose face we never see:

> we watch the bright birds in the morning
> we hope for the quiet
> daytime together
> the year turns into air
> but we are together in the whole night
> with the sun still going away
> and the year
> coming back ("The Solstice," *RT* 36)

Nearly every line is saturated with a revolving sense of time lived by the collective "we," an idyllic union constructed by the poet's fantasy of love.

If Lacan's claim is true — femininity is subjectivity proper because "[w]oman has a relation to the signifier of that Other, insofar as, qua Other, it can but remain forever Other" (*Seminar XX* 81) — then it becomes understandable why Merwin anticipates the female Other and empathizes that "togetherness" so fervently. Through an imaginary union with the woman, Merwin could obtain a kind of fortitude to transcend the rigid socio-symbolic order organized by phallic power so as to access the Other *jouissance* — an ecstatic enjoyment beyond social recognition and authorization. The goddess of love creates out of raw nature an Edenic site where being-toward-death is replaced by being-toward-infinity. Dasein is no longer conceived as burdened by care and death in an existentialistic framework but as an existent that enjoys life by living on the raw elements of nature. In "Anniversary on the Island," Merwin celebrates the isolated, independent life brought about by love:

> day after day we wake to the island
> the light rises through the drops on the leaves
> and we remember like birds where we are
> night after night we touch the dark island
> that once we set out for (*RT* 34)

The proximity of the beloved is supposed to bring ecstatic immersion and personal freedom to the self.

104   Unlike the earlier poems on islands, in *The Rain in the Trees* Merwin does not worship the natural landscape as being like the female body; instead, he attends to how time constantly renews itself in this fantastic space inhabited by the lovers alone. In "Noah's Raven," a poem in the apocalyptical 1960s, the raven regretted having returned to the old, corrupt world.① After Merwin finally settled down on the island of Maui with Paula Schwartz, the couple lived like two survivors after the biblical flood, "remember[ing] like birds where we are" (*RT* 34). They are the ravens that, enjoying themselves in the new world, have forgotten to return to the old one. The poet's creating spirit is sustained and further strengthened by this non-phallic, non-reproductive, autoerotic enjoyment:

> and lie still at last with the island in our arms
> hearing the leaves and the breathing shores
> there are no years any more
> only the one mountain
> and on all sides the sea that brought us (*RT* 34)

In this secluded garden of love created *ex nihilo*, man's libido is liberated from the "performance principle" of the capitalistic society and undergoes a "non-repressive sublimation" (170), as pointed out by Herbert Marcuse in *Eros and Civilization* (1955), a book that prophesied the liberation of Eros in Europe and the United States in the apocalyptically tumultuous 1960s. In Merwin's case, historical time is canceled out by sensuous moments, as the poet attempts to diffuse Eros to its fullest degree like Marcuse and Gary Snyder, envisioning and fantasizing a newly found world where social prohibitions are foreclosed. Readers familiar with Lacanian psychoanalysis know that foreclosure would trigger psychosis, so it is in fact a more violent act than repression.② Read in this light, Merwin's love poems can be said to be more "violent" than, for example, Allen Ginsberg's *Howl* (1956),

---

① In "Noah's Raven," the animal-speaker laments thus: "Why should I have returned? / My knowledge would not fit into theirs. / I found untouched the desert of the unknown, / Big enough for my feet" (*SF* 16).

② By foreclosing the Name-of-the-Father, the paternal function, subjects will obtain excessive *jouissance* from delusions and fantasies. Lacan proposes the foreclosure of the Name-of-the-Father as the fundamental mechanism of psychosis in *The Psychoses: Seminar III* (1955–1956).

since Merwin does not directly condemn the technocratic, postindustrial US society — he seems to live with it (if not outside it) by virtue of Eros and its fantasies.

As can be inferred from psychoanalysis, Merwin's obsessions with the receding female figure and feminine *jouissance* are heavily influenced by the relationship with his mother, from whom Merwin felt helplessly alienated throughout his adult life, as he reminisces in his essay "La Pia":

> But beyond the day by day aspect of her existence, which she made over to us consciously, proudly, without fail — though not without moments of resentment — there was always *a trackless, twilit, secret country open to no one.* (*UO* 218; emphasis added)

Echoing Freud's remark that feminine sexuality is a "dark continent" and Lacan's remark that woman has a kind of *jouissance* all to herself, Merwin's sad admission sheds some light on the entanglement of love, desire, enjoyment, and obsession in his love poems. Theoretically, it is because the m (Other) as the first love object remains inaccessible ("secret") that Merwin has to invoke her traces repeatedly through poetry. The "trackless, twilit, secret country" provides a poetic illumination on the dark zone of feminine *jouissance*. Merwin's mother here, and elsewhere too, largely functions as the very locus of knowledge, which, like a door left ajar, only admits a glimpse from the outside. Merwin's love poems can be read as a series of transferential attempts to retouch his mother's "twilit country," to overcome this alienation. After his father's death in the late 1970s, Merwin tried several times to talk more with his mother and to be more candid, only to find that "we can mention almost nothing of our own intimate lives, hers or mine... . I have grown up in the habit of being so reticent with her, that it cannot be easy now to find what we want to say to each other" (*UO* 204). But very soon Merwin would admit that the desire for knowledge was only his: "When I think of what I want to ask her now, I realize, not for the first time, that the wish to hear, the hankering for information, are almost wholly mine" (*UO* 220). In Merwin's love poems, his mother's lifelong reticence is transubstantiated into such a love object that effectively organizes the male speaker's psychic energy.

Whenever Merwin writes on love and nature, we always have a glimpse of the silent mother figure who keeps withdrawing. In a typical late Merwin poem we read:

I might have stood in orchards forever

> without beholding the day in the apricots
> or knowing the ripeness of the lucid air
> or touching the apricots in your skin
> or tasting in your mouth the sun in the apricots (*RT* 4)

In this seemingly naturalistic, blatantly erotic scene, Merwin's mother in fact looms large. The ravishing taste of the apricots, as we learn from the family poem "Apparitions, " belongs to the poet's mother:

> I wait for the smell   of parsley and almonds
> that I never imagined   otherwise than as hers (*FH* 115)

What can be more intimate, distant, tantalizing, agonizing, and haunting for a boy than the mother's smell? Merwin cannot track the "secret country" of nature, mother, and lover, for what he has is only this infinitely fragile trace, this endless and fantastic anticipation for the (m)Other, the mysterious lady "sitting in white" (*RT* 3).[①]

"The moment of green": Merwin's eroticization of flora

Merwin's shift to the sensual, erotic mode coincides with his increasing interest in nature after the mid-1970s; he fantasizes about both nature and women, confusing them intentionally until one cannot be differentiated from the other. The rivers, plants, lakes, birds, and foxes all become unmistakable objects of love and enter into poetry as the channels of libidinal cathexes. It is true that Merwin is zealous about ecologism, but his invocations of nature are so excessive, as well as obsessive, that they resemble hallucinatory symptoms that complicate a clearly defined "nature poetry." He caresses trees and plants as if caressing a woman; he aches for rivers and lakes as if they were his living lovers. For Merwin, nature is

---

① Michael Clifton has similarly noticed that "Merwin's mother also represents for him the unconscious, " stressing how the "elusive essence of Merwin's relationship with his mother" has structured the poet's visionary imagery (74). This is surely not to dismiss the influence of other figures, such as the father and girlfriends in Merwin's love poetry — all could be determinative; the mother image here simply makes clear one important phase in Merwin's work. Critics tend to consider the lovers in Merwin's poetry as "provid [ing] the mirroring function of the eternally present mother" (McDonnell 118). For a full explication of Merwin's mother as the lost love object in his later poetry, see McDonnell 102−130.

another name for whatever entices him yet constantly eludes his grasp, so his fascination with nature is "sexual" if we include in the category of sex any repeatedly failed action to obtain the desired object.[①]

In the early 1970s, Merwin dallies with the eroticization of flora in a luxurious, if not lustful, manner. Contrasting with the painful tone of most poems from that same period, "Marietta," a narrative in *The Miner's Pale Children* (1970), brings to light the other side of Merwin: warm, delightful, even vulgarly sensuous. It manifests Merwin's unquenchable longing for the natural world, where both his own and Other's desire are put on stage. The narrator journeys through a mysterious lane that "draws near to the edge of the lake" (*BF* 53). Even before meeting the hostess, the narrator has already felt the assault of desire: he has felt his "stomach contract at the nearness of the lake" (*BF* 53). Marietta, like the Virgin Mary, is a mysterious figure who has both "the heavy but graceful figure" of a woman and a face "like a girl's" (*BF* 54). She embodies the spirit that calls the poet to enjoy the natural elements:

> Then if it's an even day she leads you ... into the woods. ... leads you out into the little clearing by the backwater. ... the woods are lush and green. The path goes on to the right through more woods, around the edge of the water, where it's almost dark. And in front of you there are more trees, looking as though they grew out of a black stretch of the water itself, which is connected with the lake and the light only by a narrow inlet. (*BF* 54)

The luxuriant plants beside the water again symbolize the vast reservoir of id — unbridled sexual energy and fantasies. Under the guidance of Marietta the matchmaker, the narrator comes through this *selva oscura* (dark forest) and finally meets his Beatrice — Flora, "a girl in a white dress."

The narrative entices readers with its raw and mythic flavor. In Merwin's fantasy, Flora perfectly combines sensuous charm with natural intelligence like Mother Nature herself (Spinoza would say nature has both substance and thought, body and mind). Flora seduces the male speaker by apparently not seducing him at all: "You can see the undersides of her thighs as she sits looking around. ... She leans forward with her elbows on

---

① Žižek links sexuality to the failed repetition: "[S]exuality is ... nothing but the formal structure of failure ... when we are engaged in an activity which fails to attain its goal directly, and gets caught in a repetitive vicious cycle, this activity is automatically sexualized" (*Plague* 71–72).

her knees and you can look down inside her breasts and almost to the end of one full perfect pointed breast" (*BF* 55). The irony is that the other's eyes also gaze at the voyeur; Flora returns the gaze like a mirror: "She sees that you're looking" and "she keeps looking at you" (*BF* 55). Flora attracts the male gaze by her apparent nonsurprise and nonaction ("smiles," "doesn't move at all," "doesn't seem to notice," "goes on smiling"). As her infinite / indefinite desire baffles the male speaker, the man is always the loser in this Merwinesque play of gazes. He fumbles and fidgets before a more knowledgeable female Other: "[Y]ou hear a beating in your throat ... your mouth is dry and corners [of eyes] are stiff" (*BF* 55). The passive initiative of Flora thus impels us to regard her as nature writ small, and like nature, Flora opens herself richly, unpretentiously, and unconsciously: "She undoes the button herself" (*BF* 56).

The contrast between Flora's virtuosity in the affair of love and the male speaker's utter inexperience is spread out in a breathless and nakedly sensual paragraph. Flora finally teaches the lesson of love to the man who is already riddled with desire — as W.B. Yeats, learning of Maud Gonne's marriage with John MacBride, was "riddled with light" (125). Flora reveals to the eager amour her mysteries one by one:

> And then you undo a button at her waist and slide your hand in where it's warm and feels as though it were shining. You know your hand is cold, and you're shivering harder. You kiss again, and start to undo each other's clothes while you're kissing, and only stop when you have to, so that she can slip out of her dress and her bra while you watch, taking off your shirt and your shoes and pants. You look at her, and then, looking straight at you, she slowly pulls off her underpants and you pull off yours, with your throat almost closed up, and you let your eyes rest on the mound of brown hair and then lie down beside her and from there on start to act as though you knew what to do with everything. And she knows. (*BF* 56)

Conceiving of the female Other as possessing more knowledge on love ("she knows"), Merwin's speaker follows her silent instructions like a good student until he obtains certain subjectivity ("act as though you knew what to do with everything").

This poetic narrative reveals the inherent sexual fantasies in Merwin's much-celebrated nature writings after the mid-1970s. With the rise of ecocriticism, critics like Jane Frazier and Leonard Scigaj find in Merwin pretty much what every environmentalist wants to find: the "harmonious" coexistence of man and nature. I would contend that such oneness is only a repeated fantasy or illusion constructed to integrate or subjectivize the traces — the silent teachings and significations — of nature qua the infinite Other. At the end of "Marietta, " Merwin tells us that Flora lives upstairs, reading books most of the time, while "[y]our chest thumps as you walk across to the door and *look up the stairs*" (*BF* 57; emphasis added). The act of looking up, the stairs that vaguely recall the Jacob's Ladder that reaches to heaven, ① and the "thumping chest" — all suggest that Flora is still enwrapped in mystery, despite her proximity to and her erotic game with the male narrator who remains, to borrow from Roland Barthes's discourse on love, "the sole witness of [his own] lunacy" (*Lover's Discourse* 23).

"Marietta" foretells a series of nature poems that witness Merwin's engagement with the regional plants in Hawaii from the late 1970s to the present. In the rainforests, Merwin rediscovers the feminine Other who resists any nomenclature as Flora does (though the narrator names the girl "Flora, " he never fully penetrates the enigma behind the name). Having lived in the rainforests of Maui for ten years, Merwin was able to exclaim in the late 1980s:

> I want to tell what the forests
> were like
> I will have to speak
> in a forgotten language ("Witness, " *RT* 65).

The unnamable aspect of nature compels the poet to adopt a self-defeating posture concerning language and signification. Merwin conceives of the trees as belonging to a much earlier origin whose knowledge is even denied to his parents, the locus of knowledge commonly supposed by children. "Neither my father nor my mother knew / the names of the trees, " as the bewildered poet admits in "Native Trees" (*RT* 6). Constituting an utterly unknown dimension of existence, the archaic green obsesses Merwin in its inexplicable calling (like that of Marietta), which disrupts and traumatizes the poet's quotidian life.

---

① "And [Jacob] dreamed, and behold a ladder set up on the earth, and the top of it reached to heaven: and behold the angels of God ascending and descending on it" (*King James Version*, Gen. 28. 12). In Jewish mysticism, stairs and rungs essentially symbolize spiritual growth, as in the title of Martin Buber's *Ten Rungs* (1947) which points at the levels of religious consciousness and practice. Merwin's erotic narrative here, however, only dimly echoes the biblical legend.

"The Moment of Green, " one of the several narrative poems in *Travels* (1993), dramatizes a rather fatal call from the "green." The title itself serves as an apt epithet for Merwin's late work, fully revealing his phenomenal effort to relive in poetry the momentary and traumatic encounter with nature. The protagonist here is Gregorio Gregorievich Bondar (1881 – 1959), a botanist from Poltava, Russia. In Merwin's account, Bondar, fascinated with natural plants, leaves Russia to study botany at European universities and then goes to Brazil to "work in plant pathology" (*T* 79). He returns to Russia in 1916 during World War I without apparent reason and is thus suspected by Russian authorities to be a spy. Bondar's obsession and eroticization of flora clearly mirror Merwin's own engagement, so when Bondar recalls the regional woods in Poltava, we are not surprised to learn that:

> ... his hand grew
> pictures of her he traced the legs
> of her grasses lengthening he
> followed the lace of her veins to
> find where they opened from he drew
> the bees in her flowers and on
> her leaves the cicada one of
> her voices and the grasshopper
> part cloud part paper ... (*T* 77)

Blending human characteristics with amorphous nature, these lines are quite consistent with Merwin's "naturalistic" fantasies about Dido Milroy in "Canso, " Dana Naone in *Finding the Islands*, and Flora in "Marietta." The essence / center of nature is endlessly deferred on the synecdochic chain (legs, lace, veins, voice, grasses, bees, flowers, leaves, cicada, grasshopper, cloud) that conflates sexual allurements with natural elements.

Leonard Scigaj calls our attention to Merwin's defamiliarization of "grew" instead of "drew, " which reveals Bondar's anxiety to know nature, "that other he felt so compelled to bond with, until all distance vanishes" (209). Scigaj does not notice that such an infinitesimal "distance" from nature-Other is all that motivates Bondar's seemingly irrational decision to return to Russia during the War. Bondar is obsessed with what he could never decipher in the forest of his homeland: the illusory calling of unexplored nature. After he "had // circled the globe" Bondar comes back to see:

... the molten plain flowing past
the rim of forest and he heard
from the leaves the shimmer of sound
he recognized though he could not
begin to decipher it or
guess who it was intended for
but he heard that it was what he
had to go on listening to (*T* 81)

This is what Bondar, risking his life, has come back for: "the shimmer of
sound, " neither an audible sound nor complete silence but a phantasmal
shimmer — the Lacanian gaze as the love object. Borrowing from Jean-Paul
Sartre, Lacan elaborates on the gaze as "the sound of rustling leaves,
suddenly heard while out hunting" (*Seminar XI* 84). The gaze originates
not from the subject's eyes observing the Other but from an imaginary
feeling of being watched by this Other. Like a neurotic suffering from
auditory hallucinations, Merwin's Bondar posits an imaginary and
indecipherable gaze from the beloved flora and feels compelled to listen to it
repeatedly and desperately. This amorous and heavily cathected "shimmer"
clearly transcends mortality and historicity, crossing over the speaker's
symbolic world toward the unknown parts of nature, as he so marvels at its
uncanny indestructability: "[I]t went on after the trees / fell after deaths after
learning / after everything had been said" (*T* 82).

Whereas ecocritics unproblematically regard Merwin's nature poems as
"restor[ing] our lost sense of connectedness to the planet" (Scigaj 12) or as
establishing "a valid bond with the planet" (Frazier 24), I would read them
rather as a testimony of structural difference or a non-adequation between
man and nature. "The Moment of Green" not only establishes a bond but
also dialecticizes that bond, pushing man's love of nature to the edge of
destruction of the loving subject. In the poem the imaginary "bond" turns
out to be a "fierce devotion" that ignores all impediments in its own
dangerous *jouissance*. "So he had gone home to be shot" (*T* 76), Merwin
has announced Bondar's doom in the very beginning of the poem.

Bondar is only one of the figures seduced, tormented, and *infinitized*
by the flora. In "Cinchona, " another historical narrative in *Travels*, Merwin
recounts the colonialists' mad desire for the precious plants in Peru in the
seventeenth century. Here we meet another of Merwin's botanists, the
Englishman Richard Spruce, who feverishly launches one expedition after
another to Peru in order to transplant cinchona, which has been discovered

by the Europeans as a cure for fever, to India. The irony is striking, clearly echoing "The Judgment of Paris," in which Helen gathers flowers "whose roots are said to dispel pain" (*SF* 148). The fever-curing cinchona has become "something of value / like gold" and is

> sought stripped shipped
> to be sold in Spain carried by
> missionaries defended fought over
> killed for (*T* 45).

Richard Spruce's motivation in the mission, however, is ambiguous: officially it is "for the sake of the [British] / empire," while privately it satisfies "his devotion to / unknown flora" (*T* 46). Spurred by desire for botanical knowledge, Spruce keeps planning the excursions in spite of his "dubious health," since "he was sick again deaf / in left ear unable to walk or sit / without / great pain" (*T* 46, 48). Sick as he is, Spruce takes good care of the seedlings and cuttings, putting them on

> shaded beds to be kept watered
> by hand to root them then pack them in earth
> they knew
> and into baskets for
> the muleback journey over the mountains
> then into cases on the raft ... (*T* 48).

In these breathless and heavily enjambed lines, Merwin constructs a subject who, instead of being the master of the plant, has been continuously subjected to the plant, and in a stroke of irony, Spruce, like Bondar, has suffered from the plant he loved.

In this dreamlike and hallucinatory text, Merwin mercilessly exploits the aftereffects of Spruce's contact with cinchona, the unknown flora. As if spellbound by "the daily taste of that powdered bark," Spruce and his team defy every hardship and danger in escorting the seedlings: in the heavy rain, they cross the "savage" river and then

> a narrow sluice between snatching
> thickets the current at bends smashing them
> three times
> into the bank with such force
> that the cabin collapsed and their pilot
> once was swung by a branch
> over the roaring water ... (*T* 48–49).

Later, Spruce and his men

> grope[d] through the splintered bodies of trees
> that had saved their lives and to feel the cases
> of cuttings as though they were touching bones
> of their own after a fall ... (*T* 49).

These lines immediately recall Eve, about whom Adam once said: "This is now bone of my bones, and flesh of my flesh" (*King James Version*, Gen. 2. 23). Like Eve, the cinchona is all that is left for Spruce — the adamant Adam who lost his paradise at home — to hold onto in the dangerous forests of Latin America, for the cinchona is both his salvation and his doom. Like Bondar, Spruce and his men are also unable to provide a logical reason for their actions and sufferings. Traumatized by the flora, Spruce and Bondar obtain their subjectivity as agents of free choice and carry that choice to its tragic yet logical end.

The "undetermined fever" has driven many of Merwin's naturalists and botanists into conducting zealous researches on plants and flowers, all with unhappy results. In "The Blind Seer of Ambon, " Merwin laments the fate of German botanist Georg Eberhard Rumpf (1627—1702) who is so devoted to the study of the flora of the East Indies — with "tenacity and love" as Scigaj says (205) — that he carries on the project disregarding consecutive personal catastrophes. In the process of composing *The Ambonese Herbal*, a catalogue covering more than 1, 200 species of plants and 350 hand-drawn illustrations, Rumpf is first struck by blindness, then by an earthquake that takes away his wife and daughter, and lastly by a fire that destroys almost all his illustrations. Like Cassandra, who could literally hear the future though no one believed her prophecy, after such dire losses Rumpf, "the blind seer of Ambon, " gets finally compensated by a divine ability of hearing:

> I take a shell in my hand
> new to itself and to me
> I feel the thinness the warmth and the cold
> I listen to the water
> which is the story welling up
> I remember the colors and their lives
> everything takes me by surprise
> it is all awake in the darkness (*T* 4)

After many vicissitudes and sufferings, Rumpf strangely retains that

114 freshness ("new ... to me," "everything takes me by surprise") of the natural life as if meeting it for the first time, and by listening to it he achieves a unique salvation from nature qua the Other. In fact, Rumpf readily accepts the imaginary calling from this nature-Other, deeming it "my true calling" and admitting that his engagement with flora is hardly understood by his contemporaries: "I may have seemed somewhat strange / caring in my own time for living things / with no value that we know" (*T* 3). Unlike Richard Spruce who adventures to grab the precious medicinal bark for the empire, Rumpf perseveres in a personal project that has no immediate use-value for the European colonialists. When Rumpf says, "I named for my wife a flower" (*T* 3), he explicitly equates flora with the love object, not the object of mastery and exploitation.

In his ecstatic descriptions of natural life, Merwin usually blends erotic desire with spiritual salvation. If he sees heaven in a wild flower, as William Blake once did, it is not populated by bright angels but by charming and exuberant life forces. In *Travels*, Merwin often throws away the poetic mask and meditates on the raw force of nature with unreserved passion. Trees and flowers belong to an Edenic site where all is innocent — as innocent as the cinchona ignorant of the feverishly grabbing hands. In "The Palms," Merwin celebrates the "telluric force" of palm flowers and their dark, nonhuman vitality:

> they stand as though they had no secrets
> and one by one the flowers emerge from the sheaths
> into the air
> where the other flowers are
> it happens in silence except for the wind
> often it happens in the dark
> with the earth carrying the sound of water (*T* 87)

A Freudian reading quickly reveals the sexual import in these lines: the opening flower symbolizes the female sexual organ while the "dark" water, mother's womb, reminding us of "the bronze ferns older than seeing / unfurling above the dark springs" (*FH* 39) and also the deep, luxuriant woods found in the previously discussed prose poem "Marietta."

Merwin seems to derive unfathomable joy from such an encounter with the dark force, marveling, as Rumpf once did, that "everything takes me by surprise / it is all awake in the darkness" (*T* 4), as if there is *something* in the flower that always eludes the poet and thus entices him. In another narrative poem, "Manini,"[①] the protagonist holds pearls between his fingers and similarly remarks: "[T]here are the colors / once more and the veiled light I am looking for / warm in my touch again and still evading me" (*T* 8). What evades Manini evades Merwin as well.

Since settling down in Hawaii in the mid-1970s, Merwin has increasingly imagined or posited the omniscience of flora: she possesses a knowledge that evades him. In light of Lacan's theorem that the subject tends to fall in love with whomever he supposes to have more knowledge (*Seminar XI* 232), Merwin's obsession with the natural life on the island can be read as such a case of transference: Merwin transfers his desire for the enigmatic (m)Other to the trees and flowers. In "Field Mushrooms," the poet's and the poem's desire circulates around the knowing yet unknowable flora:

> I went on finding them
> always at evening
> coming to recognize a depth
> in the shade of oaks and chestnuts
> a quickening in the moss year after year
> a suggestion of burning
> signs of something already there in its own place
> a texture of flesh
> scarcely born
> full of the knowledge of darkness (*T* 91)

The mushrooms hide deeply among oaks and chestnuts, avoiding the light of human knowledge ("always at evening"), and like the Holy Grail, they can only be found by those who ardently seek them. The "quickening" and "burning" of the "texture of flesh" not only symbolize the raw life energy of the plants but also make visible Merwin's own libidinal drive: what really quickens and burns is not the mushroom but the poet's desire for nature qua the Other as the locus of "the knowledge of darkness." Similar to Gary Snyder who brackets nature phenomenologically,[②] Merwin has been

---

① Manini is another name for Don Francisco de Paula Marín (1774–1837), an avid Spanish horticulturist known for introducing many plants to Honolulu, Hawaii.

② See Gary Snyder's preface to *No Nature: New and Selected Poems* (1992): "There is no single or set 'nature' either as 'the natural world' or 'the nature of things.' The greatest respect we can pay to nature is not to trap it, but to acknowledge that it eludes us and that our own nature is also fluid, open, and conditional" (v).

evoking the phantoms of nature instead of trying to penetrate into nature's secret. Nature becomes this infinitely alien Thing that the subject can never categorize, thematize, and subjectivize, because it is no-thing at all, only "scarcely born."

Merwin therefore does not merely recognize or respect the alterity of nature, as ecocritics are quick to point out; he exhibits a pathological fixation on that alterity which has its own dimensions of time and space. The liberating potential of poetry ultimately resides in what is left unsaid and in the infinite promise of redemption that has arrived neither in words nor in reality. In another place the poet prays:

> let me love what I cannot know
> as the man born blind may love color
> until all that he loves
> fills him with color ("To the Rain, " *SF* 288)

Merwin's prayer to the rain presents "a love so fierce that it cannot be satisfied either with the mimetic desire of what it projects another to be or with the disinterested arrogance of presuming another merely existing to himself, " and the poem's "rage is for the sameness" (Watkins 198). In a quasi-Pauline manner, Merwin urges readers to love the unknown first and not to seek to *understand* it, because understanding already connotes mastery and limitation. Also, Merwin asks us to be open for love, since love itself is nothing but the unconditional opening toward the Other — not the manipulable, exploitable other, the other as self-image, but the *infinite* Other that paradoxically *resides* in the self but is more than the self, *atopos*, possessing "a ceaselessly unforeseen originality" as conceived by Roland Barthes (*Lover's Discourse* 34). By fostering the latent alien object in the self until it overflows one's consciousness, readers may come to realize the inherent arbitrariness of signs, symbols, orders, and generally, of all products of perceptual apparatuses. This embracing of an unknown love, tactless or blind at first sight, commits the self in an endless reattachment to such an alterity as allowing readers to reinvest themselves in the realm of the real — the coming-into-existence of what is other than the natural, the social and the logical.

Chapter 4

Wake Up in a World of Light: Memory, Grief, and Temporality in Merwin's Later Writings

Among the living American poets, Merwin has come to resemble what David Biespiel, in a review on his *Migration: New and Selected Poems* (2005), calls "poetry's Iron Man" (137): since *A Mask for Janus* (1952), Merwin has published nearly sixty volumes of poetry, prose, and translation, and his work has recently been canonized by the Library of America into a two-volume *Collected Poems* (2013). Yet unlike the critics who seek either to defend a poetics of absence in Merwin's middle period (e.g., Cary Nelson and Charles Altieri) or to laud a poetics of ecologism in his later work (e.g., Jane Frazier, Leonard Scigaj), David Biespiel is troubled by the lack of expressive urgency in Merwin's later output, as it can be difficult, as Biespiel says, to "peel away the enormous reputation [Merwin] has and get a handle on the work that's actually important" (137). Since "the handle" or the real key in Merwin's later poetry seems missing, Biespiel could dismiss Merwin's *Vixen* (1996), *The River Sound* (1999), and *The Pupil* (2001) as "placid and underwhelming": Merwin's vision in these books has simply blurred and become inconsequential (141–142). Biespiel's summery reflects a general tendency to read Merwin's later poetry in comparison with his earlier vacuum-driven style (particularly from the 1960s and 1970s) and to draw conclusions based on the quality of poetic visions and tones — how Merwinesque they are, that is, how acutely, surreally, and consistently they reveal our limitations as historical beings.

118

Though the other side of existence looms large on the periphery of human perception, we fall short of its revelation and grace in that our reading of this otherness is always already historicized or marked by a historical necessity finally attributed to certain national or global agenda.①

When critics discredit one kind of historicist reading, they often turn to another one, leaving the question of what constitutes the inner (psychic) urgency of Merwin's later poetry unsettled, perhaps even uninvestigated. When ecocritics search in later Merwin for what they have already found — a salient environmental consciousness — they have implicitly hypostasized endangered nature as the ground of Merwin's recent engagement, though it could well be the battlefield of any environmentalist. Ecocriticism on Merwin, by presupposing the (harmonious) coexistence of man and nature, largely overlooks the critiques and reformulations of existential humanism from such thinkers as Jacques Derrida and Gilles Deleuze, who regard structural difference, not group identification, as constitutive of subjectivity, and also Emmanuel Levinas, who indefatigably elicits the non-reciprocity and non-thematizability of the Other, which has been deliriously anticipated in Merwin's later works.

Certain thematic continuity informs Merwin's oeuvre from the 1950s to the present: a vast incantation of the alternative realities (nature is just one of them) that tend to disappear from the current technocratic society. From *The Lice* (1967) to *The Shadow of Sirius* (2008), Merwin has been conjuring and interrogating *the other side* of rationalized existence, searching for a more originary mode of being that resists the hegemony of totalized history — a signifying process that is all too human; anonymity has therefore remained the norm and naming, at best a designation aware of its own limit. The urge to enunciate and evoke the diachronic origins that call into question the priority as well as linearity of both personal and national histories imbues much of Merwin's writings after the death of his

---

① It is interesting to note that a recent "mock" debate between Mark Halliday and Michael Theune on the value of Merwin's *The Shadow of Sirius* (2008) centers neither on historical nor ecological issues but on whether or not Merwin has really achieved "a condition of transcendent awareness of Essential Being" (Halliday and Theune 150). Though drawing opposite conclusions, both authors seem to agree that in late Merwin the problematic "radical simplicity of timeless archetypes" clearly predominates over other less enduring concerns (160). See Halliday and Michael Theune's "*The Shadow of Sirius*: A Critical Conversation," in Weinert and Prufer 137-172.

parents in late 1970s. Beneath the invocation of natural objects, readers can feel an acute sense of loss and grief, as nature has only been summoned to fill in the abyss of subjectivity and to transcend this grief caused by the rejection / foreclosure of the Name of the Father, the very law that prohibits enjoyment within the Structure or the System.

In search of this forlorn, forbidden joy, and with a view to counter historical and ecological readings that seek to highlight certain univocal consciousness at the expense of the unconscious (what is essentially *unnamable*), this chapter ventures a psychoanalytical elaboration on Merwin's later volumes, including two important autobiographical documents, *The Unframed Originals: Recollections* (1982) and *Summer Doorways: A Memoir* (2005). Employing psychoanalysis as what Mieke Bal terms a "semiotic model" by deciphering the "traces of the unconscious and the forms it takes which disturbs coherency" (87), I attempt to elicit the latent or repressed urgency in Merwin's later output which refuses to be appropriated into any forms of historical necessity, ecological consciousness being its recently prominent form. I suggest we approach Merwin's later engagement as an urgent working-through of the dark mourning for his father's death towards ancestral origins that can only be accessed by an increasingly primordial memory. Merwin's critique of the paternal restriction commonly seen in his earlier work, e.g., "The Drunk in the Furnace" (1960), has been reversed into an uncontainable grief for the very lack / loss of paternal love, and ultimately, for time itself, although the constant renewal of time seems to promise an end to the grief for what is already lost in time.

"That patch of sunlight": Merwin's father complex

Critics clearly see the influence of a "prohibitive" father on Merwin's later writings. Examining one of Merwin's autobiographical poems from *Opening the Hand* (1983), Thomas Byers discerns that Merwin's father's "constant messages were restriction and control," and "[e]ven the poet's powerful ecological warnings may descend in part from his father's constant strictures against touching anything" ("Present Voice," 256). H. L. Hix, reading the "drama of the fall" from *The Unframed Originals*, compares the father-son relationship to that of Adam and God: "Merwin playing the role of Adam / Eve, his father playing a strict God," summarizing the pattern of many of

Merwin's poems as "the struggle between liberty and authority" (*Understanding* 114, 116). Both commentators have reduced the father's image to a stern God, a superego that prohibits and condemns. Merwin's relationship with his father, however, could be more complicated as few critics have noticed that Merwin's father, though severe and oppressive, remains *distant* most of the time: "[P]reoccupied and moody, off in his own projects and considerations," and "did not normally give any thought to my company, and occasionally spoke of being much too busy for that," and "[h]is attention to me was limited almost entirely to what I was forbidden to do" (*SD* 86, 27).

Reduced to its core, Merwin's relationship with his father is a curious mixture of both rebellion and reverence — a typical father complex. Sigmund Freud's study of the psychosis of Daniel Paul Schreber (1842–1911) offers the first detailed case of father complex that had triggered psychosis. Freud's study also brings out the interrelation between the image of sunlight and paternal function. In various delusional onsets, Schreber believes that the infinite and eternal "Rays of God" are talking to him, urging him to transform into a woman (Freud, *Case* 95). Freud interprets Schreber's paranoia as a defense mechanism against homosexual wish-fantasies for his father (*Case* 135). The sun, as Freud claims, represents a "sublimated symbol for the father," and Schreber's delusion of copulating with God can thus be interpreted as the return of his "unsatisfied homosexual affections" towards his father (130, 133). Reexamining Freud's explanation of the father complex in the Schreber case, Jacques Lacan, in *Seminar III: The Psychoses* (1955–1956), proposes the foreclosure / rejection (*Verwerfung*) of the Name-of-the-Father, the phallic function, from the Symbolic as characteristic of the psychotic structure (143–157).

In "Psychopoetics" (1984), an article that attempts a major reevaluation of the longstanding conjunction of literature and psychoanalysis, Mieke Bal, following Shoshana Felman whom she quotes in the same article, cautions critics against using psychoanalysis as an "analogical model" because such a model only seeks to demonstrate that "a literary text displays features of the psychoanalytical process," neglecting the text's potential to modify or alter that process (83). Bal suggests that this relation be "reversed" into seeing those psychoanalytical processes such as transference or repression as *problematic concepts* instead of "staged in the text" (83; emphasis added). In order to gain certain "surplus knowledge" rather than confirm the psychoanalytical conclusions, critics are invited to consider how to "make explicit in what ways the presumed subject exposes itself as existing through various psychoanalytically theorized problems" (84).

Merwin's account of his father is more than "analogical" to Schreber's complaint that his God "does not understand living men" and "was not really acquainted with living men" (Freud, *Case* 100). It modifies the Schreber case by specifying what a functional subject — unlike Schreber, Merwin goes neither paranoiac nor delusional out of imagined paternal oppression though he has been deeply troubled by his relationship with his father — can do by means of poetic utterance. In Mewin's case, helpless distance from the father predominates, and it is the father's inattention or *indifference* rather than his oppression that truly chagrins the child. During World War II, Merwin's father was physically absent, serving as a chaplain in the army, and after he came back, Merwin, with the increase of age and wisdom, no longer saw him as a restrictive, punishing God but as an Other who lacked something himself, "distant, but helplessly so, without hostility, like someone adrift in himself without oars" (*SD* 85). Behind the paternal metaphor, or the Name-of-the-Father, a signifier "replete with cultural and religious significance" (Grigg 9) that normalizes and regulates a social being's desire, Merwin discerns the father in reality as lacking, helpless and even impotent.

Yet to read Merwin's ambivalent biographical account of his father is very much like reading another Schreber case. Merwin's complaint about his father's neglect, "inadequacy, " and "loneliness" (*SD* 86), as revealed by Freudian discourse, can be readily interpreted as a complaint of love, in which the poet laments his inability to help his father out. When his father, returning from the War, proposed to spend some time together to remedy alienation, Merwin admitted that he felt " hot in the face, and uncomfortable, " and to make the drama of love more poignant and disappointing, "when the real time together started he seemed to have forgotten it, and to have returned to his distant and unapproachable self" (*SD* 86). In the Oedipal stage we witness not only a child's resentment and antagonism towards the father, as Merwin's critics are quick to find in Merwin's family poems (Hix, *Understanding* 119; Byers, "Present Voice" 264), but also *the exaltation of and the identification with the father*. Freud's studies on psychoneuroses indicate that the male child may unconsciously treat the father as a love object as the fear of the father

121

accompanies the child's desire to satisfy him. For instance, the Wolfman's fear of being gobbled up by the wolfs in his dream, as Freud proves by tortuous interpretations, can be taken as "the wish for coitus with the father" (*Case* 231), and Schreber's psychotic visions also result from his roundabout defense against the homosexual wish-fantasy for the father (139 – 141).

Freud's famous view on family romance has been critiqued on different grounds, ① yet here I am not using it to highlight young Merwin's symptomatic desire for his father, which according to psychological researches might be common for both the male and female child.② My intention is to show how this ambiguous, ticklish desire informs and structures Merwin's later work. Merwin's love for his father takes the negative form of rebellion in childhood; in youth and adulthood, distant sympathy has replaced the discontent; while after the father's death in 1977, mourning for the father comes to the foreground when the loss of the love object is acutely felt in Merwin's later poetry. As if unconsciously *working through* the psychoanalytical problematic of the paternal function, in many poems on his father, Merwin associates paternal authority with the

---

① The most vehement attack on Freud's formulation of "family romance" perhaps comes from Gilles Deleuze and Félix Guattari's *Anti-Oedipus: Capitalism and Schizophrenia* (1972), which argues for a productive, rather than prohibitive, interpretation of human desire. In the book, Deleuze and Guattari consider Freud's "tripartite formula" — "the Oedipal, neurotic one: daddy-mommy-me" — as a limited structure that has ignored ideological and social formations of the primal scene (*Anti-Oedipus* 23). Literary critics, Shoshana Felman and Mieke Bal for example, have consequently focused on the problematic conjunction of literature (textual structure) and psychoanalysis (Oedipal structure). In an early reappraisal essay "To Open the Question" (1977), Felman proposes that "[t]he notion of *application* would be replaced by the radically different notion of *implication*: bringing analytical questions to bear upon literary questions, *involving* psychoanalysis in the scene of literary analysis …" (216; emphasis original). Following Felman's implication procedure, Mieke Bal urges psychoanalytically informed literary criticism to gain "surplus information" in textual analysis and thus to "contribute to the rethinking of the subject in the socio-cultural sciences" rather than confirming psychoanalytic discourse (87).

② Freud discovers that children are largely bisexual and may treat both parents as love objects. In *Three Essays on the Theory of Sexuality* (1905), Freud ventures the view that humans have an original predisposition towards bisexuality. See Geyskens 104 – 111.

declining tendency of sunlight — the image of darkness, of *Dämmerung*. The twilit space excludes normally perceived reality and becomes the field where an acute sense of grief, as Russell Grigg says of psychic reality, "returns from outside the subject, as emanating from the real" (10). In "Sunset Water," a poem from *Opening the Hand* (1983), the speaker laments the death of the father with a haunting imagery of twilight coupled with water. As commonly found in defense mechanisms against paternal authority, Merwin posits a vulnerable and lacking father: "How white my father looked in the water / all his life he swam doggie paddle / holding hurried breaths steering an embarrassed smile" (106). Here Merwin turns the restrictions against the restrictive / distant father himself, relegating his status to a timid child faced with infinite nature. Unconscious revenge surely exists in these lines, but there is also certain sympathy for the father — "the undercurrent of tenderness," to borrow Thomas Byers's phrase ("Present Voice," 265) — as if the speaker, standing aside, wanted to help but failed to do so. As Edward Brunner observes, "Merwin's portrait of his father eludes caricature" ("Opening the Hand," 282); it rather reveals his profoundly contradictory feelings towards his father.

The second stanza of the poem reactivates the ghostly presence of the father, as if the finite father, father in flesh and blood, through his own death has become an *infinite* one. Now the son swims in this twilight zone saturated with the *absence* of his father:

> long after he has gone I rock in smooth waves near the edge of the sea
> at the foot of a hill   I never saw before
> or so I imagine   as the sun is setting
> sharp evening birds   and voices of children
> echo each other   across the water (*FH* 106)

In a stylistic discussion on these groups of poems, Edward Brunner invites readers to see Merwin's use of the caesura as a way to "understand the ambivalent emotions that structure the powerful family poems in *Opening the Hand*" ("Opening the Hand," 277). The internal caesuras in this particular stanza have indeed smoothed over the traumatic memory of the father, making the old antagonism disappear in the gently rocking rhythms. The father's image is nowhere to be found in these lines but seems *everywhere*: in sunset, evening birds, voices of children, and even in seawater. All presences convey absence, loss, and grief. The last stanza of the poem consists of a single line: "[O]ne by one the red waves   out of themselves reach through me" (*FH* 106). The Real qua the lost love object is felt in this incessant impact of waves ("one by one") and the emptiness of ego (*through* me, not *past* me), ① as immersion in water and twilight has become a way of evoking as well as healing the longtime separation between the father and the son.

Merwin's obsession with the sunlight imagery, by effectuating a reaction formation towards the severe yet distant father, offers such an exposure of what otherwise would remain a dark realm: the psychotic-like paternal imagery of grief and melancholia. By introducing the *Fort / Da* play — the first creation of meaning through symbolization of the absent referent — of the sunlight, Merwin seems to escape and simultaneously get close to the father's image in order to subjectivize the latter's severity, inattention, departure, and final death as something he could not properly subjectivize. Merwin's mourning procedure therefore modifies the classical Oedipal model of the father and the son by introducing the poetic imagery of sunlight that dissolves restriction, repression, and antagonism. In "Still Morning," a poem from *The Shadow of Sirius* (2008), Merwin resorts to a primordial memory to transcend family genealogy:

> and I am a child before there are words
> arms are holding me up in a shadow
> voices murmur in a shadow
> as I watch one patch of sunlight moving
> across the green carpet
> in a building
> gone long ago and all the voices
> silent and each word they said in that time
> silent now
> while I go on seeing that patch of sunlight (*SS* 7)

In this memory flash Merwin travels back to the pre-linguistic period when human signification and phallic function have not yet organized the child's perceptual framework. Because the young child's ego and its operational mechanisms are still immature, its psychic apparatus remains vulnerable to external stimulations that could leave long-lasting memory traces in the unconscious (Freud, *Reader* 152). This patch of sunlight is one of the early

---

① This line recalls an earlier poem "Separation," in which the loss of the beloved is expressed through a haunting presence that conveys melancholic *jouissance*: "Your absence has gone through me / Like thread through a needle. / Everything I do is stitched with its color" (*SF* 15).

stimulations that the poet cannot fully integrate through retroactive, poetic signification, for children always recognize the meaning of a symbol later than its first, natural emergence. When the passage of time has silenced all the living voices, that patch of sunlight qua the alien object stays to mobilize the poet's psychic energy. The title of the poem, "Still Morning," foretells the indestructibility of memory traces from childhood or what Jerry Harp terms "the sense of childhood timelessness" (178) if we understand *still* as the continuation of a condition.

Merwin thus has something to offer to psychoanalysis in his protean and polysemous use of the sunlight image. Biographically, this ghostly presence of light is directly related to Merwin's father, who in a sense had initiated the image in the poet's unconscious, while extra-biographically, it could well be a whimsical invention of memory since "human memory is always a matter of mediation; it is never entirely direct" (Harp 179). In an interview with Bill Moyers (2009), Merwin recollects the event of the poem as his infant baptism in his father's church in New Jersey: "I remember being held up and watching the green carpet and that patch of sunlight," and this is how the sunlight image acquired its first paternal and ecclesiastical meaning. Usually, children begin to have their earliest memories between the age of two and four, but these memories of childhood, recollected in later life, could be based on "the principle of selection": we select those memory fragments — what Freud terms "screen memories" — that bear relations to our fantasies from a later period (*Reader* 543). What we remember from childhood might be insignificant in itself, such as a patch of sunlight or a person's face, but it registers important "thoughts and impressions from a later period" (*Reader* 553). This is how memory revises the event — by unconsciously creating a fixation, not on the past traumatic event itself (the exact moment of the event remains irretrievable), but on its selective associations (metonymies) that are deposited in memory. In fact, Freud surmises that the early childhood memory might be altogether "inaccessible in its original form" (*Reader* 559); he even doubts that we could have any conscious memories from childhood:

> Perhaps we have only memories of childhood. These show us the first years of our lives not as they were, but as they appeared to us at later periods, when the memories were aroused. At these times of arousal the memories of childhood did not *emerge*, as one is accustomed to saying, but *were formed*. (559; emphasis original)

Freud's tentative formulation of the "psychoanalytical memory" (Lacan, *Seminar III* 153) reveals that Merwin's remembrance of sunlight may not be an actual occurrence but a retroactively constructed image. In his autobiographical essay "The Skyline" from *Unframed Originals*, Merwin admits that the baptism occurred when he was only "a few weeks old" (*UO* 101), and it is "unlikely that the image [sunlight on the carpet] is an actual memory, but it remains clear, and whether it comes from a dream or from suggestions or from a glimpse of the occasion itself I cannot be sure" (*UO* 102). Merwin might have selected the sunlight image as one of his earliest memories out of its association with the sacred occasion and its symbolization of thoughts and impressions about his father, that is, a distant relationship, from a much later period.

Merwin in his late phase consciously fuses three intentions — paternal, divine, and agnostic — in the description of sunlight so that the signifier "sunlight" lacks a settled signified. The fantasized divinity of the father is often traversed by the son's retrospective wisdom: "During prayers I did not dare to raise my head and look at him for long, but through other parts of the service if I fixed my eyes on him I found that an aura of light came and went around. It was a trick of the eyes, and I knew it ..." (*UO* 109). Even if Merwin confers the divine aura on his father's head he would make a disclaimer soon later, admitting that the play of light is nothing but his own boyish prank: "I learned to make that luminous phantom grow larger, more intense, spread out like rays in water, while my father's voice rose and fell ..." (*UO* 109). Although the poet once regarded his father as "a mystery, " "[t]he Minister, impressive and unknowable, " he would soon add that it was "a role concocted from the whole of his life" (*UO* 113).

Merwin's retrospective knowledge on his father's mortality and his untiring effort to make peace with his father would make that "luminous phantom" travel back and forth in his recent poetry. This spectral presence betrays Merwin's unconscious desire for the elusive father and his simultaneous defense against it. For example, in "By the Avenue, " a poem also from *The Shadow of Sirius*, Merwin remembers his father's church in New Jersey:

> ... over there among
> the young leaves brighter than the daylight
> another light through the tall windows
> a sunbeam sloping like a staircase
> and from beyond it my father's voice

telling about a mote in an eye
that was like a mote in a sunbeam (*SS* 8)

In these memory traces, the father figure is conjured up among a cluster of luminous, mystic images: numinous icons like "sunbeam" and "light" appear more than once, as the sloping staircase distantly recalls the biblical Ladder to heaven. In the poet's vision, the father seems to be placed high above in heaven indeed, yet only by hindsight does the poet realize that a mote in the eye represents no religious lesson but an optical illusion hallowing the mundane, which significantly plays down the paternal / ecclesiastic function of the sunlight by highlighting its agnostic-naturalistic aspect.

If the sunlight image accompanies Merwin's memory of his father as the Minister of God, the incarnation of the holy Other, then twilight / night / darkness enshrouds the father as an existent conditioned by mortality. The absence of light denotes the death — both symbolic and real — of the father, just as the ghost of Hamlet's dead father comes by evening to visit the guilt-stricken son. In "Waking to the Rain" from *The Rain in the Trees* (1988), Merwin suffers auditory and visual hallucinations about his dead father, who does not know that he is dead but still tries to communicate with his son:

> The night of my birthday
> I woke from a dream
> of harmony
> suddenly hearing
> an old man not my father
> I said but it was
> my father gasping
> my name as he fell
> on the stone steps outside
> just under the window
> in the rain
> I do not know
> how many times
> he may have called
> before I woke
> I was lying
> in my parents' room
> in the empty house

> both of them dead
> that year
> and the rain was falling
> all around me
> the only sound (*RT* 27)

This poem exemplifies Merwin's *infinite* mourning for the dead father: the poetic self here is emptied, paralyzed, cauterized, and "torn up from oneself, " as Levinas says of the searing power of the Other (*Otherwise* 75). The intrusion of the dead father, as the return of the Real, shatters the son's "dream of harmony, " burning him with a sense of guilt in the night of his own birthday — an overlap of life and death. The son first refuses to acknowledge the old man to be his father, but this negation does nothing but reveal his unconscious desire to get close to the father, as the father's "gasping my name" well betrays the poet's wish-fantasy to make up for his father's neglect in the early years. The "fall" of the father first puts an irony to his own symbolic status as the Minister of God; then the father figure is further reduced to a lamentable state: "outside / just under the window / in the rain, " trying to go inside but fails to reach the son. Waking up, the son feels guilty for indulging himself in egotistic sleep and failing to respond to the earnest call from the father, who in order to see the son had come all the way to a foreign land ("stone steps" hint at Merwin's stone house in rural France where he had intermittently lived for years). Written ten years after his father's death, the poem gives full release to Merwin's belated remorse and his silent, uncontainable grief.

Merwin's relationship with the paternal function is both biographically and psychoanalytically singular: it constitutes what I would call " a reverential critique": Merwin cannot help but idealize his father while at the same time he readily recognizes and accepts the discrepancy between the symbolic, restrictive father and the father in flesh and blood. He attempts to escape the former, who imposes order and law, by emphasizing the weakness he finds in the latter. The strategy is not always successful, for "[t] he dead father became stronger than the living one had been" (Freud, *Totem* 166) in that the guilt and remorse of " killing " (rejecting, foreclosing) the paternal function remains to haunt the son. In this scenario that transcends the polarity of love and hate, what Merwin truly desires, I would venture, is perhaps not the living father who is severe, distant, "flawed and human" (McDonnell 176), but the dead yet *infinite* father — the internalized, darkly radiant father.

Forbears and the light of origin

Merwin's increasing interest in his familial origins dates from the death of both of his parents in the late 1970s, and his various autobiographical writings, collected under the book title *Unframed Originals: Recollections* (1982), can be read as a psychopoetic reaction towards this loss. Merwin seeks to overcome his father complex — ambivalent feelings towards the father — by discovering irregularity, disorderliness, and Other (non-paternal) *jouissance* in his family tradition. Desiring to transcend the symbolic law of the father, Merwin relies heavily on the imago of his "libertine" grandfather. Meeting his grandfather when he was nine and was immediately "entranced, " to use H. L. Hix's word (*Understanding* 112), by his grandfather's luminous, Edenic garden, Merwin creates from his memory a vision of utopia where everything looks innocent and amoral:

> The one I was standing in was a real garden. ... And real things to eat grew there. ... The sun shone straight down into the middle of the vegetable beds and held the leaves still. ... As I looked at the vegetable beds in sunlight, with the men's voices passing over my head, I did not know how old I was. (*UO* 3–4)

As the luxuriant, naturalistic scenery offers an alternative outside the rigid moralism that the father represents, this encounter with the alterity of nature will become increasingly important in Merwin's later writings. The grandfather, like a good-hearted Eve, encouraged the boy to eat tomatoes: "'Some of them's ripe, ' he said. 'You can eat them right now'" (*UO* 6). His grandfather, as Merwin's memoir discloses, was the first to encourage him to try new things, and the line "We seek a new dimension for the world" (*FF* 11) from the early 1960s would only seem a belated echo of his grandfather's salubrious exhortation.

Mark Christhilf, a critic who valorizes the mythmaking in Merwin's poetry, dismisses the poet's autobiographical writings as basically "produced from the familiar contents of consciousness" and only touching "the surface of life" (74–75). Christhilf might be right in pointing out the questionable mystification of daily life in a "democratic nation" (74) — it is a kind of mystification without real mystery. Yet Merwin's autobiographical writings do call for a deeper reading since the author takes such pains to trace and push his family genealogy to an impossible (always anterior) origin rather than glorify the family's past by claiming its historical importance. If there were mystery in Merwin's family stories, it belongs to the mystery or magic of time itself as these stories are told through the lens of a much later period when the poet's memory has to search the past for the very event in its own construction.

In a non-mythical reading of Merwin's use of memory from the 1950s up to the '80s, James McCorkle emphasizes memory's potential to bring the disseminated parts of history together to form a certain plentitude, to "overcome silence" (*Still* 132). Particularly, McCorkle sees Merwin's family poems of the 1980s as an attempt to "recover an atavistic poetic memory," through which the family genealogy, as "a primordial form of history," could be reconstructed by the poet himself (168, 166). To locate this "primordial" or "atavist" memory, which, as McCorkle points out, is always a "conjuring of the return of apparitions" (166), it would be beneficial to consider how memory could erase the past and rewrite it according to its law of association.

The French writer and philosopher Maurice Blanchot, in a review on Marc Bernard's *Just Like Children* (1941), attributes the power of stories of childhood to "a transfiguration of the past" (*Desperate* 47), since stories or episodes in one's early life could gain extraordinary import through narrative focalization and image production. "The slimmest anecdotes," as Blanchot says, "attract the reader as if they were the reflection of some unique and poignant truth," and this is because these moments have been associated by a later memory with "the inaccessible memory of the earliest emotions" (*Desperate* 47). Such emotions, narrated and sometimes fabricated out of one's selective memory, together with their "glorious constellation" issuing from "a free and eager sensibility" (*Desperate* 47), correspond to the mythical, pre-symbolic realm that occludes, and in Dr. Schreber's case forecloses, paternal laws and restrictions. Free from the requirement of a coherent plot, well-developed characters and univocal themes, autobiography offers unique glimpses into a writer's earliest disposition and motivation by creating a telepathic connection with another self through the temporal distance between the sophisticated *now* and the innocent *then*.

In Merwin's case, this time-gap is much illuminated and clouded by a mixture of authentic recollection and idealized fiction. Merwin's re-collection of family anecdotes and origins shares certain risk or unreliability found in all autobiography as a genre: later projections are interfused with earlier memory fragments to create a halo of intimate distance. It seems that these episodes refashioned out of a luminous memory could restore both the author and reader to a more originary world, where things are said to be authentic again and, as Blanchot puts it, "natural and truthful" (*Desperate* 48). These qualities no doubt are achieved when the harsher parts of one's childhood, as Blanchot sees in Marc Bernard's narrative strategy, have been offset, glazed, and sublated by a more mature consciousness.

Critics have noticed that Merwin's grandfather is a mysterious figure in the child's imagination: the old man simply occupies an unknown zone on the outskirt of family and society (Hix, *Understanding* 109−114). What Merwin *knows* is that the grandfather once worked as a pilot on the Allegheny River — mirroring Merwin's young ideal ego as a bohemian poet — and was often drunk and absent from home, which incurred much reprobation from Merwin's Protestant grandmother and her family. General reticence, as well as a legendary aura, was fostered around him:

> When I was growing up, my father never spoke of his own father at all, outside the immediate family, and even at home there were casual references to him... . It was as though my grandfather did not exist and never had existed, or had vanished mysteriously, not only from the physical world, but from the minds of his offspring, long before I was born. (*UO* 10)

Merwin criticizes his father's family for their lack of interest in the family history and its "tiny scope," which "made it easier for them to drop him from consciousness" (*UO* 10). If the father resembles the ego that represses libidinal impulses, the grandfather in an earlier poem "The Drunk in the Furnace" stands for the return of the repressed, the boisterous id:

> Where he gets his spirits
> It's a mystery. But the stuff keeps him musical:
> Hammer-and-anviling with poker and bottle
> To his jugged bellowings, till last groaning clang
> As he collapses onto the rioting
> Springs of a litter of car seats ranged on the grates,
> To sleep like an iron pig. (*FF* 282)

In this fantastic setting, the furnace-dweller leads a pre-symbolic life that largely ignores communal, inter-subjective exchange. Merwin creates myths around his grandfather because he feels regrettably separated from him (they met only once and only exchanged a few words) and also because this ancestral origin eludes him: much of the grandfather's life is still clouded over despite the grandson's arduous excavation.

Merwin's ceaseless digging into the past could be read as an attempt to overcome the present mourning for his father, which he only escapes by forming an attachment to an earlier origin, *an earlier father*. Yet ironically, the more he seeks ancestral origins, the more mythical they seem to be, until he has to give up the whole project and exclaim the total inaccessibility of the origin or any origins. In "To the Lightning" from *Present Company* (2005), Merwin compares ancestors to the transient lightning: "Now I can believe / that you never left" (*PC* 96). The trace of the distant forebear lodges within the descendant's unconscious, influencing the latter's life and destiny in an unknown way. Like the lightning, the ancestor is the one who strikes without warning, and its knowledge brings a kind of genetic predetermination that is scarcely mistaken: "[A]ncestor // whom your children / have never remembered / not one of them / and whose illumination / they could not hope to survive" (*PC* 96). This impossible ancestral origin, as a genetic endowment, elicits a particular relationship with mystery which is only partially penetrated by science: "It is a relationship with alterity, with mystery — that is to say, with the future, with what (in a world where there is everything) is never there, with what cannot be there when everything is there" (Levinas, *Time* 88).

Merwin's contact with his grandfather resembles such lightning: fleeting, traumatic, illuminating. Indeed, Merwin did not survive this "illumination" at the age of nine when their meeting took place since in his entire writings there are endless retroactive outbursts of the contact manifested as obsessional imageries of light, water, and origin. Merwin's grandfather both completes and substitutes the role of the father as his spiritual guide. The poet himself fully acknowledges the unconscious influence of his ancestor: "[B]eginning // around us all that time / unchanged as we travelled / from whom our eyes are descended / and the things we say // whenever we see you / there is a question / we do not dare to remember / and you disappear / before there are words for it // is that from you too" (*PC* 96–97). These lines do not merely express Merwin's honoring of human history or family tradition; they are imbued not so much with a sense of inheritance as a sense of primordial loss. Like lightning, ancestral origins disappear even before there are words to question them, not to mention securing any possible answers. Words, as vehicles of human signification and representation, fail to capture the *realness* of ancestors' influence, for it is permanent yet transient, omnipresent but nowhere to be located.

In later poetry, Merwin evokes the flaming image of the origin to suggest its constitutive yet retroactive effects upon present reality. Unlike the spiritless and disheartening contemporaries, the forebears are posited as more spirited and egoless as they existed in another spatial and temporal dimension beyond our apprehension, providing an alternative out of the social life that is largely regulated by the authority and prohibition.[①]"The Comet Museum" from *The Pupil* (2001) reflects upon the prehistoric nature of the celestial body: "So the feeling comes afterward / some of it may reach us only / long afterward when the moment / itself is beyond reckoning // beyond time beyond memory" (*P* 4). The comet causes a traumatic event whose effects are not attenuated but only delayed: the repetition of *afterward* and *beyond* stress this infinite deferral. The nostalgic feeling comes from the part of psyche that has been shot through by the combusting comet, whose coming and going is truly spectral, and in this sense the comet / ancestor has come to stand for the *absent cause* of the subject — although escaping our consciousness, it shapes us towards who we are. We could never have an accurately sufficient account of our ancestral origin, for like the origin of the book, it is "the bottomlessness of infinite redoubling" (Derrida, *Writing* 374).

The trace of origins seizes the poet's imagination and drives it towards an ecstasy until that imagination collapses. The drive towards origin is surely a death drive towards otherworldliness unbound by the paternal function. Archetypal images of animals, as the infinite doubles of origin, surge from the poet's unconscious to evoke an earlier time that is diachronic with the present. In "Ancestral Voices" from *The Vixen* (1996), Merwin combines a totemic bird with the spirited, spontaneous grandfather image.[②] After describing a twilight scene, the poet is suddenly struck by the voice of a blackbird that "came believing in the habit / of the light, " and epiphanic, the blackbird, like Shelley's soaring lark, lightens the dark world as the

---

① Readers may refer to Freud's *Civilization and Its Discontents* (1930) and Marcuse's *Eros and Civilization* (1955) for an exegesis of social life organized under superegoic prohibitions.

② In the story "Blackbird's Summer" Merwin portrays a local wine merchant named Blackbird, who, similar to Merwin's grandfather, stands outside the local morals due to his fascination with wine and negligence to church service. Blackbird knew the curative power of water and retained a spiritual rapport with mysterious nature. See Merwin, *LU* 157–307.

comet burns through the night sky: "the song / of the blackbird flashed through the unlit boughs and far / out in the oaks a nightingale went on echoing" (*V* 65). These otherworldly presences clearly transcend human history, for they "were lifted here long before the first / of our kind had come to be able to listen" (*V* 65). The two birds are not only vehicles of romantic sentiment but also represent impenetrable realities in themselves, constituting a presence indifferent to human significations: "they sang / of themselves which was what they had wakened to remember" (*V* 65).

The blackbird is only one of the many totems Merwin elevates to the status of origin to counterbalance the restrictive paternal order. The *jouissance* of animal-origin finds its supreme realization in the title poem "Vixen," in which Merwin lavishes high-toned, nearly hysteric praise on the "noble animal." The vixen, similar to the comet and the blackbird, is certainly what the poet can neither hold nor escape. Invariably, behind the vixen lurks Merwin's grandfather; in a related poem "Fox Sleep" from the same book, Merwin retells the Buddhist story of an old man who had been changed into a fox for "five hundred lives" and later regained his human shape (*V* 4). In "Vixen," however, the animal does not undergo a Buddhist transformation as it only calls for a witness before what is exactly unapproachable. The poem covers the whole spectrum of Merwinian vocabulary from stasis to dynamism, earnestly eliciting the elemental mystery of the origin-Other:

> Comet of stillness princess of what is over
> high note held without trembling without voice without sound
> aura of complete darkness keeper of the kept secrets
> of the destroyed stories the escaped dreams the sentences
> never caught in words warden of where the river went
> touch of its surface sibyl of the extinguished
> window onto the hidden place and the other time (*V* 69)

This Pindaric discourse turns the vixen into an infinitely auratic being: the otherness of the vixen has been sublimated into such a status that the poet who does the praising seems to have no other existence than becoming a pure voice of this "princess" who is apparently "without trembling without voice without sound." Far from negating the poetic self, the vixen sets the self in motion towards other dimensions of space-time; in this sense, the praising of the fox has taken on what Susan Stewart, in a discussion on the poetics of praising, terms the "cognitive function": "a capacious one that calls on more than either reasoning or the application of prior terms and values" (33).

It is manifest that the vixen, the "aura of complete darkness," is "never there," never captured or absorbed by the subject through speech and reasoning, as if the animal had become the eroticized, lost sublime Thing, which the poet is compelled to find and re-find.[1] Fantasizing that the vixen was present "in the full moonlight of autumn at the hour when I was born" (V 69), the speaker entrusts his future, his want-to-be (desire), on this shimmering origin that would endlessly produce this *jouissance* towards the discovery of a more authentic self:

> ... now when your light paws are running
> on the breathless night on the bridge with one end I remember you
> when I have heard you the soles of my feet have made answer
> when I have seen you I have waked and slipped from the calendars
> from the creeds of difference and the contradictions
> that were my life and all the crumbling fabrications (V 69)

The messianic vixen clearly ruptures the continuum of one's personal life, delivering the speaker from false values, necessary lies, and dubious memories. Like the ancestral blackbird, the vixen has survived the destruction of time; though "you no longer go out like a flame at the sight of me," the speaker still acknowledges that "even now you are unharmed even now perfect" simply because this *you* comes from "the other time" (V 69).

Hölderlin at the River: another birth

Merwin's desire for diachronic origins can be reckoned as a strategy to break through the symbolic order and thus to be liberated from his unpaid debts towards his father. Merwin's predicament is then clear: he tries to salvage the lost connection with his father while simultaneously asking for a deliverance from this compulsive memory by resorting to an even *earlier origin* such as his grandfather. Between memory and oblivion there is a constant war, just as genesis and apocalypse, creation and destruction are

---

[1] In different occasions, Merwin admits that his heart had been "caught by what was never there" (*RS* 112), or "when I went looking for what I thought I remembered / as anyone could have foretold it was not there" (V 3), or "reaching into the blindness that was there" (*SS* 45), etc.

constantly opposing and transforming into each other. David Biespiel captures this dialectic in Merwin: "In Merwinworld, it's always late in the season of another year. The wind is constantly remembering and the sea is forgetting, or vice versa. Language has yet to be spoken, but it's also on the verge of being lost. The birds are singing their last songs, and the light is young" (140). The polarities in Biespiel's observation point at the warring elements and tensions in Merwin's later output. In his later stage, Merwin rarely exhibits world-weariness or resignation as found in late Eliot, nor does he trust in a cosmopolitan wisdom as late Pound but keeps that high Pindaric tone before the infinite flux of time and reality, repetitively rehearsing psychic fantasies, cleavages, deriving *jouissance* from momentary meetings, separations, and subsequent longing.

Merwin's "feverish" endeavor to relive the traumatic breakage from the paternal order can be glimpsed in "Hölderlin at the River," perhaps the most beautiful and elaborate poem in *The Vixen*. A full discussion on the poem helps understand Merwin's tortuous struggle with the father complex and the intricate mechanisms the poem has gone through in transforming psychic realities into poetic realities:

> The ice again in my sleep it was following someone
>   it thought was me in the dark and I recognized its white tongue
> it held me in its freezing radiance until I
>   was the only tree there and I broke and carried
> my limbs down through dark rocks calling to the summer
>   where are you where will you be how could I have missed you
> gold skin the still pond shining under the eglantines
>   warm peach resting in my palm at noon among flowers
> all the way I was looking for you and I had nothing to say who I was
>   until the last day of the world then far below I could see
> the great valley as night fell the one ray withdrawing
>   like the note of a horn and afterwards black wind took
> all I knew but here is the foreign morning with its clouds
>   sailing on water beyond the black trembling poplars
> the sky breathless around its blinding fire and the white flocks
>   in water meadows on the far shore are flowing past their
> silent shepherds and now only once I hear the hammer
>   ring on the anvil and in some place that I have not seen
> a bird of ice is singing of its own country
>   if any of this remains it will not be me (*V* 29)

In the first place, any reader familiar with both Hölderlin and contemporary poetry will not mistake this piece for a pastoral: neither Merwin nor Hölderlin are Virgilian pastoralists. They are hymnists and elegists; they sing of what is already gone. The river in Hölderlin's famous hymn "The Ister," as Martin Heidegger has explicated, connotes an ontological dislocation of the self, a "coming to be at home" through "a passage through the foreign" (*Hölderlin's* 29). Rivers are "remote and foreign to humans," and as origins they can induce man's self-projection with certain metaphysical violence. Heidegger goes on to explain that "[i]t is precisely that which tears onward more surely in the rivers' own path that tears human beings out of the habitual midst of their lives, so that they may be in a center outside themselves, that is, to be excentric" (*Hölderlin's* 28). Apart from *ekstasis*, the river also connotes a returning to the origin: "[T]he river can never forget the source, because in flowing … it itself constantly is the source and remains the locality of its own essence (*Hölderlin's* 138).

Like Hölderlin, Merwin is also a troubadour of the elements of light, water, and fire, a devotional rather than a confessional poet. Merwin's line "I wanted to be far away like the surface / of a river" (*V* 29) could also have been written by Hölderlin. The first-person narrative, however, fuses Merwin's own psychic fantasies with Hölderlin's legendary madness about rivers. The poem begins with a dream at night: an alien Thing, "the ice," is following the dreamer. Ice, "the whiteness that we could not bear" (*FF* 227), attracts the speaker for its extreme coldness that tears the self out of its cozy inwardness. When the speaker "recognized its white tongue," the ice came to hold him "in its freezing radiance," as Merwin's Hölderlin did not survive this illumination at all but went through an Ovidian transformation, suffering the psychotic vision of broken limbs and dark journeys.

To further evoke the origin, Merwin introduces memory traces by the end of the fifth line. The speaker now wistfully apostrophizes summer, which is synonymous with the poet's youth, for both summer and youth shine gloriously yet transitorily. In the summer of 1948, Merwin first left the U.S. for Europe at the age of twenty-one, so that summer would serve as the prototype on which all later poems on summer are modeled. He then broke away from paternal authority, wandering around Europe as his grandfather had wandered on the Allegheny River two generations earlier. He would reap the guilt and pain of separation later; at the moment he was full of ecstasies and expectations. In retrospect, Merwin believes he was

138 following the call of some unknown origin at the time, which is recorded in his *Summer Doorways: A Memoir* (2005), a memoir about his departure and first years in Europe. The book begins with an intimation about unknown origins: "A summer descends to us from earlier years, heir to ancestors it never knew" (*SD* 3), and at the end of the book we read: "I would have the luck to discover, to glimpse, to touch for a moment, some ancient, measureless way of living, of being in the world ... evanescent like a work of art, an entire age just before it was gone, like a summer" (*SD* 216). Hölderlin's calling for summer therefore echoes Merwin's first breakage from the socio-familial life in the exploration of a more liberal, spontaneous way of living, "ancient" and "evanescent" it may seem. For Merwin, the notion of summer exactly constitutes what Heidegger calls a "passage through the foreign" (*Hölderlin's* 29), drawing the self out of its habitual location and initiating its transmutation.

Along with summer, the poem summons other images that are heavily loaded with Merwin's childhood memories. The pond image activates the libidinal fixation on water that Merwin has had since childhood, especially in Scranton, Pennsylvania, where he first tried to sail on Fiddle Lake. According to Merwin's memoir, in the first summer in Scranton the Merwin family lived far from the city, in the woods. When Merwin's father was absent during the week, "leaving his list of prohibitions hanging in the air," Merwin would take to the lake: "I love the lake, the rowboat, the sunlit rippled sand in the shallows ... and all that they allowed me to imagine, as I had never loved anywhere up until then, and I counted the days there, trying to keep them from slipping away" (*SD* 30). Merwin's obsession with lakes is largely a rebellious strategy against the symbolic restriction as he frankly confesses: "Some of my discontent and claustrophobia in those years took the form of feeling far away from water" (*SD* 27). The "still pond," the "rowboat," and the "sunlit rippled sand" all convey Merwin's youthful desire for spontaneity.

This partly explains why Merwin would present Hölderlin as attached to *other* callings. Hölderlin looked "far below" and saw the "great valley" that may hint at the impending yet unknown death. Merwin's Hölderlin here has witnessed the death of those around him: "[B]lack wind took / all I knew." The killer-wind represents both the external cosmic force that annihilates the individual and the uncontainable psychic force that strives for the infinite commonly found in Romanticism. Merwin here uses the wind image to suggest what both impels humans and wears them down: a scourge of the soul like the lightning, wind violently wipes the slate clean for the re-inscription of a new self.

When Merwin drives his Hölderlin towards despair, he does not forget to prepare the light of salvation. The later part of the poem reveals Merwin / Hölderlin's desire for a heterogeneous origin to compensate for the loss of the love object. Having mourned both lost youth and family members, Hölderlin beholds the heterogeneous morning in its freshening view. The connection between "mourning" and "morning" actually goes far beyond their identical sound. First, morning puts an end to mourning by introducing a new time series, as morning might offer salvation to the mourning subject mired in guilt and remorse. Second, mourning expresses grief for the bygone mornings and the inaccessible origins, parents, and ancestors as love objects. Third, morning completes and consummates mourning, as dawn consummates the vigil overnight. Merwin's later work can be felicitously described as a marriage of mourning and morning: the poet incessantly laments the death of his parents and ancestors and the loss of his own youth yet at the same time ecstatically declares an alien beginning, constantly evoking nature as the antidote to grief.[1]

The drive towards total oblivion and final death reaches its climax via Hölderlin's *infinite* vision in later parts of this alexandrine-like elegy (some lines resemble the 12-syllable, 2-hemistich pattern while others do not). The "foreign morning" scenery is void of human sorrow: the sailing clouds, "the black trembling poplars," and "the sky breathless around its blinding fire," presumably the heavenly light that had struck Hölderlin and driven him mad for forty years. The shepherds here are not the passionate ones of Christopher Marlowe's pastoral but rather remain "silent." The otherworldliness of the scene is further conveyed by the distant "hammer / ring on the anvil" and the singing of "a bird of ice" in a place that the speaker could not see. The sounds of inanimate metal and the strange bird call for nothing but the dissolution of the self, which is explicitly stated in the last line: "[I] f any of this remains it will not be me." A nature poem on

---

[1] For instance, Merwin's speaker often becomes fearless by transforming himself into an enduring entity: "[F] rom the beginning I would be older than all the animals / and to the last I would be simpler / frost would design me and dew would disappear on me / sun would shine through me / I would be green with white roots / feel worms touch my feet as a bounty / have no name and no fear" ("A Contemporary," *FH* 12).

the surface, "Hölderlin at the River" discloses Merwin's desire for the lost object and his drive towards what is other than self / ego, the heterogeneous origin, and "an *other* birth and an *other* essence" (Derrida, *Of Spirit* 107).

It is through such a radical alterity initiated in what Sean Joseph McDonnell calls "intrapsychic space" (159) that Merwin's portrait of Hölderlin can be best understood. Refusing the Name-of-the-Father that constitutes a normally functioning social being as prescribed by psychoanalysis, Hölderlin wandered outside his socio-familial world (he lived alone in a tower for thirty-six years, during which period his mother and sister never visited him) and pursued a kind of mystic *jouissance* in the withdrawal of both ancient deities and the Judeo-Christian God. Has not Merwin experienced a similar other-birth, the same pleasures and pains of not only encountering the strange but also becoming the Stranger himself? Merwin's passage through the foreign — through repeated departures and journeys — sets in motion such a fundamental dislocation of the self that in later poetry he keeps asking himself about what has actually happened to him, what he has really lost and kept through numerous breakages and separations.

This rite of passage and the process of rebirth have preoccupied Merwin after the 1980s when the mourning for his father began to gnaw at his spine. The poet attempts to ward off this compulsive memory by resorting to an origin earlier than memory, which only aggravates his grief, because the possibility of such an origin is already constituted by memory. The freezing radiance and blinding fire, which cause Hölderlin's grief and are also its remedy, are both originary and mnemonic. Memory completes the rite of passage and spiritual rebirth, since all journeys, to a certain degree, are journeys of the mind. In "Memory," Merwin travels back through memory to an origin other than human:

> Climbing through a dark shower
> I came to the edge of the mountain
>
> I was a child
> and everything was there
>
> the flight of eagles the passage of warriors
> watching the valley far below
>
> the wind on the cliff the cold rain blowing upward
> from the rock face
>
> everything around me had burned

and I was coming back

walking on charcoal among the low green bushes
wet to the skin and wide awake (*RT* 58)

Drawn by some unknown force, the child came to the mountain where he saw the traces of primordial liberty ("flight of eagles") and ancient bravery ("passage of warriors"), and like Hölderlin he observed the gaping valley below. The scene uncannily echoes both the journey of Odysseus ("the wind on the cliff the cold rain") and the sacrifice story of Isaac from the Old Testament ("everything around me had burned"). Merwin, however, might not have these prototypes in mind when he wrote the poem; he might simply be recollecting a childhood journey into the unknown wilderness to escape paternal control. Towards the end of the poem, the child was traumatized, "wet to the skin and wide awake," unable to return to the old self. The title of the poem suggests that memory is perhaps nothing but the inscription of this encounter with the alien both inside and outside consciousness.

The effort to recapture the traces of otherworldliness by travelling at night through the "dark passage" (*RS* 15) certainly has its rewards as the poet beholds the anonymity of the world before it is illuminated by logos and order. "Wakefulness is anonymous. It is not that there is my vigilance in the night; in insomnia it is the night itself that watches" (Levinas, *Existence* 66). At night, one directs one's desire not to any object but to the dark, objectless, and anonymous space, to the ghostly "wands of the auroras," which provide a precise image for the dialectic of desire and origin.[1] Driven by who-knows-what for the unnamed, distant otherness, Merwin's night-traveler experiences the familiar alienness of the world:

I remember waking at the rivers
to see girders of gray sleepless bridges
appearing from sleep out of a current
of cold night air velvet with the secret
coal smoke of those small hours and nobody
on night roads the few words of toll-keepers
old complaints of gates and cables the bark

---

[1] "Wands of auroras," in its Stevensian overtone, visualize man's metaphysical desire for the infinite: the far, shadowy light, inaccessible, uncontainable, dancing, beckoning, withdrawing.

> of bridge floors leaping up from under us
> and the swelling hiss of a surface just
> beneath us not loud but while it was there
> nothing else could be heard except as calls
> far off in some distance (*RS* 126)

The end of this poem, "Traveling West and Night, " points to some vague yet compelling otherness beckoning the traveler to continue the Hölderlinian wandering. Many of Merwin's recent poems on nightly passage exemplify desire's objectless propelling; the traveler does not know what he truly wants, nor could he identify the "calls / far off in some distance, " yet he follows the call without hesitation. The Prodigal Son "had to leave to be able to find" (*FF* 161), as Merwin wrote in the 1950s, yet what Merwin found during all those years away from his family, from the American continent, however, still remains undefined, because strictly speaking, desire, being the metonymic movement of signifiers, lacks an object. When Merwin, traveling in some foreign land, stays awake at midnight, he must have felt acutely the enigma of human motivation. Mark Christhilf understands Merwin's " world-traveler" as motivated by an urgency to "resist self-complacency" (70), yet in Merwin's later poetry this drive has been greatly accentuated by a daily necessity to deal with loss and grief and a nightly attraction into the anonymous. If there is grief in the silent sound of rain, this grief will be over when morning comes and the traveler is again on the road.

Crossing the shadows: grief and morning

The opposition between the father as the phallic sun and the grandfather as the amorphous river, between ego and id, between the socio-symbolic life and the real or imaginary origins, finally erupts as a tension between finitude and infinity in Merwin's late writings. The side of life that has been given meaning would embrace its infinite underside, which by resisting phallocentric function provides the *real* impetus for human actions. In later poetry, Merwin plumbs the infinite depth of human existence, for the *in* of infinity, for Levinas, designates the " depth of an undergoing that no capacity comprehends" (*Collected* 163).

Evolving from a lifelong obsession with the chiaroscuro of light and darkness, Merwin's *The Shadow of Sirius* revolves around the unknown side of existence that escapes univocal meaning. Sirius is the Dog Star, the most luminous one in the sky, twenty-five times brighter than the sun; Merwin curiously writes about its shadow that no one on earth has ever seen. Merwin explained the title to Bill Moyers:

> We are the shadow of Sirius. There is the other side of — as we talk to each other, we see the light, and we see these faces, but we know that behind that, there's the other side, which we never know. And that — it's the dark, the unknown side that guides us, and that is part of our lives all the time. It's the mystery. That's always with us, too. And it gives the depth and dimension to the rest of it.

The shadow of Sirius thus symbolizes the depth of the human psyche, which paradoxically contains the uncontainable exterior, as, again, Levinas's philosophical discourse lends a perspective: "The infinitely exterior becomes an 'inward' voice, but a voice bearing witness to the fission of the inward secrecy" (*Otherwise* 147). Although memory, desire, and grief are expressed through words, a large part of them still belong to the realms outside language and signification, which is also why they seize upon the poet so urgently and fiercely through that "inward voice." The son's cry that "but it is the world, / Father, that I do not understand" (*FF* 109) can be supplemented by "it is myself, Father, that I do not understand." Any interrogation of the world turns out an interrogation of the self, not of its imaginary identity and illusionary wholeness, but of its ontological abyss, its irreducible strangeness that eludes the thematization of language.

Ever since *The Moving Target* back in the early 1970s, Merwin has repeatedly resorted to the unnamed calling, although he has not quite figured out what that calling means for him. What corresponds to the calling is the infinite as well as infantile longing for the beyond of naming, language, meaning, and phallic function. In the late 1990s, Merwin admitted that "I thought I was getting better / about that returning childish / wish to be living somewhere else / that I knew was impossible" (*RS* 125). He is not "getting better" actually, nor does he outgrow his childhood. The fist poem from *The Shadow of Sirius*, "The Nomad Flute," begins wistfully as ever: "You that sang to me once sing to me now / let me hear your long lifted note / survive with me" (*SS* 5). The speaker identifies himself with the calling of the Other, which is manifest in another poem "Calling a Distant Animal" from the same book: "Here it is once again this one note / from a string of longing // tightened suddenly from both ends / and held for plucking" (*SS* 44). The poet compares himself to an instrument playing the music of longing, whose note can only be heard in a more ancient space-time and echoed only by "the silence it calls to." This "string of longing" aptly sums up Merwin's poetic stance as an Orphic bard, a nomadic singer driven by inner forces he knows little about but feels palpably. The infinite silence to which the note addresses does not reduce the addresser's zeal, for he has already recognized the silence not as a failure of response but as the only valid response to another even more primordial silence.

Calling expresses loss and grief, two main driving forces in Merwin's later poetry. The lyric self is able to acquire certain proximity to the lost love object via repetitive calling when the improbable articulation of such loss activates a passionate, as well as pathological, movement of words around that silent kernel, as if all loss can be remedied by this mere saying.[①] Like the unseen shadow of Sirius, loss and grief are invisible to us, who see only the positive side of the star, not its negative, dark side. As Merwin tells Bill Moyers in the same interview:

> One of the great themes that runs through poetry, all poetry, and I think is one of the reasons for poetry, one of the sources of poetry, one of the sources of language, is the feeling of loss. The feeling of losing things. Not being able to hold, keep things. That's what grief — I mean, grief is the feeling of having lost. Of having something being out of reach. Gone. Inaccessible. And I think that that's a theme that runs through much of all poetry.

The icy calls for Hölderlin, for the lightning and the summer days: all originate from the same loss. Unable to enunciate loss that is on the edge of language and knowledge, a "groundless country" or an "unmapped imperium" (*PC* 34), Merwin untiringly calls upon its stand-ins. In a poem for his dead dog, Muku, which means "complete darkness" or "night without moon" in Hawaiian, Merwin denies the possibility of any positive knowledge about loss: "Now you are darker than I can believe / it is not wisdom that I have come to // with its denials and pure promises / but this absence that I cannot set down" (*SS* 45).

---

① Slavoj Žižek usefully distinguishes "loss" from "lack" for their different relations with desire: "[L]ack is co-substantial with desire, while loss designates the moment at which desire loses its dialect ... by being transfixed by some positive object which is missing... . [T]he subject possesses [the lost object] in the very mode of loss" (*Plague* 195).

The light of knowledge, as the word *enlightenment* indicates, sinks infinitely in this groundless country of loss, and its resultant mourning presents a yearning that outlasts one's life, acquiring a posthumous life for its own sake:

> back of the same sky
> that lights the days as we watch them
> what do you want it for
> this endless longing that is only ours
> orbiting even in our syllables
> why do you keep calling us as you do
> from the beginning without a sound
> like a shadow ("To Grief " *PC* 33)

This longing, being endless, does not die as one's life ends; it walks like a specter in broad daylight in its afterlife, disturbing and traumatizing the living. In "No," a poem about pure negativity, Merwin conjures the grieving voices of the dead to haunt the living:

> Out at the end of the streets in the cemetery
> the tombstones stared across the wheeling shadows
> of tombstones while the names and dates wept on
> in full daylight and behind them where the hill
> sheared off two rusted tracks under a black
> iron gate led up out of pure darkness
> and the unbroken sound of pure darkness
> that went on all the time under everything (*SS* 21)

Merwin intimates that what underlies our daily life is something we choose to ignore, because we are afraid of confronting the "pure darkness" which supplements light / logos / order as its undesirable other. Attending to the whimpering grief of the dead, the poet readily embraces the constitutive negativity (darker sides) of our existence.

Merwin explains to Moyers about his belief in the good darkness, which "is not the threatening dark, but the nourishing dark. The nourishing darkness. That there's that we all take with us." As James Wright and Robert Bly who write in a similar vein have recognized, "nourishing darkness" connotes a dormant pregnancy that offers a poet vision, energy, and wildness. Darkness evokes loss and grief, yet it also pacifies them. In "Curlew," Merwin appreciates darkness from the angle of a bird: "When the moon has gone I fly on alone / Into this night where I have never been // the

eggshell of dark before and after / in its height I am older and younger //
than all that I have come to and beheld / and carry still untouched across the
cold" (*SS* 59). There is neither fear nor sadness in these lines, and grief, if
implicit, has been attenuated by the originary darkness that renews and
engenders life.

Under the shadow of Sirius, the unseen and unknown side of
existence, Merwin searches for the light of that "foreign morning" that once
freed Hölderlin from the bondage of memory and grief, and since the
1990s, Merwin has anticipated the heterogeneous morning urgently,
ecstatically, almost religiously. Edward Brunner once points out the
problem of time scale in Merwin's later poetry: "Along with physical and
social boundaries that dissolve, time also becomes fluid, approaching the
condition that it enjoys in nature" (*Poetry* 282). As the origin-Other,
morning is a categorical imperative: morning must come at the end of
hallucinatory mourning and involuntary memory. It consummates grief and
therefore overcomes it. Impersonally, morning cares not for human loss,
and its presence means nothing but a prehistoric birth. In a poem to his
wife, Paula Schwartz, Merwin declares the overcoming of all grief with the
coming of a new time sequence:

> the worn griefs will have eased like the early cloud
> through which the morning slowly comes to itself
> and the ancient defenses against the dead
> will be done with and left to the dead at last (*SS* 84)

The light of morning releases Merwin from the "ancient defenses against the
dead": the symbolic debts to his father and grandfather, from whom he
feels hopelessly alienated. For Merwin, morning bestows a beginning that is
diachronic with the past, a heterogeneous present that is pure surprise,
exigency, and release.

Throughout his later writing, Merwin continues to envision *the other
side* of perceived, known existence, avowing that "[t]he foolish thing is to
take that world which we have made as the real, total, absolute final
world" (*RM* 335), prioritizing and problematizing the unknown through
presenting the incessant calling of / for an ever-receding origin. The spiritual
"aura" of Merwin's recent work rests, on the one hand, on what Walter
Benjamin formulates as "the unique phenomenon of a distance"
(*Illuminations* 222), while on the other, it corresponds to a returning
specter in the sense of both Levinas, "The aspiration *for the return* is the
very breath of the Spirit" (*Entre Nous* 135; emphasis original), and

Derrida, who similarly emphasizes "the returning [*revenir*] of a spirit" (*Of Spirit* 91). Merwin's compulsive journey in his later career towards the salvation of origins is not a lucky trip but a difficult pilgrimage combining self-erasing gestures and existential decisions. In his ardent desire to approach the impenetrable beginning, Merwin has come to create an authentic spiritual discourse that elevates the lost otherness to the founding necessity of personal freedom. The guarding of *other* origins that transcend family genealogy and identity archeology thus becomes a suitable poetic critique of any self-assured knowledge of tradition, heritage, and history, for, as Merwin's later project prophesies, something surely will burst out from that knowledge.

Conclusion

Merwin's poetry, from the 1950s to the present, strikes readers as a vast, continuous incantation of the alternative realities that tend to disappear from the current technocratic society. Merwin conjures and interrogates the other side of the rationalized existence, searching for the pre-symbolic mode of life that has escaped the hegemony of human language and signification. "Merwin's poems assume that language cannot determine experience" (Biespiel 140). To resist the conscious control of the writing process, which he deems as the ramification of a technological society, Merwin resorts to the prototype of the biblical waif, the tradition of the troubadours, and other inspirational sources such as European surrealism and Asian Zenic poetry. The urge to enunciate the "dumb reality which is *das Ding*" (Lacan, *Seminar VII* 55), to evoke the ultra-phenomenal and the spiritual continues to inform Merwin's writings after he settled down in Hawaii in the late 1970s. He has not compromised his desire to reach out for the "new dimension" of the world; his obsession with alterity has only been transferred to the female form, to the flora and ancestral origins. The poetic self clings tenaciously to the timeless memory traces from childhood to counteract its socio-historical determinations.

Merwin's struggle with the phallic function enters into his poetry through psychoneurotic mechanisms. Much of his work can be simply read as a symptom sent to the Other, not the symbolic, big Other founded on the Name-of-the-Father that confers identity within the familial-social system, but the *real* Other, the traumatic Thing which resists signification, which spellbinds the poet by its staging of appearance-as-disappearance. Through poetry Merwin seems to have maintained an impossible relationship with this pre-symbolic entity: *"Das Ding* is that which I will call the beyond-of-the-signified. It is as a function of this beyond-of-the-signified and of an emotional relationship to it that the subject keeps its distance and is constituted in a kind of relationship characterized by primary affect, prior to any repression" (Lacan, *Seminar VII* 54). Bruce Fink explains Lacan's sentence as: "[The Thing] is the object from which the subject keeps his or her distance, not getting too close or too far away either. *The subject comes into being as a defense against it, against the primal experience of pleasure / pain associated with it"* (95; emphasis original). If the subject gets too close to the Thing, his symbolic world will collapse in excessive *jouissance*; if too far, he will be reduced by the symbolic order to a mere automaton deprived of subjectivity.

This study indicates that Merwin prefers a closer, thus more precarious, relation with the Thing. The basic message we hear from Merwin's corpus is that the poet-speaker refuses to compromise on the question of desire by having a fixation of libido on the primal trauma of a non-understandable alterity. Merwin's infantile confrontation with the external stimuli that he cannot comprehend or master disrupts his integration of the symbolic order and triggers psychoneurotic symptoms in his poetry afterwards. Reliving the primal trauma throughout his poetic career, Merwin attempts to subjectivize the Other's desire, to "assume the place of the cause" (Fink 62) and becomes what he has always already been: a poet of "what is not there." The constant projection of the self is paradoxically accompanied by the discovery of an earlier, interior otherness that keeps returning to disrupt as well as organize the poet's subjectivity. Thomas Byers's comment that Merwin compels readers to "envision relationships to the other ... that are grounded in the value of its difference from us" (*What I Cannot Say* 114) can be supplemented by the observation that the constitutive difference / otherness arouses in the poet a psychic process of finding and refinding the Lacanian object.

Refusing to totalize or thematize the experiential world under the phallic function — the function of signifiers — Merwin has nevertheless subjected himself to the unsignifiable Other which miraculously resides in the self but cannot be contained by the self. Obsessed by this uncontainable, phantasmal otherness surging from the inside, Merwin takes on the responsibility to articulate the Other's absent presence that constitutes subjectivity proper. Poetry for Merwin thus resembles an urgent cry at finding oneself "penetrated," as it were, by a knowing yet unknowable

Other who has already withdrawn from the horizon, so the self and the Other, as we have seen in Merwin, Levinas and Lacan, do not form a totality but an infinitely diachronic or displaced non-relationship. It is exactly this interplay of contact and noncontact, interiority and exteriority, proximity and distance, that creates the kinesis in Merwin's writings. Thomas Byers's summary that Merwin "seeks a place for the self ... in an essentially non-human order" (*What I Cannot Say* 105), which represents critics' consensus on Merwin's poems of the 1960s, thus seems to have missed the kaleidoscopic fantasies in his staging of the sublime quest for what is other than the dichotomy of human / non-human.

Since *The Moving Target* (1963) Merwin's endeavors have been so unpredictable, unprogrammatic, and so narrowed down to the essentials that Edward Brunner's claim that "Merwin appears to have no style at all, or to take on whatever style suits the moment" seems fully justified (*Poetry* 286). If "[t]o live with the unknown ... is to enter into the responsibility of a speech that speaks without any form of power" (Blanchot, *Infinite* 302), then the erasure of any dominative style would coincide with a passive exposure of the self before the infinite when exteriority, the void-Thing, overtakes, pierces, and suffuses the subject. Such a Levinasian-cum-Lacanian irruption of exteriority in the interior precludes the mediation of style, which is the conscious ordering of the intellect commanded by the phallic function. Assertive style, directed by instrumental reason, runs the risk of miring one deeper in what Merwin calls the "ego-bound, historical, culturally brainwashed, incredibly limited moment" (*RM* 329). Rather, Merwin follows a "transparent" style, an impersonal, "suspended regard" in order to evoke the "inexorable splendor, " "the processions of an immeasurable continuum" ("Preface, " xii, xiii). The luminosity of Merwin's poetic space and its chiaroscuro of light and shade come from his desire to capture the ephemeral, to let the hallowed Other, which keeps withdrawing after the first encounter, shine again in its "inexorable splendor": rivers, lakes, creatures, flowers, lovers, parents, forebears, and origins. As James McCorkle says, "[Merwin's] vision has an emergent corollary: the counterpunctual epiphany of a numinous world" ("Merwin" 1044). The poet's transparent style is problematized, however, by the ego's traumatic fissuring when it is confronted with infinite revelations and sudden illuminations from the numinous world.

Highly suspicious of man's manipulation of signifiers to solidify ideology, Merwin would disagree with Victor Shklovsky's equation of art with technique. If art strives to give full liberation to man's desire, drive, Eros, and spirit, it then refuses to be aligned with repressive mechanisms such as teleological design of forms found in academic poetry prevalent in the U.S. in the 1950s. If in his early phase Merwin was still under the grip of formalism, since *The Moving Target* he has rejected the closed form and significantly reduced his conscious control of the writing process by relinquishing punctuation which "assume[s] an allegiance to the rational protocol of written language" (*SF* 1) and other structural patterns, linguistic designs, rhetorical schemes that are correlated with the paternal / authorial function. Rhetoric in general, as Merwin sees it, "has been a dirty word in the discussion of poetry in the language for several decades" because its function is to "impose" an end in art, not to "question" it (*RM* 314). Paring away the ostentatious impositions and persuasive ornaments, Merwin in his middle and later periods has brought poetry back to its "naked condition, " "where it touches on all that is unrealized" (*RM* 299).

Probing into the uncanny core of the poetic process, Merwin attempts an evocation of desire in the unconscious ("all that is unrealized"), and as he said in a 1981 interview, he never got away from that "spooky feeling about poetry, " without which poets are just playing "intellectual games" (*RM* 347). He surely does not intend to denigrate human intellect that fosters sensibility; he simply insists on the origin of poetry as the impersonal spirit that "no one knows where it goes" (*RM* 295). The poet does not intellectualize or domesticate the alien spirit in the self; he follows it faithfully and calls upon it repeatedly, even obsessively, and finally, to become or incarnate that spirit himself. Merwin rewrites the modernist imperative to make it new as a returning to a spiritual locus where authentic poetry originates: "True originality has to do not with trying to be new but trying to come from the place from which all renewal comes. The meaning of originality has to do with origin, the place where something comes from" (Elliott 18). Repetition and spontaneity are united in that each *tuché* with the creative spirit opens up a new horizon yet at the same time repeats and re-inscribes the former efforts in a differed / deferred way.

A mechanism contrary to the paternal function, poetic process seldom comes by authorial design; for Merwin, it happens in its unduplicatable, tremendous moment as chance work, the *tuché* with the timeless origin, and he would certainly agree with Alain Badiou who says, "The poem presents itself as a thing of language, encountered — each and every time — as an event" (233). Under the proximity of the infinite moment, poetry, as

152 a highly cathected movement of words, approximates the point where all motion becomes stasis, just as Merwin exclaims: "I really want a poem to make the world stop, for a matter of a few seconds" (Elliott 18). In this situation, poetry evokes what resides in the self but can no longer be contained by that self — a surging, propelling desire / drive to respond to the present moment. Poets are those who are possessed by words and more importantly, by a desire / drive that words can only approximate. In "On Open Form" (1969), Merwin elaborates form as "the setting down of a way hearing how poetry happens in words" and "testimony of a way of hearing how life happens in time" (RM 299). Such happenings are not to be circumscribed, categorized or thematized but only recorded as testimonies to the Other qua the rupture in the socio-symbolic order. Far from an expected and rationalized discourse, poetry originates from the traumatic contact with the uncontainable exterior, from an event that re-coordinates one's existent fantasy-frame and symbolic relations with others.

How do we evaluate this poetics of "infinite" obsession with the Other, this sublime hunger that does not call for satisfaction but its own starvation? What can this devotion to the unnamable Other make happen in a civilization characterized by global technocracy and military power? How can we imagine a radical passivity towards the Other without ironically turning it into a melodrama of victimization and self-glorification? Postwar American poetry has been a highly contested area for the ethical as well as political issues apropos the ambiguous status of the Other. The full discussion on these questions exceed the present study, and I will simply mention the confessionals and the Beats — two groups manifestly engaged in transcending the Name-of-the-Father — in contrast with Merwin's own project to bring out a poetics of infinite opening.

Poets writing in the confessional mode, Sylvia Plath and Anne Sexton, for example, resort to an aesthetic of antagonism by depicting the Other as essentially phallocentric and crippling (e.g., Plath's "Daddy" and Sexton's "Her Kind"). Their feminist efforts at transcending the Name-of-the-Father are problematized by self-dramatization and an imposed hostile totality of self and Other. Relying on the authoritative father as the conferrer of identity, confessional aesthetics cancels the possibility of radical otherness beyond the paternal function. Despite their violent protestations, both Plath and Sexton are reluctant to abandon the liaison with the phallic function, which is seen in their clinging to a rhetorical / authorial poetics to achieve persuasively pathetic effects. Their poetic spaces open more towards an antagonistic tension than anonymous exteriority. "Daddy" ends with a defiant curse on the father, and "Her Kind" constructs the speaker's ideal ego as opposed to a traditionally conceived femininity. The full trust in language to depict antagonism between the two sexes actually undermines the confessionals' more radical, political potentials.

Another direction at transcending totality is offered by the Beat poets, Allen Ginsberg for instance, who displays a Whitmanian all-embracing attitude towards multiplicity. Ginsberg's equalitarian gesture however, to borrow Jonathan Culler's observation on Whitman, "constitute[s] the object as another subject with whom the poetic subject might hope to strike up a harmonious relationship" (qtd. in Byers, *What I Cannot Say* 111). For Ginsberg, personal freedom is based on the belief in the self's ability to choose among different objects of representation for the more or less politically oriented agenda. The anti-culture, anti-intellectual engagement on one hand affords Ginsberg raw materials for his incantations and denunciations of the capitalistic society, while on the other hand it orientates his poetics towards the same antagonistic logic that has characterized the confessionals. Both Ginsberg and Plath have over-politicized (antagonized) the poetic space at the expense of privacy, and in doing so they have risked their aesthetics to the logic of identity and sameness.

Different from Ginsberg and Plath, Merwin seems more withdrawn from public spheres. There is fierceness in Merwin, but it does not consist in openly condemning the dominance of the Name-of-the-Father but in the continuous exploration of what has escaped the paternal function and signification ("the other side of despair"). Merwin tries to "touch on all that is unrealized" rather than criticize what is already realized as socio-historical data. Then, Merwin's imagination is basically non-antagonistic; even in his overtly political poems of the 1960s, readers still feel a psychotic detachment from present reality when the poet-speaker confesses that "I found untouched the desert of the unknown, / Big enough for my feet. It is my home" (*SF* 16). Making one's home in "the desert of the unknown" entails a radical rupture with the current social, cultural, political, and ideological assumptions.

The obsession with psychic process and constant becoming, which invalidates naming, would endow Merwin's poetics, quite unexpectedly, with a unique political potential. Incessantly undermining the bedrock of ideology — the belief in sameness — Merwin compels readers to imagine

153

the beyond-of-the-signified that keeps sliding away from their perceptual apparatuses. Forming a picture of that fleetingness from memory traces, readers are able to evoke the primordial happiness and thus to reflect upon the distance between present life and prehistoric origin. Contemporary life, marked by the market and overshadowed by nuclear weapons, may begin to investigate the limits of its own totalizing logic. Unlike Plath and Ginsberg, Merwin does not defy the father's name; he recognizes it, respects it, and plays it down at his own emotional cost. What ideology cannot tolerate is not open defiance but the exclusion of its very structure.

Merwin's writings are so diversified in their styles, concerns, and motifs that any single approach would seem reductive and restrictive. The psychoanalytical and philosophical readings of Merwin, while revealing the essential dynamics, have left unsaid other important aspects such as his explorations of Hawaiian history, which occupies much of his later career, his practice of Zen Buddhism, which shapes his later poetry toward Eastern spiritual meditations, and the way his aesthetics of the open form relates to other contemporary poetics, for example, the projective verse of the Black Mountain practitioners. My examination of the desire of / for the infinite in Merwin's works has only made the first step towards the larger question of spirituality in contemporary poetry, and its diverse psychological, ethical, and political implications. As this study on Merwin's poetical work suggests, becoming more mindful of the unarticulated, unrealized side of existence, we may come to stay with a poetry that aims not only at a criticism of life but also at impossible creation and pure fascination.

Works Cited

Altieri, Charles. *Enlarging the Temple: New Directions in American Poetry during the 1960s*. Cranbury: Associated University Press, 1979.

—. "Situating Merwin's Poetry since 1970." Nelson and Folsom 159–197.

Andersen, Kenneth. "The Poetry of W. S. Merwin." *Twentieth Century Literature* 16.4 (1970): 278–286. *Academic Search Premier*. Web. 7 December 2015.

Badiou, Alain. "Language, Thought, Poetry." *Theoretic Writings*. Ed. Ray Brassier and Alberto Toscano. New York: Continuum, 2004. 233–241.

Bal, Mieke. *On Meaning-Making: Essays in Semiotics*. Salem, OR.: Polebridge Press, 1994.

Barthes, Roland. *A Lover's Discourse: Fragments*. Trans. Richard Howard. London: Penguin, 1990.

—. *Le degré zéro de l'écriture*. Paris: Seuil, 1972.

—. *The Pleasure of the Text*. Trans. Richard Miller. Oxford: Blackwell, 1990.

Beach, Christopher. *The Cambridge Introduction to Twentieth-Century American Poetry*. Cambridge: Cambridge University Press, 2003.

Benjamin, Walter. *Illuminations: Essays and Reflections*. Trans. Harry Zohn. New York: Schocken, 1968.

—. *Reflections: Essays, Aphorisms, Autobiographical Writings*. Ed. Peter Demetz. Trans. Edmund Jephcott. New York: Schocken, 1978.

Benston, Alice. "Myth in the Poetry of W. S. Merwin." *Poets in Progress*. Ed. Edward Hungerford. Evanston: Northwestern University Press, 1962. 179–204.

Biespiel, David. "Iron Man." *Poetry* 187.2 (2005) 137–142. *Academic Search Premier*. Web. 7 December 2015.

Blanchot, Maurice. *Desperate Clarity: Chronicles of Intellectual Life, 1942*. Trans. Michael Holland. New York: Fordham University Press, 2014.

—. *The Infinite Conversation*. Trans. Susan Hanson. Minneapolis: University of Minnesota Press, 1993.

Bloom, Harold. Introduction. *W. S. Merwin*. Ed. Harold Bloom. New York: Chelsea House, 2004. 10–16.

Bly, Robert. *American Poetry: Wildness and Domesticity*. New York: Harper & Row, 1991.

—. *Selected Poems*. New York: Harper & Row, 1986.

Bowers, Neal. "W. S. Merwin and Postmodern American Poetry." *The Sewanee Review* 98.2 (1990) 246–259. *Academic Search Premier*. Web. 7 December 2015.

Brunner, Edward. "*Opening the Hand*: The Variable Caesura and the Family Poems." Nelson and Folsom 276–295.

—. *Poetry as Labor and Privilege: The Writings of W. S. Merwin*. Urbana: University of Illinois Press, 1991.

Bryson, J. Scott. *The West Side of Any Mountain: Place, Space, and Ecopoetry*. Iowa City: University of Iowa Press, 2005.

Buber, Martin. *Ten Rungs: Collected Hasidic Sayings*. Trans. Olga Marx. London: Routledge, 2005.

Byers, Thomas. "The Present Voices: W. S. Merwin since 1970." Nelson and Folsom 250–275.

—. *What I Cannot Say: Self, Word, and World in Whitman, Stevens, and Merwin*. Urbana: Illinois University Press, 1989.

Carroll, Paul. *The Poem in Its Skin*. Chicago: Big Table, 1968.

Christhilf, Mark. *W. S. Merwin the Mythmaker*. Columbia, MO: University of Missouri Press, 1986.

Clifton, Michael. "Breaking the Glass: A Pattern of Visionary Imagery in W. S. Merwin." *Chicago Review* 36.1 (1988): 65–83. *Academic Search Premier*. Web. 7 December 2015.

Contoski, Victor. "W. S. Merwin: Rational and Irrational Poetry." *Literary Review* 22.3 (1979): 309–320. *Academic Search Premier*. Web. 7 December 2015.

Davis, Cheri. *W. S. Merwin*. Boston: Twayne, 1981.

Dean, Jeanie S. "Re-seeding the Burnt Wasteland: W. S. Merwin's *The Rain in the Trees*." *Passions of the Earth in Human Existence, Creativity and Literature*. Ed. Anna-Teresa Tymieniecka. Dordrecht: Kluwer Academic Publishers, 2001. 81 –

100. Web. 7 December 2015. <http://link.springer.com/chapter/10.1007%2F978-94-010-0930-0_7>

Deleuze, Gilles. "The Simulacrum and Ancient Philosophy." *The Logic of Sense*. Ed. Constantin. V. Boundas. New York: Columbia University Press, 1990. 253−279.

—. and Félix Guattari. *Anti-Oedipus: Capitalism and Schizophrenia*. Trans. Robert Hurley, Mark Seem, and Helen R. Lane. Minneapolis: University of Minnesota Press, 1983.

—. and Félix Guattari. *A Thousand Plateaus: Capitalism and Schizophrenia*. Trans. Brian Massumi. Minneapolis: University of Minnesota Press, 1987.

Derrida, Jacques. *Adieu to Emmanuel Levinas*. Trans. Pascale-Anne Brault and Michael Naas. Stanford: Stanford University Press, 1999.

—. *Of Grammatology*. Trans. Gayatri Chakravorty Spivak. Baltimore: Johns Hopkins University Press, 1997.

—. *On the Name*. Trans. David Wood, John P. Leavey, Jr., and Ian McLeod. Stanford: Stanford University Press, 1995.

—. *Sovereignties in Question: The Poetics of Paul Celan*. Ed. Thomas Dutoit and Outi Pasanen. Trans. Thomas Dutoit, et al. New York: Fordham University Press, 2005.

—. *Of Spirit: Heidegger and the Question*. Trans. Geoffrey Bennington and Rachel Bowlby. Chicago: University of Chicago Press, 1987.

—. *Writing and Difference*. Trans. Alan Bass. London: Routledge, 2001.

Eliot, T. S. *Collected Poems, 1909−1962*. New York: Harcourt Brace, 1963.

Elliott, David. "An Interview with W. S. Merwin." *Contemporary Literature* 29. 1 (1988): 1−25. *Academic Search Premier*. Web. 7 December 2015.

Felman, Shoshana. *The Claims of Literature: A Shoshana Felman Reader*. Ed. Emily Sun, Eyal Peretz, and Ulrich Baer. New York: Fordham University Press, 2007.

Fink, Bruce. *The Lacanian Subject: Between Language and Jouissance*. Princeton, NJ: Princeton University Press, 1995.

Folsom, Ed. "'I Have Been a Long Time in a Strange Country': W. S. Merwin and America." Nelson and Folsom 224−249.

—. and Cary Nelson. Introduction. Nelson and Folsom 1−18.

Frazier, Jane. *From Origin to Ecology: Nature and the Poetry of W. S. Merwin*. Cranbury: Associated University Press, 1999.

Freud, Sigmund. *Introductory Lectures on Psychoanalysis*. Trans. James Strachey. New York: Norton, 1966.

—. *The Penguin Freud Reader*. Ed. Adam Phillips. London: Penguin, 2006.

Works Cited

—. *Three Case Histories*. Ed. Philip Rieff. New York: Simons & Schuster, 1996.

—. *Totem and Taboo*. Trans. James Strachey. London: Routledge, 2008.

Geyskens, Thomas. *Our Original Scenes: Freud's Theory of Sexuality*. Leuven: Leuven University Press, 2005.

Goethe, Johann Wolfgang von. *Selected Poems*. Ed. Christopher Middleton. Trans. Christopher Middleton, et al. Vol. 1 of *Goethe: The Collected Works*. Princeton, NJ: Princeton University Press, 1994. 12 Vols.

Grigg, Russell. *Lacan, Language, and Philosophy*. Albany: State University of New York Press. 2008.

Gross, Harvey. "The Writing on the Void: The Poetry of W. S. Merwin." *The Iowa Review* 1.3 (1970): 92–106. *Academic Search Premier*. Web. 7 December 2015.

Guy, Sandra M. "W. S. Merwin and the Primordial Elements: Mapping the Journey to Mythic Consciousness." *Midwest Quarterly* 38.4 (1997): 414–423. *Academic Search Premier*. Web. 7 December 2015.

Hallberg, Robert von. "Authenticity." *The Cambridge History of American Literature, Volume 8: Poetry and Criticism 1940–1995*. Ed. Sacvan Bercovitch. Cambridge: Cambridge University Press, 1996. 123–159.

Halliday, Mark and Michael Theune. "*The Shadow of Sirius*: A Critical Conversation." Weinert and Prufer 137–172.

Harp, Jerry. "All of Memory Waking: Word and Experience in W. S. Merwin's *The Shadow of Sirius*." Weinert and Prufer 173–183.

Heidegger, Martin. *Being and Time*. Trans. John Macquarrie and Edward Robinson. New York: Harper & Row, 1962.

—. *Hölderlin's Hymn "The Ister."* Trans. William McNeill and Julia Davis. Bloomington, IN: Indiana University Press, 1996.

—. *Poetry, Language, Thought*. Trans. Albert Hofstadter. New York: Harper & Row, 1971.

—. *On the Way to Language*. Trans. Peter D. Hertz. New York: Harper & Row, 1971.

Hirsch, Edward. Interview with W. S. Merwin. *The Paris Review* 102 (1987). 1–26. Web. 7 December 2015. <http://www.theparisreview.org/interviews/2692/the-art-of-poetry-no-38-w-s-merwin>

Hix, H. L. "'This Simple Test': A Thematic Continuum in Merwin's Middle Period." Irwin 68–74.

—. *Understanding W. S. Merwin*. Columbia, SC: University of South Carolina Press, 1997.

Hoeppner, Edward Haworth. "A Nest of Bones: Transcendence, Topology, and the Theory of the Word in W. S. Merwin's Poetry," *Modern Language Quarterly* 49.3 (1988): 262−284. *Academic Search Premier*. Web. 7 December 2015.

—. "Shadows and Glass: Mirrored Selves in the Poetry of W. S. Merwin and John Ashbery." *Philological Quarterly* 65. 3 (1986) 311 − 330. *Academic Search Premier*. Web. 7 December 2015.

Homer, Sean. *Jacques Lacan*. London: Routledge, 2005.

Howard, Richard. *Alone with America: Essays on the Art of Poetry in the United States since 1950*. Enlarged edition. New York: Atheneum, 1980.

Hughes, Ted. "The Horse." *Sharkpack Poetry Review*. Web. 5 June 2015. < https: // sharkpackpoetry.com/2012/10/22/poem-ted-hughes-the-horses/ >

Irwin, Mark. "A Conversation with W. S. Merwin." Irwin 47−52.

—. ed. *Many Mountains Moving: A Tribute to W. S. Merwin*. Boulder, CO: Many Mountains Moving, 2001.

Kalaidjian, Walter. "Linguistic Mirage: Language and Landscape in W. S. Merwin's Later Poetry." Nelson and Folsom 198−223.

King James Version. Bible Gateway. Web. 5 June 2015. <https://www.biblegateway.com/versions/King-James-Version-KJV-Bible/>

Lacan, Jacques. *Écrit: A Selection*. Trans. Bruce Fink. New York: Norton, 2002.

—. *The Seminar of Jacques Lacan, Book III: The Psychoses*. Trans. Russell Grigg. New York: Norton, 1997.

—. *The Seminar of Jacques Lacan, Book VII: The Ethics of Psychoanalysis*. Trans. Dennis Porter. New York: Norton, 1992.

—. *The Seminar of Jacques Lacan, Book XI: The Four Fundamental Concepts of Psychoanalysis*. Trans. Alan Sheridan. New York: Norton, 1998.

—. *The Seminar of Jacques Lacan, Book XX: On Feminine Sexuality, The Limit of Love and Knowledge*. Trans. Bruce Fink. New York: Norton, 1999.

Lazer, Hank. "For a Coming Extinction: A Reading of W. S. Merwin's *The Lice*." *ELH* 49.1 (1982): 262−85. *Academic Search Premier*. Web. 7 December 2015.

Levinas, Emmanuel. *Collected Philosophical Papers*. Trans. Richard A. Cohen. Dordrecht: Martinus Nijhoff, 1987.

—. *Entre Nous: Thinking-of-the-Other*. Trans. Michael B. Smith and Barbara Harshav. New York: Columbia University Press, 2006.

—. *Ethics and Infinity: Conversations with Philippe Nemo*. Trans. Richard A. Cohen. Pittsburg: Duquesne University Press, 1985.

—. *Existence and Existents*. Trans. Alphonso Lingis. The Hague: Martinus Nijhoff, 1978.

160

—. *God, Death, and Time*. Trans. Bettina Bergo. Stanford: Stanford University Press, 2000.

—. *Otherwise Than Being: Or Beyond Essence*. Trans. Alphonso Lingis. Pittsburg: Duquesne University Press, 1998.

—. *Time and the Other*. Trans. Richard A. Cohen. Pittsburg: Duquesne University Press, 1987.

—. *Totality and Infinity: An Essay on Exteriority*. Trans. Alphonso Lingis. The Hague: Martinus Nijhoff, 1979.

Libby, Anthony. "Merwin's Planet: Alien Voices." *Criticism* 24.1 (1982): 48-63. *Academic Search Premier*. Web. 7 December 2015.

—. "W. S. Merwin and the Nothing That Is." *Contemporary Literature* 16.1 (1975): 19-40. *Academic Search Premier*. Web. 7 December 2015.

Lieberman, Laurence. "W. S. Merwin: Church of Ash." *Irwin* 96-105.

Marcuse, Herbert. *Eros and Civilization: A Philosophical Inquiry into Freud*. 1955. Boston: Beacon, 1966.

McCorkle, James. "Merwin, W. S." *The Greenwood Encyclopedia of American Poets and Poetry*. Ed. Jeffrey H. Gray, et al. Vol. 4. Santa Barbara: Greenwood Press, 2005. 1044-1048.

—. *The Still Performance: Writing, Self, and Interconnection in Five Postmodern American Poets*. Charlottesville, VA: University Press of Virginia, 1989.

McDonnell, Sean Joseph. "I with No Voice: Absence, Presence and Intersubjectivity in the Poetry of W. S. Merwin." Diss. University of California, Davis, 2003. *ProQuest*. Web. 7 December 2015.

Merwin, W. S. *The Book of Fables*. Port Townsend, WA: Copper Canyon Press, 2007.

—. *The Ends of the Earth: Essays*. Washington, DC: Shoemaker & Hoard, 2004.

—. *Finding the Islands*. San Francisco: North Point Press, 1982.

—. *The First Four Books of Poems*. 1975. Port Townsend, WA: Copper Canyon Press, 2000.

—. *Flower & Hand: Poems 1977-1983*. Port Townsend, WA: Copper Canyon Press, 1997.

—. Introduction. *Twenty Love Poems and a Song of Despair*. By Pablo Neruda. Trans. W. S. Merwin. London: Penguin, 2004. vii-xviii.

—. *The Lost Upland: Stories of Southwest France*. New York: Knopf, 1992.

—. *The Mays of Ventadorn.* Washington, DC: National Geographic Society, 2002.

—. Preface. *Transparence of the World.* By Jean Follain. Trans. W. S. Merwin. Port Townsend, WA: Copper Canyon Press, 2005. xi−xiv.

—. *Present Company.* Port Townsend, WA: Copper Canyon Press, 2005.

—. *The Pupil.* 2001. New York: Knopf, 2002.

—. *The Rain in the Trees.* 1988. New York: Knopf, 2008.

—. *Regions of Memory: Uncollected Prose, 1949 − 1982.* Ed. Ed Folsom and Cary Nelson. Urbana: University of Illinois Press, 1987.

—. *The River Sound.* New York: Knopf, 1999.

—. *The Second Four Books of Poems.* Port Townsend, WA: Copper Canyon Press, 1993.

—. *Selected Translations 1948−1968.* New York: Atheneum, 1969.

—. *The Shadow of Sirius.* Port Townsend, WA: Copper Canyon Press, 2008.

—. *Summer Doorways: A Memoir.* Washington, DC: Shoemaker & Hoard, 2005.

—. *Travels.* 1993. New York: Knopf, 2003.

—. *Unframed Originals: Recollections.* 1982. Washington, DC: Shoemaker & Hoard, 2005.

—. *The Vixen.* 1996. New York: Knopf, 2006.

Molesworth, Charles. "W. S. Merwin: Style, Vision, Influence." Nelson and Folsom 145−158.

Morton, Timothy. *Ecology without Nature: Rethinking Environmental Aesthetics.* Cambridge, MA: Harvard University Press, 2007.

Moyers, Bill. Interview with W. S. Merwin. *Bill Moyers Journal.* 26 June. 2009. Web. 5 June. 2015. <http://www.pbs.org/moyers/journal/06262009/watch.html>

Nelson, Cary. "The Resources of Failure: W. S. Merwin's Deconstructive Career." Nelson and Folsom 78−121.

—. and Ed Folsom, eds. *W. S. Merwin: Essays on the Poetry.* Urbana: University of Illinois Press, 1987.

Neruda, Pablo. *Twenty Love Poems and a Song of Despair.* Trans. W. S. Merwin. London: Penguin, 2004.

Newman, Amy. "Radiance and Regret in W. S. Merwin's 'One Story.'" Irwin 124−129.

Olson, Charles. "Projective/Verse." *The Norton Anthology of Modern and Contemporary Poetry.* Vol. 2. Ed. Richard Ellmann, et al. New York: Norton, 2003. 1053−1061.

Otto, Rudolf. *The Idea of the Holy*. Trans. John W. Harvey. London: Oxford University Press, 1936.

Perkins, David. *A History of Modern Poetry: Modernism and After*. Cambridge, MA: Harvard University Press, 1987.

Perloff, Marjorie. "Apocalypse Then: Merwin and the Sorrows of Literary History." Nelson and Folsom 122-144.

Pinsky, Robert. *The Situation of Poetry: Contemporary Poetry and Its Traditions*. Princeton, NJ: Princeton University Press, 1976.

Pound, Ezra. *Personae: The Shorter Poems of Ezra Pound*. Ed. Lea Baechler and A. Walton Litz. New York: New Directions, 1990.

Ramke, Bin. "Returning to the Place of Loss." Irwin 133-136.

Ramsey, Jarold. "The Continuities of W. S. Merwin: 'What Has Escaped Us We Bring with Us.'" Nelson and Folsom 19-44.

Rilke, M. R. *The Selected Poetry of Rainer Maria Rilke*. Trans. Stephen Mitchell. New York: Vintage, 1989.

Rueckert, William H. "Rereading *The Lice*: A Journal." Nelson and Folsom 45-64.

Scholes, Robert. "Reading Merwin Semiotically." Nelson and Folsom 65-77.

Scigaj, Leonard. *Sustainable Poetry: Four American Ecopoets*. Lexington: University Press of Kentucky, 1999.

Smith, Daniel. "Deleuze and Derrida, Immanence and Transcendence: Two Directions in Recent French Thought." *Between Deleuze & Derrida*. Ed. Paul Patton and John Protevi. New York: Continuum, 2003. 46-66.

Smith, Dinitia. "A Poet of Their Own." *New York Times*. 19 Feb. 1995. Web. 5 June 2015. <https://www.nytimes.com/books/99/04/04/specials/merwin-own.html>

Snyder, Gary. Preface. *No Nature: New and Selected Poems*. New York: Pantheon Books, 1992. v.

Stepanchev, Stephen. *American Poetry since 1945: A Critical Survey*. New York: Harper & Row, 1967.

Stewart, Susan. *The Poet's Freedom: A Notebook on Making*. Chicago: University of Chicago Press, 2011.

Toliver, Carl Clifton. *W. S. Merwin and the Postmodern Environment*. Diss. University of Texas, Austin, 1997. *ProQuest*. Web 5 June. 2015.

Trakl, Georg. *Poems and Prose: A Bilingual Edition*. Trans. Alexander Stillmark. Evanston: Northwestern University Press, 2005.

Vendler, Helen. *Part of Nature, Part of Us: Modern American Poets*. Cambridge, MA:

Harvard University Press, 1980.

Virgil, *Aeneid*. Trans. Allen Mandelbaum. New York: Bantam, 1981.

Watkins, Evan. "W. S. Merwin: A Critical Accompaniment." *boundary 2* 4.1 (1975): 186−199. *Academic Search Premier*. Web. 7 December 2015.

Weinert, Jonathan and Kevin Prufer, eds. *Until Everything Is Continuous Again: American Poets on the Recent Work of W. S. Merwin*. Seattle: WordFarm, 2012.

Wilson, Reed Daniel. "Words on a Journey: Vision and Religion in the Poetry of W. S. Merwin." Diss. University of California, Los Angeles, 1988. *ProQuest*. Web. 5 June 2015.

Wood, Renate. "Looking for the Unknown: W. S. Merwin's 'Finding a Teacher.'" Irwin 160−168.

Yeats, W. B. *The Collected Poems of W. B. Yeats*. Ed. Richard J. Finneran. New York: Simon & Schuster, 1996.

Zahavi, Dan. *Husserl's Phenomenology*. Stanford: Stanford University Press, 2003.

Zhang, Ziqing. *A History of 20th Century American Poetry*. Changchun: Jilin Education Publishing House, 1995. (张子清:《二十世纪美国诗歌史》,长春:吉林教育出版社,1995。)

Žižek, Slavoj. *The Abyss of Freedom*. Ann Arbor: University of Michigan Press, 1997.

—. *On Belief*. London: Routledge, 2001.

—. *Did Somebody Say Totalitarianism?: Five Interventions in the (Mis)use of a Notion*. New York: Verso, 2001.

—. *Enjoy Your Symptom: Jacques Lacan in Hollywood and Out*. New York: Routledge, 2008.

—. *The Fragile Absolute: Or, Why is the Christian Legacy Worth Fighting for?* New York: Verso, 2000.

—. *The Metastases of Enjoyment: Six Essays on Women and Causality*. New York: Verso, 2005.

—. *Organs without Bodies: Deleuze and Consequences*. New York: Routledge, 2004.

—. *The Plague of Fantasies*. New York: Verso, 1997.

—. *The Sublime Object of Ideology*. New York: Verso, 1989.

—. *The Ticklish Subject: The Absent Centre of Political Ontology*. New York: Verso, 1999.

—. *Violence: Six Sideways Reflections*. New York: Picador, 2008.

—. *The Žižek Reader*. Ed. Elizabeth Wright and Edmond Wright. Malden, MA: Blackwell, 1999.